REBELLIOUS

Poisonous Passions
Book Three

Mae Thorn

Dragonblade Publishing, Inc. is an imprint of Kathryn Le Veque Novels, Inc.
P.O. Box 23
Moreno Valley, CA 92556
ceo@dragonbladepublishing.com

Produced in the United States of America

First Edition June 2022
Trade Paperback Edition

ARE YOU SIGNED UP FOR DRAGONBLADE'S BLOG?

You'll get the latest news and information on exclusive giveaways, exclusive excerpts, coming releases, sales, free books, cover reveals and more.

Check out our complete list of authors, too!

No spam, no junk. That's a promise!

Sign Up Here

www.dragonbladepublishing.com

Dearest Reader;

Thank you for your support of a small press. At Dragonblade Publishing, we strive to bring you the highest quality Historical Romance from some of the best authors in the business. Without your support, there is no 'us', so we sincerely hope you adore these stories and find some new favorite authors along the way.

Happy Reading!

CEO, Dragonblade Publishing

Additional Dragonblade books by Author Mae Thorn

Poisonous Passions Series
Notorious (Book 1)
Dangerous (Book 2)
Rebellious (Book 3)

For Suzanne. You saved my life.
And for my dad. You never gave up on me.

CHAPTER ONE

T HE CRACK OF gunfire sent Lynette flinching back into the carriage seat. She was thrown into the side as the horses cried in confusion and halted the carriage's progress. Shouts rang out in the night, echoing in her shocked mind.

"Where is it?" a man asked just outside the carriage door. "We know this is Greymore's carriage." The voice was like the crunching of glass from his throat.

"My lord isn't here," the driver pled. At once, Lynette regretted borrowing the carriage without the accompaniment of its owner.

"Then who do we have here?" the man said and thrust the door open. The lower half of his face, up to his eyes, sported a torn scarf. A cocked hat rested low on his forehead. A highwayman.

The man grunted at the sight of her. "His doxy, then."

Her anger unseated her fear, and Lynette's jaw dropped. "I am nobody's doxy. Release us, you fool."

He tilted his head at her. "Hand over your purse, and I'll consider it."

She folded her arms. "I will do nothing of the sort."

"We were told Greymore was transporting contraband through here. A pretty wench like you is the perfect cover."

"You were told wrong." Viscount Greymore a smuggler? She

should have hired a coach after all. Surely the man was doing her no favors by offering his carriage.

"Dixon, we found it," a voice called from behind the man. Dixon turned toward the voice as another man in a similar disguise came into view. He halted as he saw Lynette in the carriage and turned to Dixon. "Send her away. We've found Greymore's stash under the carriage."

Lynette stared at the men with wide eyes. She was going to throttle Greymore for this.

"But, sir, she looks like she has a bit of coin herself." Dixon's low tone became a grating whine.

"Do it. Now."

Dixon gave her one last look and slammed the carriage door shut. The men gave a chorus of shouts outside before their hoofbeats faded.

What seemed like hours passed before she could relax back into the seat. She let out a long, steadying breath, and the carriage door opened once again. The driver peered in with an oil lamp, and his other hand wiped his bald head. Blood smeared from a cut along his forehead.

"Are you well, miss?" His brows drew down as he anxiously studied her for injury.

"Yes. A bit shaken up is all."

He steadied himself against the carriage. "We were lucky. Only a few cuts and bruises, though the footmen are both out. We should have posted a guard, but my lord didn't think the bloody Wyvern would rob him." He shook his head.

"The Wyvern?"

"Aye. You just met the most notorious blackguard in England."

She blinked at him in confusion. "That highwayman is named after a flying worm?"

"He's not just some highwayman. He's a thief and murderer a hundred times over. You can be sure of that. A pirate by land and sea."

She peered out the door over the driver's shoulder uneasily. He hadn't seemed so dangerous at the time. Of course, Dixon had been receiving most of his ire. Suddenly, she couldn't wait to see Briarwyck again.

"When can we be off?" Her eyes darted back to the driver.

He grunted and motioned with his head to the front of the carriage. "As soon as the men wake up. Unless you want travel companions."

"By all means, let me help you load them so we can be out of here."

He stared at her with a dead expression but assisted her as she stepped down from the carriage. He came up from behind with the light, and she squinted toward the front of the vehicle. A cloud of road dust rose behind her. She sneezed and slapped at the cloud until it settled.

The crack of a pistol froze her in place. The underbrush rustled to the side of the road, and the driver shouted at her to get down. Her body slumped against the carriage, and he pulled at her skirts to get her to drop to the ground.

Another pistol rang out in the darkness, and fire exploded through her arm. She cried out at the shock and was, at last, compelled to fall to the dirt. She grasped the screaming wound, her eyes darting around for the shooter. The underbrush moved in the lamplight, and she could just make out his features.

Dixon stalked out of the darkness with his sword held high. He must have abandoned his pistols, shots spent. Her driver rose above her, his sword ready. Dixon paused before slamming his boot into the older man's chest. A whoosh of air escaped his mouth as he fell.

"Now, doxy, give me your purse." Dixon beckoned with his hand.

"Make me."

His hand paused between them as he considered her refusal. He extended his sword this time and raised the tip to her wound.

"You should have that looked at—that is, if you survive. Give me the purse, and I won't open you up from your belly to your pretty neck."

"Is that a promise? I don't respond well to threats."

He twisted his wrist, and the fire heated into lava oozing down her arm. She gasped but kept her searing gaze on his, daring him to kill her. Movement flashed behind him, and another to his side. They were surrounded, but by whom and why? She hadn't heard their approach as she had Dixon, and the driver lay sprawled across the road. Anyone sneaking up on Dixon had to be an ally. At least, for a time.

She raised her chin and spit as high as she could, hitting his chest. "I won't be giving you anything."

"You foolish girl. There are worse things for me to take than your purse." He leaned forward and grabbed for her. Grimy hands hoisted her by the front of her dress, and her feet grazed marks over the dirt. She shrieked in his face as loud as she could. He flinched and nearly dropped her.

She spotted him then, just behind Dixon. His hazel eyes narrowed over the scarlet scarf covering his face. He raised his arm, and steel flashed as he struck down on Dixon's neck. Lynette dropped. Her legs crumpled below her, sending her backward, where her head slapped the carriage wheel.

She closed her eyes against the sudden jolt. Out of her dull awareness, she registered that he stood over her, watching her.

"You should have given him your purse." The scarf muffled the Wyvern's voice.

Lynette tried to look up at him, but the blur of motion sent her head reeling back to find the carriage wheel once more and into unconsciousness.

A horse moved beneath her. The pounding hooves were in tandem with her headache, creating a steady stream of pain. Fire throbbed through her arm at the movement. She lashed out once to regain some sense of control, but a hand grasped her wrist, keeping her from striking.

"Easy. You're safe now," the man riding with her said.

She swallowed back the cotton in her throat. "The Wyvern?"

"Gone now. Your men will be all right, but you need a doctor." His voice turned soothing, and she fought against threatening sleep.

"Briarwyck?"

He placed a firm grip on her head and steadied her back with it. "No time. Briarwyck is too far. Rest now."

She attempted to nod but decided against it and shut her eyes until the rocking motion soothed her to sleep. She dreamed of a winged serpent flying beside their horse as they raced away from a band of armed men. Their pursuers were a blur of activity thundering behind them. The serpent reared its head and gave a shrill cry from deep in its throat, sending echoes along the valley.

Then she was falling, the horse gone. The serpent carried her in its mouth, and a fang clamped down on her arm. Its breath was a sweltering bath that sent her sinking further. A low rumble shook its chest, and she wondered if it would engulf her in fire. The growl formed into words as it spoke.

"Harpy, it's just a scratch."

A cold weight pressed against her head, and she shivered into the warmth of the cushions below her.

"If you die in this bed, leaving me to deal with my brothers, I will kill you."

She snorted in response and fell back into the fire and flight of her dream.

Moments, dreams, heartbeats passed. She shrieked as the fire was engulfed in an icy torrent. Her eyes flew open. An elderly woman stood over her, pushing her down with admirable strength into a tub of frozen water. A bony hand forced her under the surface.

She clawed at the hand as her lungs pleaded for air, only to be released just as her chest threatened to explode. She gasped and coughed over the edge of the tub, sending streams of mucus and water raining to the tiled floor. The woman slapped the middle of her back as though she was trying to expel more than water.

Lynette lifted her head to peer up at her and met a tanned, dried-up face pinched in permanent disapproval. The severe tightness of her silver-blue bun seemed to harness her wrinkled features in place. Her thin lips frowned down at her and forced Lynette to look away.

She struggled to gain her feet, but the old woman forced her back with a stern hand, trapping her in the tub. Her limbs wobbled, and she doubted she would have stood on her own anyway. She slouched over the tub and allowed the chill to overwhelm her until her body shook in spasms. At last, the grip on her shoulder eased. The woman patted her and motioned for her to rise. Her arm protested as she pushed herself to her unsteady legs, and a tight bandage encompassed her arm.

The woman grunted and sighed with each of her failures until, finally, she pulled Lynette from the water, hands below her arms like she was hoisting a toddler. The tiled floor proved warmer than the tub, and she found her footing just as the woman released her. The woman thrust a towel into her hands, and she wrapped it around her shoulders as she shivered. Her arm protested at the pressure, but the pain was preferable to the cold.

A knock sounded just outside the room. An empty space inhabited where a door should be to a connecting room. A bright-toothed smile met her gaze and dropped. She clutched the towel closer, preserving whatever remained of her modesty. The man peering around the corner drew away, shielding his eyes.

He cleared his throat. "Rycroft wants to know how the patient is holding up. He asked me to assist in any way I can." His words were hurried, but Lynette caught the hint of an accent she didn't recognize. It gave his voice a musical quality.

"Good." The woman spoke from behind her.

Lynette took a step toward the newcomer. "Why is Mr. Rycroft here? And, for that matter, where is here?"

"You're at Rycroft House, ma'am."

She stopped midstride a few paces from him. "Why am I at Rycroft House? I should be at Briarwyck."

He kept his hand raised as he spoke. "I told you on the ride over Briarwyck was too far. This was the closest place. It was lucky we found you when we did."

She narrowed her eyes at the hand shielding his face.

The other woman tsked behind her and placed a plush robe over Lynette's toweled shoulders. Lynette wrapped it around her gratefully and tied the garment in place. As the ice in her veins thawed, the biting pain in her arm became less of a nag and more of a cry.

She grasped the area and turned back to the man. "I'm decent enough. You were the one who brought me here?"

He lowered his hand with slow caution. Once he was satisfied, he dropped it the rest of the way. "We brought you here."

"Why didn't the Wyvern kill me too?"

His wide grin reappeared. "Who knows? I think I may have scared him off. Probably didn't want to get caught."

The woman cackled behind them and ushered her out of the room. The man moved aside as they passed, revealing a bedroom decorated in yellow and cream. The bed at the center took up much of the room. An armoire sat against one wall, and a mirrored dressing table rested at another, holding a single unlit lamp. Her gaze snapped to the window, where light streamed in through the fabric of the curtains.

"How long was I unconscious?"

"A few days. You hit your head." He tilted his own head at the rumpled bed, and he shifted his weight. "I shouldn't be in here. There are no other female servants though."

"Then are you a servant?"

"You mean because I'm black?" He smirked and crossed his arms over his chest.

She bit her lip and struggled for words. "No, I didn't mean that. I'm sorry. I meant because you were sent to assist me."

He winked at her. "Relax. I've been called far worse. No, I'm not a servant or slave. I'm just a friend of Rycroft's."

"He has friends?"

He laughed, shaking his head. "A few, not many. I'm Isaiah Howell, by the way. I assume your name isn't Harpy?"

She took in a quick breath. "Of course not. I'm Lynette Wolcott." She attempted a curtsy out of habit but lost her balance, and the other woman reached out to steady her. A bony finger poked her toward the bed, and she sighed loudly before complying. She seated herself and gazed back at Mr. Howell.

Mr. Howell gestured to the woman. "Your tormentor is Mrs. Johns, the housekeeper. I'd keep an eye on her."

Mrs. Johns's frown twitched up slightly to what must have passed for a smile. She pointed a knobby finger at him and shook her head. Lynette thought it to be some old joke between them. Mrs. Johns seemed to be a woman of few words.

"Is there anything I can get you, Miss Wolcott? Dr. Pascoe said you should rest, try not to move around too much. Mrs. Johns has been battling your fever since you arrived."

"From the gunshot? Who is Dr. Pascoe? Where are my clothes? I need to get to Briarwyck." She gazed over the room again, knowing her clothing wasn't there.

"I believe Riley is still looking for suitable clothes for you, but he gets sidetracked. The dress you were wearing was ruined."

She shook her head. "Who is Riley?"

"Never mind, you'll meet him later. You need to rest now. Briarwyck can wait." He motioned to the bed.

Mrs. Johns moved toward her, and Lynette hastened to push her feet under the covers, yelping at the pain piercing through her arm as she did so. Mrs. Johns grunted in approval and moved off to straighten the adjoining room. Mr. Howell had started to leave.

"Mr. Howell, wait," Lynette said.

He stopped and met her gaze. "Yes?"

"Has word been sent to Briarwyck? I must not worry my sister. You see, she is in a delicate state. Already she has taken a fall, which is why I was rushing back to her." She exhaled her words on one breath.

"I don't know. Rycroft mentioned something about sending a message to your family. Try to rest, Miss Wolcott. I'm sure your answers will come. The roads are not what they once were, though, and who knows what the Wyvern will allow?"

CHAPTER TWO

M R. HOWELL'S REASSURANCES did nothing to ease Lynette's mind. She tried resting, but the pain in her arm grew to the pounding of a sledgehammer. Mrs. Johns sat at her bedside, staring down at her like a carrion bird perched on a stool. It raised the hair on the back of her neck.

Rycroft had to see sense in her sending a note to Delia. Her pregnant sister could no longer travel and would not be able to come to Rycroft House. She doubted Delia would trust a letter from Rycroft, and a message from Lynette would be a welcome reassurance. Her brother-in-law, William Travers, Viscount Carrington, was still in Bath on business with his brother, Mr. Hugh Travers. She didn't know where to reach them or if they would come if she did. The rest of her friends in England were preoccupied in London, too far away to be of much help.

Her fate rested with Mr. Maxwell Rycroft, a man who threw up her guard. She was grudgingly grateful to him for aiding her from the side of the road, though she suspected much of that was due to the amicable Mr. Howell and not Rycroft. Still, she would have to deal with the man.

When she thought she could handle it no more, she peeked through slit eyes at the woman beside her. The stool was vacant and the room empty. Darkness painted the curtains, but a low burning candle cast an amber glow from the dressing table.

She raised her chin and swung her feet to the floor. When she pushed up from the bed, her arm threatened to collapse into flaming jelly. She gritted her teeth against a scream. Any sound could alert Mrs. Johns from whatever shadow the woman inhabited.

Her gaze caught on a folded nightgown the mysterious Riley must have found. It wasn't what she needed, but it would have to do. She wasn't about to wander around in nothing but a robe. Her nightgown on, she fastened the robe over herself for good measure.

Her mess of waist-length black hair hampered her progress, and she searched the dressing table for anything to pull it back. The best she found was a wide-toothed comb, which she tugged through her snarled hair before tying it back in a knot.

She reached for the doorknob and turned. It wouldn't budge. She narrowed her eyes at the offending lock and tried again. It protested against her hand. Why lock the door?

Maybe she had missed a second door. She hadn't noticed an exit while she bathed, but she decided to check to be sure.

Sure enough, only one door led out of her room.

The single window was nailed shut, probably years ago, if the chipped paint proved anything. She peered out, her nose to the glass, and shielded her eyes. The moon offered scant light, but the shadows revealed nothing. No way would she chance jumping into that void below. Better to wait.

Her arm throbbed with the moving about, but she pushed the feeling to the back of her mind. She tugged at the door of the armoire, expecting it to be locked, but it swung open with little effort. The contents were shaded, and she fetched the light off the dressing table. The cabinet was empty save for a bar to hang clothes.

She let out a loud sigh and moved to the two long drawers below the cabinet doors. The top drawer contained extra linen for the bed and bath. She rustled through it and found nothing else. The bottom drawer was slightly less useless. A lone book rested in the deep recess. She wondered, absentmindedly, why the linens hadn't taken up the larger space. She leaned down to pull out the book and read the title by the low light—the *Odyssey*.

She snorted.

The book seemed fitting, since she'd thrown a copy of the *Iliad* at Rycroft back at Briarwyck. Had Rycroft placed the volume in her room on purpose? She was sure it was some kind of coincidence, but her trapped state made her wonder all the same. At least she had a sort of weapon now. Though, she doubted it would prove effective against the inhabitants of the house.

Lynette dropped the book on the pillow next to hers and sat on the edge of the bed. She studied the bandage on her left arm. Blood had soaked through. Should she change it? Wash it? What would she use? She wished Delia were here to advise her. Lynette hadn't paid much attention when her sister had rambled on about healing and herbs. Of course, except when it had come to poisoning the king's officers.

A sour weight grew in her stomach.

No, she wasn't going to do this here, not now. It had happened, it was over, and there was no going back. Maybe this was why she was here, why she'd been shot by Dixon to be left to die only to be rescued by the one man she would rather never see again.

It had an irony to it.

She wished she had her cards to consult if only to relieve her boredom. They had served her well in the past, but she thought she knew what they would say now. They'd say she'd lost. The universe would balance itself out, and she was past due. This time, though, she hoped she would give it a fight.

Her stomach growled as she waited. By the time the door opened, she was pacing the width of the room. Mrs. Johns's presence sent pinpricks down her spine, though she did not decline the cool glass of brandy she offered.

Mrs. Johns tilted her head to the bed. "Rest, Mary."

"Excuse me?" Who was Mary?

The woman guided her to bed and covered her with far too many blankets for the summer temperatures.

"Mrs. Johns, can't I have something to eat, please?"

The woman's lips pressed into a thin white line. She nodded once and left the room with a click of the lock behind her. Lynette's glass rested on the dressing table, well out of her reach.

She stared at the glass, willing it to come closer, but she didn't want to be ushered back to bed. This woman was exhausting. Who was Mary? Lynette must have heard her wrong. She couldn't imagine any reason the otherwise silent woman would call her Mary.

A dozen minutes later, Mrs. Johns returned. She set a small plate of cake next to Lynette on the bed. Lynette had expected broth, maybe porridge. Cake to the hungry was a beautiful sight, and Lynette ate with abandon. It was dense, meaty, with no particular taste she could identify. She finished in a few bites and looked up to Mrs. Johns for more. The old woman handed her the brandy. She sipped slowly, pushing the last of the cake down.

"What was that? It was delicious."

Mrs. Johns gave her a patient nod. "Your favorite."

She squinted at the woman. The words were clear but made little sense to her. She had never had that cake before, and she certainly didn't know this woman well enough for her to know her preferences. Something was wrong.

More than wrong. On her next sip of brandy, she struggled to swallow. She coughed, handing the glass back to Mrs. Johns before she could drop it. Her mouth was smaller. No, her tongue was bigger. *Oh no, not again.*

She grasped her throat and forced herself to take slow, even breaths. Panicking would only make it worse. Without Delia, she would have to push through this. With as much calm as she could gather, she addressed Mrs. Johns.

"What was in that cake?" Her words came out a garbled mess of syllables.

"Favorite."

Lynette closed her eyes, trying not to focus on the narrowing space in her mouth. "Mrs. Johns, I need a doctor. Get Mr. Howell or Mr. Rycroft." She drew out her words, carefully forming them around the obstacle.

Mrs. Johns grunted but began her slow shuffling to the door. She tried the knob, forgetting she had locked it. She patted her dress, searching for the key, but found it looped around her waist with a ring of other ones. How was this woman in charge of housekeeping?

She lifted the ring and seemed to consider each key in turn.

Lynette made a tiny whimper, feeling the familiar tightness in her chest.

She would do this. She could do this.

At last, Mrs. Johns appeared to locate the key. She pushed it in the keyhole, but it only went in partway. She twisted the key with the same result.

Deep breaths.

It will pass. It has to pass.

Mrs. Johns moved her fingers over the next key and tried it. She grunted as her efforts met with success. Lynette threw her legs off the bed and pushed her way past Mrs. Johns.

Lynette pounded the walls as she went, unable to yell for help. Mrs. Johns muttered something behind her, but she ignored her. The paintings shook as she made her way down a long hall.

Her head grew lighter as she reached a staircase. Not knowing where to go, she attempted a step. At that moment, her vision blurred, and she lost her footing.

In the half moment between balance and falling, her stomach crowded into her chest as the panic won.

The rush of stairs came up to meet her. Shock slammed into her palms as they slapped the surface. Her body rolled along the thin carpet until she flopped, unceremoniously, onto her back.

And breathed.

She groaned, and hurried footsteps came toward her. She blinked up at the blurry figures materializing above her. The one closest to her was shaking its head. His head. She squeezed her eyes closed and open. The man leaning over her was missing his shirt. Her gaze scanned the surface of muscle and scar, not knowing what she saw but enjoying the view. Her eyes widened when her gaze met Rycroft's.

She tilted her sore head to the side. This was not how she had wanted to confront him.

The pain rekindled along her arm. She breathed in. She suspected her fear had outweighed the actual danger—a notion she had no intention of disclosing.

"Can you move?" Rycroft asked.

She mentally assessed her body. Aside from her previous injury, her hands and shoulders stung from taking the weight of her fall. Her back ached into her awareness as it rested across the landing. Her body was covered in bruises. She tested an arm and let it fall back to the floor. Maybe she could sleep here.

"Give me your hand."

She faced him once more and blinked up at him. The other people had departed, save Mr. Howell. He stood silently behind Rycroft.

"Must I?" she asked.

"Do you want to stay there forever?"

She sighed. "Your housekeeper is trying to kill me." Her tongue had taken over now, making the words a jumbled mess of sound.

"What?"

She slowed down and repeated herself.

He scoffed. "Mrs. Johns is harmless. What is wrong with your mouth?"

"Figs. Allergic to figs," she explained in as few words as possible.

He offered his hand again, and she took it without hesitation. The floor was starting to grow on her, an uncomfortable thought. He pulled and grasped her shoulder with the other hand as he eased her to her feet.

She winced as lightning raced down her arm to her fingers. Her free hand steadied her on the stair railing, and she peered up the stairs. She hadn't fallen far. Luckily, the landing created a break before continuing down further.

"Can you walk?" Rycroft asked.

She tested her feet and stepped forward in answer.

"We'll make sure you get back without falling on your fool head again. Lead on."

She cast a scowl at him but did as he said. She couldn't argue with him there. Her aching body took the steps one foot at a time and leaned heavily on the railing, though it was more from fright than actual need. When she made the top of the stairs, she stopped, unsure which way to go.

He came up to her side and gestured to her right.

She tried her voice again. "Briarwyck?"

"Yes, I know. Howell told me you want to send a message. I've taken care of it, but it's still early for a response." His voice was impatient.

She gripped his arm. "No figs."

"Right. Mrs. Johns will take care of that." He gazed down at her holding his arm but didn't protest. She pulled her hand away. It must be her addled brains.

She swallowed around the bulk in her mouth. "Locked?" She indicated the door to her room.

"I'm sure Mrs. Johns left the empty room unlocked." He moved to the door as if to test it.

She waved to get his attention and shook her head.

He aimed a smirk at her. "I won't go in there. I didn't take you for the modest type, especially after my conversation with Howell."

Howell laughed but kept to himself.

She took a slow, steadying breath. Why didn't he understand her? She stepped through the door and paused to choose her next words. If she had a piece of paper or a chalkboard…

Rycroft and Mr. Howell watched her with matching grins.

What was wrong with these men? She had just tumbled down the stairs, most likely waking them from their sleep. How was this amusing? She could have died.

"Room a prison," she said.

Rycroft cocked his head. "Is Mrs. Johns being overbearing?"

She nodded frantically and pointed to the lock.

He raised a hand to his chin and stroked it thoughtfully. "Has she been locking you in?"

She nodded with slow emphasis.

"Why, that must be quite difficult. Perhaps she was trying to make sure you don't fall down the stairs or get lost in the house? Perhaps she wanted you to rest and not bother yourself?"

Her face froze, and her hands dropped numbly to her sides.

"Little Harpy, that is what I pay her for. She is supposed to lock the door."

Before she could blink, Rycroft shut the door. She reached out as she heard the click of the lock and pounded on the door.

"Get some rest. We don't need you wandering the halls, killing yourself tripping over air."

The scuffling of feet told her they were leaving.

She pounded again on the door. "Please."

"Sweetheart, you're a guest here. I promise I'll unlock the door when the sun is up. Until then, we would all like to sleep."

She dropped her fist. His promises meant nothing to her. She was not going to get out this time, but there would be opportunity enough. Mrs. Johns would be easy to overpower, and they couldn't keep her here forever. Delia would send someone.

If Rycroft had sent the letter.

How was she supposed to believe a man whose own brothers didn't trust him? From her experience, he was a thief and most likely worse. At present, she didn't have much choice, but tomorrow, she would make damn sure she got out of this room.

CHAPTER THREE

ORTUNATELY, IT WASN'T long after the door was locked that
Mrs. Johns returned. The woman's sudden presence took
Lynette off guard, and she was unprepared to take advantage of
the open door. The housekeeper bore a tray, and Mr. Howell
carried a small square table, which he set just inside the door. He
stayed in the hallway as the door shut behind Mrs. Johns, who
arranged the table at Lynette's bedside.

The woman offered her a mug that reminded her of Delia's
concoctions, and she studied it with worn eyes. Mrs. Johns urged
her to drink. She shrugged, a rise and fall of her shoulder, and
tipped the mug to her lips. They would have killed her by now if
they wanted to.

It was sweet. Maybe honey? Her impression became of an
old, grassy taste and texture. She upended the mug, wanting to be
done with it.

Her eyes widened. The swelling was already receding. A
wave of relief rushed over her, and her chest loosened. She
thanked Mrs. Johns for the tea. The woman nodded and gestured
to the bowl of broth before turning to leave her to the sparse
meal. Lynette frowned at the bowl and thought back to the cake
she would never have. She took up her spoon as she watched her
escape open and close.

After her meal, she idled her time away, reading passages in the *Odyssey* and staring at the ceiling. Mrs. Johns had left her a lit candle, and it gave scarce enough light to make out the words on the pages.

A steady stream of sunlight grew beyond the curtains as she fantasized about strangling Rycroft. She found her injuries had lessoned to a dull ache. It must have been something in her drink.

A light tap unsettled her silence. She bolted upright and wondered if she was hearing things. A second tap confirmed the first. "You can come in. I can't very well open it."

The knob struggled on the locked door, then silence. The lock clicked, and a mass of dark curls peeked in at Lynette. The girl's grip fell as she opened the door, leaving it to swing toward the wall.

She was about Lynette's age and of a slim build as she was. Her tight curls crowded around a lightly freckled face the color of rich caramel. She wore a simple floral-patterned gown and carried a similar garment in her arms.

She made a pretty curtsy. "Miss Wolcott, I'm Margaret de Lacey. I came to welcome you to our home. Also, I brought you something proper to wear." Miss de Lacey's eyes were silver-gray like light reflecting on dark water.

Lynette returned the curtsy, unsure what to say in the unusual circumstances. "Thank you. I was told Mrs. Johns was the only other female in the household."

Miss de Lacey sighed and shut the door behind her, leaving it unlocked. "My brother says he doesn't wish to burden me. In truth, I'm bored senseless here. Instead, Mr. Howell offers to help you." She shook her head. "Men don't understand what it's like to be female in a strange place with stranger people."

"Your brother?"

"Max." Miss de Lacey tilted her head, and a small smile tugged at her lips. "Though we aren't related by blood. Forgive me for being blunt. Max's mother was not the only one unfaithful to her marriage. De Lacey is my mother's surname." Miss de Lacey stepped toward her and gestured to the bandage wrapped around Lynette's arm. "Let me check that for you. Mrs. Johns is an admirable healer, but she has to sleep some of the time."

Miss de Lacey studied the bandage and wound beneath. Lynette had nearly forgotten the injury. The throbbing had gone down, and the swelling in her mouth had occupied her thoughts.

"You were lucky. The ball took some of you with it but didn't hit anything serious. I think it should heal nicely, though there'll be scarring. Your fever seems to be over as Mrs. Johns assured me. I wanted to help sooner, but Max is a stubborn man. I confess he doesn't know I came to see you." Miss de Lacey slid the bandage back into place.

"Miss de Lacey, I don't mean to sound ungrateful, but do you know why your brother would lock me in here?"

The girl avoided her eyes and bit her lower lip. "Max is...complicated. I know he doesn't wish to cause you harm. He can be a bit paranoid at times. I think you'll have to ask him yourself." She held the dress out to Lynette. "Will this suit you?"

The dress came complete with underclothes and shoes and was embroidered with tiny yellow flowers with green stems. Lynette tried the clothes with her help, finding them a good fit, but the shoes slipped off her heels.

Miss de Lacey screwed up her lips as she studied the shoes. "They will have to do for now. I can try to get Riley to find you some better ones, but I don't know that I trust him to, since he can't tell the difference between a dress and a nightgown."

Miss de Lacey brought her attention to Lynette's hair. They opted for a simple, loose style to avoid the soreness of Lynette's scalp. Miss de Lacey insisted Lynette accompany her to breakfast, though Lynette had no interest in socializing with her jailers. In the end, her stomach made the decision for her, and Miss de Lacey assisted her down the stairs as a precaution.

They were halfway down when they encountered Rycroft going the opposite way. He was fully dressed this time, to Lynette's disappointment, wearing a well-tailored linen shirt and brown waistcoat and breeches. His Hessians were scuffed up but well polished. He stared at the women before resting his disapproval on Miss de Lacey.

"I asked you not to bother yourself with her." Ire altered his tone.

Miss de Lacey wound her arm more firmly in Lynette's. "This is my house too, and I don't appreciate your locking up guests."

"I was just coming to ask her down to breakfast. I thought Mrs. Johns had the keys. Where is she?"

"Max, Mrs. Johns needs rest. She's doing the work of five, and if you haven't noticed, she's getting old. I told her to sleep." Miss de Lacey spoke as though she was scolding a child. "Now, shall we go down to eat before Howell eats everything?"

He scoffed but turned on his heel and led the way to the food.

The green, patterned carpet of the upstairs gave way to the tiled floors of the downstairs. The way to the dining room was airy and bright, adorned only by a few landscape paintings and an unremarkable bust she couldn't identify. The dining room consisted of a long table that seemed as light and unimposing as the rest of the decorations. The room let in the natural light of the windows and faced a garden in an expansive yard. Mr. Howell was seated at the table, his plate stacked high with eggs and hog's pudding.

Breakfast was not as varied as she was used to at Briarwyck, but it left a comfort behind she hadn't experienced since home. She kept to the simple foods, avoiding another shock to her abused body. She was spreading a scone with clotted cream when Rycroft gasped.

"You're not putting your clotted cream on first, are you?"

She smirked and continued to spread the cream. "What of it?"

He shook his head. "You've been in Cornwall too long. Doing everything backward. Maggie will have to work hard to correct Carrington's bad influence on you."

She set down her knife and gazed at him through lowered lashes. "I'm not sure she will have much time to. Have you heard from Briarwyck?"

He avoided her gaze and faced Miss de Lacey. "You hear that? Our guest is trying to run away already. Never mind she was shot and almost broke her neck on the stairs."

Miss de Lacey gave him an irritated look and addressed Lynette. "Please do stay for a while. I don't get any female company. Max has his…friends over, but really, all I have is Mrs. Johns. I'm sure you're aware of her friendly manner. In truth, I think Max is right. You need a bit more rest before traveling."

"He didn't seem worried when my friend Abigail was injured near here." Lynette took a jab at him from their previous acquaintance.

"Have you ever tried to keep that girl in one place?" He shook his head. "Besides, I would have been pummeled by my brothers if I hadn't taken her back."

"What exactly do you think will happen if you don't take me?"

"Nothing of the sort. This is a different situation. I have Riley taking care of it as Howell can tell you."

Mr. Howell sighed. "I was in the room when he sent Riley. You have nothing to worry about."

"You see?" Rycroft helped himself to more of the sausage. "Is there anything else you would like? I'm afraid we didn't find your bags. I assume the driver took everything in the carriage when he fled."

"The driver left me?" The nerve of the man, though she couldn't judge him too harshly. She would probably have done the same. "What about the footmen?"

"It was an unfortunate situation. Greymore will be rather angry. It's too bad we won't get to see it when he learns of his misfortune." He thoughtfully nibbled the sausage at the end of his fork.

She raised a brow. He hadn't answered her questions. She would have to pursue it later. There was nothing she could do about it now anyway.

"My shoes could use a better fitting."

He nodded in a distracted way and said nothing.

"I can't help but ask, Who is Mary, and why does Mrs. Johns keep calling me that?"

Rycroft stiffened, and his hands clenched into fists. Mr. Howell and Miss de Lacey stayed silent, studying Rycroft's reaction. His hands slowly uncurled, and he regarded Lynette with a cool calmness that reminded her of her brother-in-law, Lord Carrington.

"Mary was my mother." He paused. "Mrs. Johns was her housekeeper as far back as childhood. Try not to take offense. She means well, but she gets confused." He rose from the table. "If there is nothing else, I have business to attend to. Maggie can send word to me if you think of something."

Mr. Howell sighed loudly and rose with him. Rycroft remained silent at his friend's displeasure and left the room on swift legs. Mr. Howell excused himself and trailed behind him.

Miss de Lacey met Lynette's gaze. "I know I can't keep trying to apologize for my brother, but you'll have to excuse his rudeness. He hasn't spent much time in civilized company of late. I must warn you not to mention his mother. He took her death hard."

Lynette tilted her head to the side. She was boiling over with questions, but the tired look in Miss de Lacey's eyes stopped her from asking. It was clear Rycroft had cherished the memory of his mother when he had gone to such lengths for the Travers family heirloom, a necklace promised to his mother upon Rycroft's birth. His pain, at that moment, had seemed raw like an open wound. Mary Rycroft had died years ago, but to her son, the loss could have happened yesterday.

Miss de Lacey continued, "Max and Howell should be gone much of the day. I can show you around the house, unless you would rather rest?"

"I think I would like to see some of the house, though I'm not sure how far I can walk." She swallowed the rest of her tea, hoping it would help with the trip. She didn't know how she had made it to the dining room, but she couldn't pass up getting a look around. It meant she may plan a route of escape if she became trapped again.

Plus, her fidgety limbs required release. She needed to get a glimpse into Rycroft's life. The man puzzled her. He lived with a sister who wasn't his sister, a mad old woman, and a band of friends that seemed to share his eccentricities. She thought the Travers family was unusual. Or maybe this was normal and her American family was odd.

Miss de Lacey wisely chose to start downstairs. Lynette leaned into her arm as they walked. They lingered over the portraits in the drawing room, and Miss de Lacey described each in painful detail. Lynette's eyes caught on a portrait Miss de Lacey had skipped over before moving on to the pictures of the two half brothers she shared with Rycroft. They resembled Miss de Lacey more than Rycroft, though they were both pale-skinned. It was a wonder he had been recognized as a third son. Henry Rycroft must be a tolerant man to take in his wife's son and his bastard daughter.

"What of your mother?" Lynette asked before she thought better of it.

Miss de Lacey seemed undisturbed by her question and continued to study the portraits. "Mother doesn't have a portrait. Don't misunderstand though. There was never a chance to commission one. My father loved my mother. I'm told I look something like her, but I never knew her as my mother."

"I'm sorry."

Miss de Lacey waved her apology away. "Never mind that. She died giving birth to me, and I have no memories to mourn." She faced Lynette. "She was a slave in Barbados. If my father hadn't stolen me away, I would be too. In a way, my mother died for my freedom."

"But couldn't Henry Rycroft purchase your mother? Set her free?"

Miss de Lacey shook her head. "Her master would never

allow it. My father and her master were not on good terms. Still aren't. There is tension between the families, since they believe I'm stolen property. When I said I don't get much company, I mean I'm isolated from everything. This house was built to be secluded."

Lynette stared at her, trying to absorb these revelations. "Your mother's master—he's still looking for you? After all this time?"

"He holds grudges. Maybe he imagines me as a child still. Easy to control. Max wanted to keep me from meeting you, but I'm tired of being afraid."

"I thought slavery was unsupported in England. That slaves couldn't be forced to leave." Lynette had admired this country for this very reason. It was something the colonies lacked. They sought freedom from British rule yet refused to grant it to their slaves. She found their reasoning hypocritical and morally lacking.

Miss de Lacey gave her a small, sad smile. "Yes, and I hope that holds true."

Lynette studied her. "Why are you telling me this? I'm a stranger to you and your brother. I could run and tell your location as soon as I leave here."

Miss de Lacey's eyes widened a fraction. "Do you mean to? I know I'm taking a chance. A big one, considering your relations. I trust my instincts with people though, and I trust Max would have left you lying in the road if he thought you were any danger to me."

"I would never. The thought sickens me. Not to mention I owe Mr. Rycroft my life. Why are my relations such a risk?"

Miss de Lacey took a deep breath. "Forgive me. I didn't mean to sound rude. It is no wonder you didn't understand me. I forget you're not so familiar with the sad story. You see, your being here is a danger in itself. When Miss Riverton was in residence, I had to keep to my room. Max was afraid she would let something slip to the Travers family. Again, he worries you may learn too much."

Lynette narrowed her eyes. "Why does that matter? Lord Carrington and Mr. Travers would never wish any harm on a young woman. I don't think I judged them wrong."

"The brothers are not such a problem. They are probably as unaware of my situation as you. No, it's their father—Max's father—the Earl of Aberlane. He can't know I'm at Rycroft House. He was my mother's master."

CHAPTER FOUR

L YNETTE STARED HARD at Miss de Lacey. She had met Lord Aberlane upon her and Delia's arrival in England, and he seemed pleasant enough, though her acquaintance had been a brief one. Yet Lynette had trouble seeing him as the source of Miss de Lacey's problems. She suspected there was more to the story, but it was cruel to deny a father the raising of his child.

"I had no idea." She shook her head. "There isn't much talk of slavery at Briarwyck. Or the plantations in Barbados."

"Or course not. Most people don't confront the evils of slavery until they're staring them in the face. I don't remember plantation life myself, but I have my father and brothers to fill in the details. That is more than enough for me."

Miss de Lacey gave her a small smile and brought her attention to the portrait Lynette was drawn to. It showed a fine-featured woman with upswept black hair and striking hazel eyes. The artist had captured her expression as one of warmth and acceptance, a woman one would want to befriend.

"Mary was the only mother I knew. You do look somewhat like her." Miss de Lacey pointed to the woman's features. "You're small like her, and your hair is similar. I wouldn't have considered the resemblance if Mrs. Johns hadn't taken to calling you Mary. You can see why Max reacted the way he did. Perhaps that's why I feel I can trust you."

"Really? I don't see a resemblance. Her eyes are such a beautiful shade, nothing like mine."

"Yes, I've always admired her eyes. They are like Max's, or had you noticed?" Miss de Lacey favored her with a lazy grin.

Lynette's cheeks heated. Of course she had noticed. She had noted far more about his appearance than she was comfortable admitting. She wasn't going to reveal this to Miss de Lacey or let him become aware of it. The last thing she needed or wanted was another scoundrel thinking he could take advantage of her.

She grasped for a different subject. "Miss de Lacey, I'm getting rather weary. Would you be so kind as to escort me back to my room?"

"Yes, enough of this sad business. You must be exhausted. Forgive me for selfishly keeping you. Let me show you back to your room so you may rest before dinner." She laced her arm through Lynette's and led the way. "Please, call me Maggie. Nobody calls me Miss de Lacey. It feels strange."

"All right, Maggie. You should call me Lynette." She tried not to pry, but she wanted to ask what had happened to Mrs. Rycroft. This feud was a puzzle to her. How did two families become so entangled in bad feelings? She suspected there was a long history between them but refused to let her curiosity get in the way of this new friendship.

It would be difficult to return to Briarwyck and face Lord Carrington and Hugh. Maggie believed they were both probably unaware of her, but she had said herself she was isolated from the rest of the world. Lynette needed to see her sister and consult with her on what she knew. Did Delia already know? She couldn't believe her brother-in-law would condone his father's actions.

It was easier to believe Lord Aberlane would hunt down Maggie. She knew little about him, but she thought Maggie told the truth. To Lord Aberlane and many other slave owners, Maggie and her mother were property, not people. It wouldn't matter to him if a family was taken apart, since he didn't see it as a family from the beginning.

As much as she told herself otherwise, she had grown tired from their short walk. By the time they reached her room, her arm was throbbing and her legs were ready to give out. Maggie sent Mrs. Johns to make some of her tea, and they assisted her to bed. She wouldn't make it back to Briarwyck in this state. She would be lucky if she made it to dinner.

Her prediction proved correct, and she missed dinner, but so did everyone else. A storm had built as they had during much of that summer. Rycroft and Mr. Howell had not yet returned, and Maggie sent up food to her through Mrs. Johns with a note telling her they would likely see the men in the morning and it was better that Lynette rest anyway.

Lynette took a place by the window to watch the storm and eat her dinner of beef stew and crusty brown bread. She snuggled into a blanket while the thunder rumbled through the house. The sporadic flashes of lightning moved over the countryside at the house's front.

Her meal was near completion when a man on horseback raced toward the house, leaning low into the saddle. He was blurry in the shadows, but a single rider in this weather was cause for concern. She dropped her spoon into the bowl and carried the oil lamp into the hall.

As she neared the stairs, arguing came from below, but the conversation was muffled. As Lynette drew closer, Maggie's insistent British accent became clear.

"Don't you dare. I forbid it."

A man muttered something.

"Riley's here. You can't possibly think he'll allow it," Maggie replied in her echoing voice.

Lynette rushed forward, but this proved to be futile, as all her strength went into reaching Maggie. The man dripped into the hall. His clothes clung to his body. It was Rycroft. Her gaze darted away from him as he turned to her. She peeked back at him, and his face was worn like he'd been coughed up by some beast inhabiting the countryside. His clothes were loose over the body she had, once again, been admiring. When he met her gaze, his brows lifted.

A scarlet scarf hung laxly from his neck.

Her eyes widened, and she shot back as fast as her legs would take her. She turned midstride and gained speed as she went. Rycroft cursed behind her and caught up without much effort. He grabbed her arm and made her face him.

"I don't have time for this right now. Stay here, and I'll explain everything to you." His sharp hazel eyes willed her to obey.

"As you explained before? Are you the Wyvern? I almost died because of you." She was ready to drop to the ground, but every instinct told her to flee this place.

"Never mind. I need to help Howell. Can I trust you not to do anything foolish while I get help for my friend?" He held on to her shoulders as much to steady her as to get her attention.

"Mr. Howell? What did you do to get your friend hurt?"

He sighed and dropped his head. "I'll tell you when we get back if you promise not to run off. I need to take Mrs. Johns and Riley with me to help him. Stay here with Maggie. Or will you force me to lock you in your room again?"

"You are not taking Mrs. Johns." Maggie moved to his side. "She would catch her death out there. Take me. I know just as much as Mrs. Johns does about healing."

He shook his head. "You know I can't do that."

"That's ridiculous, and you know it. Besides, you said yourself he isn't far. What harm could come of it? You have Riley and Bosworth to aid you."

"You women will be the death of me. Fine, Maggie, come with me. We're wasting time. He may already be dead considering whether Bosworth can follow directions." He released Lynette's shoulders.

Maggie rushed off, presumably to get ready.

"Stay here." His stern voice reminded her of a man ordering a hunting dog. He spun on his heel back toward the entryway.

She followed him where another man donned a long coat. This must be Riley. He was half a head shorter than Rycroft with flaming orange hair and gangly limbs. He scowled up at Rycroft as he put on his broad hat.

"I'm gone for a week, and you try to kill my grandmother." Riley's deep voice didn't align with his appearance.

Hadn't he been sent to talk to Briarwyck? Had Rycroft lied about that too?

"Mrs. Johns is a tough old woman. A little rain wouldn't hurt her. Besides, if you hadn't lingered on your way back, maybe you would have been here to look out for her." Rycroft watched for Maggie's return.

Riley scoffed. "Now you're being unreasonable. I need my entertainment."

"I assume you took care of it? I'd hate to find out you spent the whole week in a pub." Rycroft's tone dropped, tinged with a warning.

"What do you take me for? It's settled."

Rycroft grunted to the other man as Maggie reappeared in a cloak. She carried a bag with her, Mrs. Johns following her to the door. Riley kissed his grandmother on the cheek, and she spoke to him in firm, angry tones in a language Lynette couldn't understand. Riley's face reddened to match his hair, and he hurried to appease her in the same language.

Maggie noticed Lynette watching and gestured for her to come closer. "Mrs. Johns will be here to assist you if you need any help. We should be back within the hour, but I hope you will choose to sleep." Her tone was firm but motherly, and she nodded as though Lynette had given her agreement.

Rycroft gave her another stern look before the trio exited, leaving her to the company of the old woman at her side. Mrs. Johns shooed her toward the stairs, and they made their way at a crawling pace to Lynette's room. She exaggerated her weakness for the benefit of the other woman and hoped she would be left alone with this new opportunity to flee.

Either Mrs. Johns believed she needed the rest, or she was tired herself. Lynette was left alone in her room when her door lock clicked. She nearly screamed in frustration. Rycroft must have told her to lock Lynette in. Mrs. Johns was a confused older woman, but she was loyal and handled directions well.

To be fair, Lynette had every intention of escaping while they were gone. If she were Rycroft, she would have locked the door too. How was he to know whether she would tell everyone about Maggie and his identity as the Wyvern? She would never turn on Maggie, but she hadn't decided what to do with this new information about Rycroft.

If the stories were true, Rycroft was a notorious blackguard. From her experience, he was a thief and smuggler. He had also killed Dixon to save her, but it had been with such ease she wondered at his past. Not to mention Dixon would not have attacked her if it weren't for Rycroft robbing them. Would he have acted the same if she weren't connected to his half brothers? Or would she have ended up another victim?

She grasped her throat. She couldn't trust he wouldn't keep her locked up or end her life when he returned. As much as she appreciated Maggie, she didn't think Maggie had control over Rycroft. Lynette wasn't going to stick around to find out.

She waited long enough for Mrs. Johns to get out of earshot and stripped the bed of its blankets. The action sent a searing pain through her arm, but she ignored it. This might be her only chance, and Lynette wasn't going to let the pain and exhaustion win. She pushed the bed toward the window. It didn't budge. She tried again, using her body against the large frame. It gave and moved short of an inch.

This wouldn't do. She would have to try her luck with the length of the blankets. She tied the two slimmer blankets together, tightening them as much as her arm would allow, and fastened them to the bedpost. She needed more length if she was going to hobble away from the house in one piece after dropping from the second story.

Her arm throbbed anew, but she continued to tie the rest of the bedding together, adding the contents of the armoire to the long chain. When she could delay no more, she rechecked the window, but it was sealed beyond hope. She used the chair to wedge the door shut and lifted the small table over her head.

The table shook above her, and her arms threatened to give out. Her wound screamed for mercy. She released the wood against the window pane, and the window shattered under the table's weight. There wasn't time to celebrate. The crash could be heard for some distance. She threw her makeshift rope out the window with a silent plea it would be enough. The rope dangled, but its length dropped away into the shadows.

It would have to do.

She closed her eyes as she swung her leg through the window, being sure to move the broken glass away. She held the rope in a death grip and tried not to think of what might happen if her arms gave way.

One step. The rope lengthened under her weight. She gasped as she fell, dangling from the window.

She took a deep breath, and her heart pounded in frantic beats. She wouldn't make this. Her grip already threatened to leave her.

Her body dropped again, hands burning from the slide. Her skin would suffer, but this may be the only way.

Another drop; her heart stayed above her with the fall.

As she was no longer sheltered from the storm, the rain splattered her face now. Her hands slipped more freely, but she continued to hold on. Her stomach rose to her throat when she reached the bottom of the rope, and the ground was nowhere in sight.

She dangled for a long second, and the slick rope made her decision for her. She dropped into the darkness beneath her.

The ground came up to greet her, the impact smacking her feet to the side. Pain in her arm sent a cry from her throat as she tumbled over a patch of ground cover. When she finally stopped, she allowed a brief moment of celebration that she hadn't fallen to her death. She inhaled a delicious gulp of air.

Aside from during the flashes of lightning, it was impossible to see. She cursed herself for not finding a way to bring the lamp or even a candle, but that would have been a mistake too. Light would give away her location. She would have to make her escape the best she could before day.

She rolled over and pulled her legs underneath her body. Her arms shook as she tried to support her weight, and with the burning in her fingers, she guessed they were raw and blistered. She forced a great shove and straightened her legs to stand.

In a burst of pain, she toppled back to her knees. She must have injured her ankle in the fall. The urge to curl up on the ground and cry nearly overwhelmed her, but that would only make matters worse. She crawled.

With the occasional flash of light, she guessed a general direction and made for it. There was a silhouette of trees against the sky, and if she reached it, she would at least have shelter, maybe a hiding place. The ground shifted to mud, making her arms wage a battle against the earth.

She trudged on.

She contented her mind with imagining telling Delia about this foolish adventure. They would laugh about it, sipping tea in the garden. She thought of beating Rycroft with her one remaining shoe, the other having fallen somewhere under the window. Then she thought of Maggie and hoped she would see her again. Perhaps Delia could do something about Maggie's circumstances. After all, Lord Aberlane was her father-in-law.

In her musings, Lynette missed the drop-off in the ground. The area beneath her ended in a steep decline. She slid with the mud before she could stop herself. She hadn't the will to scream. Her body halted to nestle in some type of furrow along her path. Her attempts at regaining her crawl failed and drenched her further in mud. Instead of bursting into tears, she let out a hysterical giggle and couldn't stop. She'd likely die here. What were the chances anyone would find her before the rain drowned her?

CHAPTER FIVE

T HE MUDDY WATER inched up on Lynette's sides. A scream caught in her throat. All that came of her efforts to escape was more mud to line her new bed. After a time, she contented herself with sitting up. At least the chilled rain soothed her injuries, and the mud lent support to her ankle as well. Even if she were never found, she could settle back into the soft hole.

From time to time, lights came from the house, but the storm drowned out her cries. She no longer cared if the inhabitants of Rycroft House discovered her. She would take her chances. This storm would kill her if she didn't get assistance.

At last, a light came near enough to reveal a figure slipping in the mud in her direction. She called out, and the figure halted as though gauging the location of her voice. She called again, and the person came more quickly toward her. She hoped it would be Maggie or the new man, Riley. With her luck, it was Rycroft.

He frowned as he shone his lamp down on her predicament.

"Fool woman. Didn't I tell you to stay put?"

"You can lecture me as much as you want later. Help me out." She held back her tears.

"What if I just left you there?"

"You wouldn't."

He smirked. "What makes you so sure? It's a convenient ditch to bury you in."

Her frustrated tears mixed with the rain streaming down her face. Would he truly leave her to die? He could. Nobody would know what had become of her.

She pasted a plea on her features. "Kill me if that's your intention, but do it now. I was only afraid of what you would do once you returned. Get it over with. If you let me out, I promise I won't run again."

He ran his free hand over his dripping hair. "Why would I kill you after all the trouble Mrs. Johns has taken with you for the past week? I thought maybe you would do something like this, and I was only trying to keep you from the storm. At least you were going in the right direction. Did you know Rycroft House sits on a cliff?" They shook their heads simultaneously. "I didn't think so."

"What do you mean, a week? It has been barely a couple of days."

He sighed and set his lamp down near her head. "You were out for days, and you have been here for almost a week." He crouched next to the edge of the hole.

Her eyes widened. If that was the case, her sister must be frantic with worry. If Riley had gotten a message to Briarwyck, wouldn't there already be someone to bring her back? She knew it was less than a day's ride.

"What of Briarwyck? Have they sent word?"

He reached down to her before answering. She gripped his hand with her good side, and he pulled her up with the help of his other hand on her arm. His closeness sent her skin abuzz, and she hurried to release him once he had her settled across the grass.

"We haven't had any word. Riley reassures me he went directly to Briarwyck. He's reliable, though he gets distracted easily. When he tells me he's done something, then I consider it completed. There could be any number of reasons they haven't sent anybody. He didn't have a reply from them, since he was assured they intended to bring you home. My note mentioned you could rest here for as long as you needed. I assume they took that to heart." He studied her muddy form, though she doubted the scant light did him any good. "Now, Miss Wolcott, can you walk?"

She shook her head just as the lamp went out. Everything went black.

He let out a long breath. "Crawl toward my voice."

She scooted with hands thrust out in front of her as she went. Her hand hit something.

He yelped. "That was my eye."

She lowered her hands to the ground. "I'm sorry."

"Don't be sorry. Just give me your hand again."

He caught hold of her wrist and pulled her closer. He held on to her as he regained his feet. Her eyes still had not adjusted, and she wondered if they would. They no longer had the benefit of the lightning, and the moon was closeted away in cloud cover.

His hands traveled along her body. Her breath caught in her throat as he moved below her shoulders, and his hands closed under her arms. He made a low grunting sound as he settled her against his chest. One hand supported her back while the other lifted her legs.

She was grateful for the darkness as she realized how she must appear. Her clothes were soaked through, clinging to her body. Of course, his sight didn't mean anything if he could feel her through her clothes. Her cheeks heated, and she turned her head into his shoulder. He lent warmth to her body, and she sighed against him.

"You're slipping. Put your arm around my neck," he said.

She met his gaze and found his face inches away. Her own face bloomed scarlet, and her heart fluttered. She hung her arm behind his neck and clasped it with her aching one. She flinched at the motion but kept quiet, not wanting to upset him further.

"How is Mr. Howell?" she asked.

He ambled forward and slipped where he lost his balance in the mud. "He'll live. Thanks to Maggie. I hate having to put her in danger for no reason. We might as well have taken Mrs. Johns, since she's worse off than she would have been."

"What do you mean? What happened to her?"

"What do you think happened to her? She went looking for you, terrified she had lost you in the storm. She feared she disobeyed me somehow. A ridiculous notion, but she's soaked through. Maggie is looking after her now. Might I also add, not a good impression to make with Riley. You think I'm a scary figure? Riley will slit your throat before you can blink."

Lynette was at a loss for words, not wanting to apologize yet again. She held in her tears from before and gazed up at his face now illuminated by the house. He met her eyes as he reached more solid ground near the entrance.

Her chest clenched tight. "What can I do? Let me make it right."

She sensed him considering her words as his gaze roamed her face. When he shifted her weight, his gaze dropped to her chest. His eyes darted away, and he cleared his throat, drawing attention to her discomfort with the closeness of their bodies. He was as soaked as she was, albeit not as muddy. Her body hummed at every inch of flesh she touched through his sodden clothes. Her body flamed, and she clenched her eyes shut, hoping foolishly that it would hide her.

"For now, you can rest. I wouldn't be surprised if you opened your wound. There may come a time when you can help with the other invalids, but you need to be able to walk for that. I wouldn't bother to speak with Riley. You'll have to make amends through Mrs. Johns. That is, if he doesn't kill you first. Maggie though…" He broke off, considering his words. "You hurt my sister. For that, I should have left you in that ditch."

His words struck her like a blade slicing through her belly. She hadn't wanted to hurt Maggie. What she must think of her. Did she believe Lynette would betray her? Lynette's excuses for climbing out the window had disappeared back in the pit. Maybe he should have left her there. He was right. She was a fool.

When they reached the entrance, the house was quiet. She

caught sight of Riley carrying something up the stairway, and she cowered into Rycroft's chest. He noticed her reaction and let out a low laugh that rumbled through him. It should have irritated her, but instead, it set her more at ease. She couldn't explain her body's reaction to him, but somewhere between the muddy grave and the house, she had come to trust him.

He moved in the opposite direction of her room. She gazed the other way and back at Rycroft.

"Where are we going?"

He sighed, putting all his irritation and impatience into one exhale. "We haven't the time to fix the window in your room, and there's only one other room made up. Mrs. Johns is too worn to clean, and Maggie is helping Howell and Mrs. Johns. Bosworth is still with the horses, and I'm fairly sure Riley isn't going to leave his grandmother for you. That leaves me."

They reached the entrance to a room, and he settled her feet down before unlocking it. He pushed open the door with his foot. She leaned heavily on him as he inched through the dark and stopped to light a lamp set on the mantelpiece. The dim light revealed an expansive room in accents of rose and gold. A lady's room that housed a large, canopied bed opposite the ornate golden fireplace. Two wall-length windows occupied the far wall, covered by thick floral curtains. The rest of the furnishings consisted of a matching floral divan set before the first window, a vanity table between the two windows, and a square bedside table.

He guided her to sit on the divan while scanning the room. A tension settled between them that Lynette could only fill with words.

"What room is this? It seems too nice to be for guests."

He seemed not to hear her as he studied the portrait above the fireplace. It was a picture of him and his mother, probably the last they'd had painted. He didn't look much younger in the painting. She realized too late her question may drag up new problems, but he seemed calm enough.

"My mother's. It's meant for the mistress—I mean—lady of the house." She wondered if he was expecting someone or if he regularly let his playthings stay here? Or even worse, he intended to sleep with her. It was a vulgar idea to keep mistresses in his mother's room. Maybe he had meant his father's mistresses? That was no improvement. He faced her, scanning her expression and state of undress.

He seemed to have read her thoughts. "We don't normally have people stay in it, but Mrs. Johns keeps it clean in Mother's memory. A sort of shrine. I don't think she'll mind you sleeping in here for now, since she's confusing you with her." He glanced away. "I'll find your nightgown, but Maggie will have to get you another dress and see to your injuries. In the meantime, I do have a basin you can use in the adjoining room."

He removed a key ring from his pocket and unlocked a door set beside the fireplace. It opened into an equally large master bedroom in dark blue. She stared past him as he went to get the water. They would practically be sleeping in the same room. She cursed herself once again for climbing out the window. If this ever got out, she would be ruined. It didn't help there wasn't a decent chaperone in the house.

He had disappeared into the room, and he must have left by another door when he came back carrying her nightgown and the promised washbasin. He set them down at the vanity and looked to her.

"I ran into Maggie on the way. She'll be here soon. Can I get you some tea or cake? Right, no cake. Maybe bread?" He rubbed the back of his neck with his hand, and his gaze danced from her to the door. It would have been funny if she weren't so conscious of her immodesty.

Her skin itched in awareness, and she attempted to smile. "No, no cake. Please. Tea would be most welcome, but you don't need to trouble yourself."

"No trouble. Tea it is." He hurried out before she could respond. Why was he so civil suddenly? She'd expected a lecture or at least more of his previous foul mood. If he was trying to make her feel guilty, he was going about it the right way. She could handle any manner of yelling from him, but nice? She didn't know what to think.

She peeled off her mud-soaked clothes, paying careful attention to her ankle. Lynette's sore hands slowed her. Once down to her shift, there was a light tapping on the door. Maggie peeked her head in before entering and closed the door behind her.

"Oh, Maggie, I'm so sorry," Lynette said.

Maggie's face was expressionless when she set down her bag. She remained silent as she searched through it, pulling out bandages and a canister of ointment.

"I would never have told anyone. I just..." Lynette fell short of what she wanted to say.

Maggie raised a hand. "Stop. You're making it worse."

"I appreciate everything you've done for me. It isn't you. When I found out about Rycroft—" She shook her head. "I couldn't think of anything but escape."

Maggie's lip curled up on one side. "I mean, you keep tugging at your bandage. Stop it."

Lynette stared down at her hand. Sure enough, she was pulling at the worn cloth. She dropped her hand. Maggie made her way over to her side, her expression half-hidden by her lowered head. The air returned to her arm as Maggie removed her bandage. She sucked in a breath as Maggie dabbed at it.

"We haven't had this much excitement for weeks. I think you may give Max a heart attack." She suspected Maggie was trying to distract her, and she welcomed any interruption of her guilt.

"It can't be good for Mr. Howell. What happened?"

"To be honest, I no longer ask. I'd be worried sick if I knew what they were about. He was stabbed, but it wasn't as bad as Max thought. You know how men tend to exaggerate injuries. A cold turns into the plague. In any case, Howell is sleeping now. He won't be spreading terror through the countryside with Max for a while."

"What of Mrs. Johns? How is she?"

Maggie clicked her tongue. "Mrs. Johns is just soaked through. A little cold, maybe, but nothing a roaring fire and a cup of tea can't heal. Is Max trying to make you feel guilty about all this? Think nothing of it. Your arm is healing nicely." Maggie had finished with the new bandage and knelt to examine her ankle.

"It doesn't appear broken. A bandage will make it feel better. Try to keep it rested. There is a bellpull by the bed, though I can't be sure anyone will hear you. I'm sorry Max doesn't allow any more servants."

Once her ankle was wrapped, they replaced her shift with the nightgown. Maggie moved to the front of the fireplace and stared at the vacant opening. "Are you warm enough? It seems too hot in here for a fire."

A knock at the connecting bedroom door prevented her from answering, and Maggie opened it. "It's about time. Why are you coming through here? What is this I hear about you frightening Lynette?"

He grunted and passed Maggie the tea.

"Max, it isn't proper. Give me the keys, and I'll lock you out." Maggie held out her hand. He dropped them in her palm and started to turn away. "I'm not finished with you. What did you think Lynette would do, scaring her like that? It would have been better if you stopped locking her in. At least then she wouldn't be injuring herself falling out of windows."

"Look, little sister, this is my house too. How was I supposed to know she would do something so insane in this storm? Clearly I underestimated her desperation. Now can I please rest?"

"One minute." Maggie held up her finger. She gestured for Lynette to join her at the door. Lynette frowned at her but was able to limp her way over to the siblings. Maggie took her hand in her own, placed the key ring in Lynette's palm, and closed her fingers around them.

Rycroft watched with wide eyes. "Why?"

"I like Lynette, and I hope she will come to be a friend. If she

42

can't trust us, then she will surely try to leave again. I don't believe she means us any harm, and this is a chance for her to prove it."

He crossed his arms. "She'll likely kill me in my sleep or poison our brandy."

Lynette paled at his words. He couldn't possibly know what had happened in New York, what she had done. She grew light-headed and leaned into Maggie for support. Rycroft moved forward to help brace her when Maggie went to set the tea down.

He leaned his head down to Lynette. "I didn't mean that. I'm sorry."

She shook her head as he led her over to Maggie. They helped her get under the blankets, not caring for propriety in her distress. Maggie hugged her about the shoulders and then stood, Rycroft at her side.

Maggie slapped at her brother. "He makes terrible jokes. Think nothing of it."

She kept silent and stared off beyond them. She barely noticed as they let themselves out. Maybe it was true that killers could sense other killers. What would Maggie think if she knew Lynette had killed a man? In New York, she had friends, but they were always more Delia's friends than hers. She enjoyed Maggie's company and hoped she could count her as a friend too.

What if Rycroft found out? Would he throw her out for endangering his sister? She didn't think he would turn her in, since she knew he was the Wyvern. She supposed that was the advantage of knowing he was guilty of far worse crimes than her. Not exactly a soothing thought for spending the night next to such a dangerous man.

CHAPTER SIX

LYNETTE ELECTED TO stay in her room the next day. She reasoned she didn't want to walk on her ankle and trouble the rest of the household. Maybe they would forget her in her little corner. Better yet, Delia would send someone for her to end this ordeal.

No luck. Maggie came in search of her as soon as breakfast was over.

"We missed you at breakfast," she said by way of greeting. She insisted on examining Lynette before giving her the food she'd brought.

Maggie rewrapped her ankle and shook her head as she went. "It shouldn't be paining you. The swelling has gone down. Have you been able to walk on it?"

Lynette shrugged. She couldn't lie to Maggie after she had put so much trust in Lynette. Besides, the pain was mild compared to the ache in her arm. She was making excuses not to leave the bed, but she couldn't convince herself to confront them.

"What is it? Does Max bother you that much? Or Riley, maybe?"

"No, it isn't them."

"Then Max doesn't bother you?" Maggie gave her a funny, wavering smile.

"Goodness, Maggie. It isn't Max—I mean Mr. Rycroft." She

wrinkled her nose at her mistake.

Maggie's smile only widened. "Right. Then what is it?"

"It was something he said, something I can't talk about."

"You mean his little joke? Why would that bother you so much?" Maggie lowered her brows. "Did someone kill someone dear to you?"

Lynette let out a long, steadying breath. She wanted to tell her, needed to tell her. Her tongue was frozen in her mouth as she grasped for the words to confide in Maggie the way she had trusted her.

"I... I can't tell you."

"Why not? I don't mean to pry or anything, but it would prevent me from upsetting you in the future." Her smile faded, and her posture stiffened.

"Too many people could get hurt. My life and freedom could be at stake." Her words were out before she had fully considered them. Her friend's face fell like she'd been slapped.

"Of course. I understand that all too well." Maggie rose from her perch on the bedside.

"I didn't mean that. It isn't that I don't trust you."

Maggie narrowed her eyes at her. "Then what did you mean?"

She didn't know. She wasn't ready for this kind of conversation and didn't know if she ever would be. New York needed to stay in New York. How was she to explain this without offending Maggie? She stared after Maggie as she hastened out the door.

"I left some clothes for you if you feel the need to escape again."

Lynette flinched as the door shut.

What was she doing? She had just met Maggie, and their friendship had been fast forming. Maybe it was too much, too soon. She would be minus a friend before she even got the chance to have one. She used these thoughts to prompt herself out of bed and examined the clothes Maggie had left her. A beautiful teal silk dress sat on the divan. It must have been another of Maggie's. She had already ruined one of Maggie's dresses, and she'd responded by giving her a better one.

She bit her lip and steadied her limbs.

She dressed with more ease than she wanted to admit and silently thanked Maggie for including stays that fastened in front. She wanted to cry when she put on the matching teal kidskin slippers. They were the most comfortable shoes she had ever put on. Maggie had left combs and ribbons on the vanity table. Her arm forgotten, Lynette made quick work of her hair, tying back the thin onyx strands in a simple half updo.

Before she knew it, she was rushing into the hall. She almost collided with Rycroft when he exited his room.

He took a step back to examine her appearance, not bothering to hide his interest. "Feeling well now?"

"Much better, thank you." Her eyes lowered to examine the shoes.

"How do you like the clothes?"

She gazed up at him curiously. "They're beautiful."

"Maggie thought you would look good in them." He glanced down at her feet. "It was fortunate she remembered she still had them. Do they fit?"

"Yes, very well." She considered her words with care. "Mr. Rycroft, why do you concern yourself with my attire?"

"My sister came storming out of your room and almost ran me down. I was just making sure it wasn't the clothes. You see, I gave her those a few months back. The shoes were the wrong size, and she didn't have other matching shoes at the time. She's particular about that. Funny, isn't it? Stuck in this house."

She caught the warning in his voice. He must be angry with her too, and this wasn't about the clothes at all. She moved as though to go past him, but he didn't stand aside. She stared up at him, challenging him to say more.

"I don't care if you like Maggie or me. Don't pretend you do. She doesn't deserve it." His gaze jumped between her eyes and her lips. She wouldn't step back to give him the satisfaction of knowing he had made her uncomfortable.

She kept his gaze dead on and forced him to stare back. "What about you? Should I pretend to like you only to smash your illusions under these slippers?"

His lips grew into a lazy grin. "Sweet, you don't have to pretend. I know you like me."

Her mouth dropped open, and her cheeks flamed.

He burst into laughter and leaned against the wall with both hands as he lowered his head in mirth. She rushed past him and didn't slow her pace until she had reached the stairs. She realized too late she had no idea where she was going or even where Maggie would be.

She sensed more than heard Rycroft come up from behind her. He stopped beside her at the top of the stairway and watched to see what she would do. The amusement still played along his features.

"Maggie is likely with Athena. That is where she goes when she gets upset." He spared her the embarrassment of asking.

She tilted her head toward him. "Who's Athena?"

"Athena is her mare. Do you want me to show you the stables? Maybe you will decide to steal one of the horses this time?"

She lowered her gaze, refusing to respond to his goading.

"Follow me. Just do me a favor and don't take Hermes. He's part of the crew, and it took a good deal of trouble to get him." He skipped down the stairs, not bothering to slow his pace for her.

She had the urge to lash out, push him down the stairs. Instead, she called down to him. "Was it trouble to steal him, or trouble to steal the money for him?"

He halted on the steps and stared back at her with a dumbstruck expression. "I paid for him. I don't lack for money." He continued descending the stairs.

"I'm surprised at you." She caught up to him as they reached the ground floor.

His chuckle echoed off the walls. "I never said I paid fairly. It's bad luck to ride a stolen horse in my work."

"Who says that? How ridiculous. Why would it be bad luck to ride a stolen horse to rob people?"

He dropped both feet to the floor and looked back at her. "I say that. Riding a stolen horse would be like tempting fate. She may turn her head once, but you can't be sure she will do so again." He made sense in a roundabout sort of way.

She followed him out into the yard and tried not to watch his movements too closely. The man had a bit of a swagger like a conceited cat. It wouldn't do if he caught her staring at him, and she would never hear the end of it. Lynette needed to get back to Briarwyck.

When they reached the stalls, Rycroft led her to a burly man patting down one of the horses. Rycroft introduced him as Bosworth. There was no sign of Maggie. Maybe she had already come and gone.

Rycroft tensed. "Have you seen Maggie poking around?"

Bosworth scratched his head and looked up to the sky as though in conversation with some higher power. "She came through not ten minutes ago. Took Athena."

His jaw clenched. "What do you mean, she took Athena?"

The big man rubbed at his face. "Boss, I'm sorry. There was no stopping her."

"You're telling me you couldn't stop a small female from riding off when I specifically told you not to let her ride alone? Give me one reason not to gut you."

"You know how she gets. She was in a temper. What should I have done? Restrain her? I can't hit a woman. Even if I had, you would have beat me after she did." Bosworth threw out his hands.

Rycroft considered him for a moment and then nodded. "You make a valid point."

Lynnette stepped between them. "But where did she go?"

Bosworth's gaze went to her briefly and back to Rycroft. "I think she intended to head to the coast. I would have followed her, but she warned me against it. I was about to come up to the house when you came."

"Right." Rycroft sounded unconvinced.

"Does she do this often? Ride off on her own?" she asked him as he moved off to one of the horses, a dark-brown stallion with a white blaze.

"Only once before. We agreed one of the other men or I would accompany her when she goes riding. It took some convincing, but she usually keeps her word once she gives it. This isn't like her."

"Let me go with you. This is my doing, and I need to make it right with her."

He shook his head as he saddled the horse. "You're supposed to be injured. It would be faster if I went alone. You'd never keep up, and I don't fancy Riley or Bosworth would want you to ride their horses."

"Nonsense. Let me go alone, then. She will think I don't care if I don't go." She moved around to the side of the stallion.

He stepped between her and the horse. "You? Take Hermes? Didn't I just warn you against that? Besides, we have no more sidesaddles. You are wasting my time." He pulled himself up in the saddle and glared down at her. "Move off."

"Rycroft, please?"

He held out his hand, and she hesitated, sensing some sort of trick.

He rolled his shoulders back. "If you want to go, you'll have to ride with me. I will probably catch hell from Maggie and Mrs. Johns for letting you ride at all."

"Then why are you letting me?"

He sighed. "I don't know. My brothers will probably kill me for all the injuries you seemed to attract here. Call it a test run for your return to Briarwyck. Now give me your hand."

She put her foot in the stirrup and let him pull her up. She sat sideways in front of him, almost in his lap. This wouldn't do. Why did she let herself get into these compromising positions?

She shifted around, trying to find a better fit. "Let me face forward. I'd like to see where we're going."

The corner of his mouth twitched. "Sweetheart, if you're trying to reclaim some sort of modesty, you aren't going to get it with your skirts hiked up."

She sucked in a breath and held back from screaming at him. He was getting a good laugh at her expense, but he said no more as he led the horse out into the yard. He was an experienced rider, which made all too much sense if he robbed people on horseback.

He started slow and built speed as he made sure she was secure in front of him. She soon forgot his close presence and marveled at the rush of the air through her hair as it tumbled down. She wasn't as interested in horseback riding as her sister, but she could appreciate the beauty of Hermes as he raced toward the coast.

Never had she allowed herself to ride with this much speed and abandon. It was reckless, like tempting death. She laughed wildly, and for a moment, she no longer felt the pain from her injuries or the guilt that always haunted her. The crushing weight was lifted, and she could float along with Hermes. Even what was left of her pain seemed to disappear in the winds.

She peered back at Rycroft and sensed the same thrill that resonated through her. He stole a glance at her and winked before letting Hermes fly faster. She could fit a lifetime in that moment. A different lifetime, maybe. One where she wasn't a killer and Rycroft wasn't a detested villain.

The moment ended when Rycroft slowed and brought Hermes up to a stop. He helped her slide to her feet and jumped down. He scanned the area and bent down a few feet in front of them.

"What is it?" Lynette asked. "Why are we stopping?"

He lifted a shoe to her, a purple slipper not unlike her own. "This is Maggie's. She never wears proper riding clothes. I spend a fortune on dresses, but she doesn't usually lose her shoes."

"What do you mean?"

He examined the ground around the shoe. He strode forward and stopped at times to look around him. He gave a sharp whistle, almost as if by rote, and Hermes trotted up to follow him. He gestured for Lynette to follow him as well.

When she caught up, he mounted Hermes and pulled her up after him. His lips were a thin, tight line, and his eyes kept darting along the terrain. She didn't dare to ask what he was about. The set of his jaw made him appear determined, angry. The thought of this man angry was as comfortable as that of confronting a lion.

They rode on in a frantic manner. This wasn't the carefree Rycroft of before but the dangerous Rycroft people whispered of behind closed doors. She wondered briefly if he was insane but decided she wasn't helping herself by thinking so.

He cried out and set the horse toward a more determined course. A horse stood on the hillside, nibbling the underbrush. The mare was what she would have pictured for Maggie. A sleek palomino with an expensive-looking sidesaddle that complemented its golden coat. Her rider was nowhere in sight.

Hermes pulled up next to Athena, and Rycroft dismounted to grab the other horse's reins. He scanned the ground, but he appeared to have given up when he faced her. His brows knitted with worry.

"Someone must have taken her. There are other horse tracks but not much in the way of footprints. She couldn't have gone far on foot if she had the chance. She wouldn't have abandoned Athena anyway."

"You're sure she wouldn't walk off on her own? The horse seems mild enough."

He shook his head. "She loves every minute of being with that horse."

"You think it was Lord Aberlane?"

His eyes widened. "She told you everything, then?"

"At least everything about herself. Nothing about you."

He scoffed. "No, she wouldn't have. She doesn't like to talk about my activities. It probably would have saved us some trouble if she had." He reached up to her and helped her dismount. The touch of his hands sent a thrill through her body. "I don't know who took her. To be honest, several people besides Lord Aberlane would love to get me back."

"Why am I not surprised?"

He released her and stepped back. "I'm not so sure you didn't tell anyone. You have had the opportunity. How do I know you didn't send word to the earl?"

She clenched her teeth. "You can't be serious. I adore Maggie."

He studied her face with a suspicious cast to his eyes. "I don't think you intend Maggie any harm, but that doesn't mean you didn't help with her kidnapping. Were you meeting someone outside the house? Your injuries seem to have improved quite remarkably since your gallant climb from your window."

"You found me in that muddy ditch yourself. When would I have gotten the chance to talk to anyone?"

He grabbed her arm. "You could have climbed down there yourself." He yanked up her sleeve, causing a stretching sound that threatened a rip. His hands roamed over her bandage, and he examined the wound. She didn't protest, hoping it would put his suspicions to rest. "It's doing better but not as well as your ankle."

"You still don't believe me." Her sharp gaze clashed with his. "Maggie herself said my ankle wasn't as bad as it felt at the time. Why would I risk my neck to climb out of a window to talk to someone when I didn't previously know Maggie existed? How would I have even scheduled a meeting?"

"You're trying to get back at me for taking the Travers jewels."

She scowled at him. "That is a thin excuse, and you know it. I gave up on that stupid necklace a long time ago. Not that I believe you have any right to it. You're a blind fool. It would serve you right if I turned you in."

"Well, go on, then." He tossed her the reins to Athena. "Run back to Briarwyck and tell them all about the Wyvern and Maggie. Tell them about how we tortured you by forcing you to eat fig cake and pushing you down the stairs. Don't forget to tell them how you fell out of a window and nearly drowned yourself in a puddle."

CHAPTER SEVEN

LYNETTE STOOD FROZEN as Rycroft rode off toward his house. She arranged herself carefully next to Athena and stepped up as best she could. Her arm didn't want to support her weight, and she teetered in the saddle. Athena danced under her but stilled when Lynette soothed her with a few calming words.

She angled the horse south for a heartbeat but guided her back to follow Rycroft. He was some distance ahead of her, and she was already gaining on him. He wasn't going nearly as fast as he was on their trip down. She dared to believe he allowed her to catch up to him.

"Rycroft, please stop."

He glanced back at her and shrugged but slowed the horse's pace. Athena pulled up even with Hermes.

"I don't know why you'd think I'd betray you. I want to help find Maggie. I can't bear to think she could be in danger right now."

He sighed. "Try to keep up."

With that, he set his horse forward with the speed she had identified with Hermes. Athena seemed to understand her task and set to match her companion. Lynette wasn't sure she wouldn't fall to her death, but she let the horse race forward. Perhaps if she died, it would be her punishment for associating with nefarious individuals.

As soon as they reached the stables, Rycroft shouted orders to his men. Bosworth rushed to take the horses, barely giving Lynette the chance to get down. Riley met them on the way to the house, and Rycroft sent him scurrying away with messages. To Lynette, it sounded as though Rycroft was assembling an army.

He deserted her upon entering the house, presumably to check on Howell. She stood in place, windswept and lost. She settled on finding Mrs. Johns, which proved a difficult task. The housekeeper would have been easy enough to locate if Lynette were familiar with the layout. At last, she located her in the kitchens. Mrs. Johns stirred what appeared to be a stew. Maggie was right. The woman did too much work for one servant.

Mrs. Johns greeted her with a grunt.

"I'm sorry about escaping. I didn't mean to cause you trouble. None of that matters now though. Maggie was taken."

Mrs. Johns stilled her stirring, and her gaze scanned Lynette's face.

"It's true. Rycroft has gone mad."

Mrs. Johns nodded slowly and let the spoon drop against the side of the pot. She wiped her knobby hands on her apron and guided Lynette out into the hall. They met Riley before the entranceway, readying to leave again. Mrs. Johns said something to him in their unknown dialect. Riley eyed her and said something back to his grandmother. Mrs. Johns snapped at him with a few words, and he agreed. Mrs. Johns left them in the hall.

"Come along." Riley gestured for her to follow him.

She raised a brow. "Where are we going?"

"Well, Miss Harpy, if you insist on helping locate Maggie, then you need to be ready. I'm to gather the men. While I'm gone, you can start packing bags. We need a week's provisions." He looked her up and down. "That's your only outfit?"

She sighed.

"I'll get you some better clothes. No dresses. I think I have some of my nephew's things still."

She sucked in a breath. "You want me to wear boys' clothes?"

"It won't do for us to travel with a girl. Besides, my grandmother insisted on it. Change your mind?"

"No. No, of course not. I'm just surprised. What else?" Her mind whirled with the turn of events.

"Grandma will help you with food and supplies. She isn't as fit as she was, and things will move faster if you assist her. Most importantly, stay out of Max's way. If he thinks you're delaying him in any sense, he'll take your head off. I assume you know what I mean."

She stared forward, mute, as he gave her directions to his room and instructed her on where the items would be. What had she gotten herself into? She needed to get back to Briarwyck, not join a band of ruffians. But she couldn't abandon Maggie. It was her fault her friend had stormed off.

Riley's room was precisely what she expected. Clothes and papers were strewn everywhere, and the smell of old cheese permeated the air. She was in and out of the room as fast as she could manage. She found the breeches and a loose-fitting shirt, but none of the waistcoats would fit around her bust properly, making it all too obvious she was female. She settled for a long overcoat to cover as much as she could. Lynette completed her assemble with another pair of ill-fitting shoes—boots this time—from the unnamed nephew, a colorless scarf for her face that she left loose around her neck, and a wide-brimmed hat that narrowly fit all her hair. It took her the better part of an hour to braid her hair closely enough to her scalp.

When her transformation was complete, a dainty young man looked back at her in the mirror. She could have passed easily as a fop if she had the right clothes—a pity. Perhaps she could pass by Rycroft's notice as well—small chance of that.

By the time she made it to the kitchen to help Mrs. Johns, the old woman had completed much of the packing. She nodded approvingly at Lynette when she entered the room. They worked silently side by side. Lynette got the sense she had passed some sort of test with the old woman when she was rewarded with a warm smile after Riley came to collect her.

Riley raised a brow at the show of affection, but he didn't comment on it and gestured for her to follow him. "If you mean to go through with this, there are a few things you must know."

She agreed absently as they made their way to the stables.

"We don't use our birth names. You can call me Wren. When Howell joins us, he goes by Jackal. It would be better if you don't talk to Max, but if you have to, call him Wyvern."

"Why Wren?" She hurried to keep up with his long strides.

"Max fancies I'm good luck. I'm sure you are aware he has dubbed you Harpy?"

She sighed. Why was it she got the most unflattering of names? "Couldn't I go with something else? Wouldn't Harpy draw attention to my being female?"

"On the contrary, many of the men go by feminine names. It is a bit of a joke to Max. Keeps them on their toes. Besides, it's better not to try to go against his whims."

They reached the barn, where Bosworth was already readying the remaining horses. Riley stopped in front of a saddled Athena, whom Lynette was meant to ride.

"Riley—I mean, Wren—does this mean his men don't know who he is?"

"No, most of them know. We've found it's better to cast our identities aside. It's good for our purposes, but it may be bad for you. Men tend to do things they wouldn't normally do when they forget their names. Do not trust any of them, and do not let them know you're a woman. It would be wise if you stayed by my side."

She put her hands on her hips and frowned at him. "Then why bother to go at all?"

"I have been asking myself that same question. It isn't too late for you to go back." She heard the hope in his voice and resented the fact he implied she was useless. If a hardy old woman like Mrs. Johns thought she could be of some use, she would show this man and, more importantly, show Rycroft she could bring back Maggie.

For answer, she pulled herself atop Athena. To her humiliation, her arm failed her. A hand pushed her backside and took the opportunity to squeeze her unguarded behind. Once she was mounted, she rounded to slap Riley but came face-to-face with those dancing hazel eyes as Rycroft blocked her hand with his own. His amusement warmed her cheeks.

"That was uncalled for, sir." She filled her voice with as much ire as she could muster.

He cocked his head. "Indeed. I apologize. Perhaps you would like me to escort you back to the house? Or are you determined to flaunt yourself before a group of rowdy men?"

Her jaw grew slack. She wanted to lash out at him, but he had a point. "I can take care of myself. Maggie deserves that much from me."

He scoffed. "I warned you." He turned his anger on Riley. "What do you mean by bringing her along? She'll be trouble, a distraction to the men."

"Sir, she looks male enough to me. Your eyes are clouded."

Rycroft's sharp stare prompted Riley to continue hastily, "No offense, but I'm more afraid of my grandmother than you."

"This is that witch's doing?" He paused. "I should have known you wouldn't have come up with this stupid idea."

"Careful now. You're talking about my grandmother."

"That doesn't make her any less of a witch. Keep the Harpy out of my hair. She's going to be bad luck as it is. We'll have to keep her off the ship. You'll be my second until Jackal rejoins us." He continued listing off orders she could scarcely follow, his voice becoming muffled as he donned the scarf. She did likewise as the four of them exited the stables. Lynette and Bosworth took up the rear, and they rode south at a brisk pace that was at once uncomfortable to her unaccustomed body.

An hour later, she was surrounded by the strangest ragtag lot of men she had ever seen. Wren stayed by her side but didn't keep her from constantly second-guessing her disguise or her safety. They were split into groups to search different leads. Some of the men came from near Briarwyck in the southwest and claimed the way south was blocked off by flooding from the rain. It wasn't bad enough to cause concern, but Maggie's kidnappers could not have taken her that way.

The Wyvern would send one group by sea, a likely route if Maggie's kidnappers took her back to Barbados. Another group would check the rival smugglers, and a third group would check the way to London and the east. Some of the ground was already covered for them by the flooding, but still they had a lot of area to search.

He assigned Wren to lead the group to Bideford, where they had a ship docked, meaning he would send her with one of the other groups. A giant of a man called Bull would lead the men east with Bear, whom she knew as Bosworth. That left the Wyvern to lead the group against the rival smugglers.

When his gaze finally landed on her, he seemed a bit surprised she was still there, or maybe he had forgotten her entirely. "Harpy, you're with me." He gestured to the group behind him. She flinched at the moniker but did as he requested.

She stole a glance at Wren, who shrugged at her and beckoned the Wyvern to speak to him alone. Wren talked too low for her to hear, but the Wyvern's response was clear.

"No. You've the best chance with the *Mary*. I've a mind to strangle someone, and I can't do that on a ship." He meant to move away, but Wren gripped his arm, saying something else in his low voice. The Wyvern's eyes narrowed at Wren's hand, and a low growl escaped his teeth.

The other men watched this exchange with a mixture of fascination and horror. Wren's eyes widened above his scarf, but his grip never softened. She considered interfering but thought better of it. She would only make matters worse.

"I need to be able to reach everyone by messenger and nearby for when Jackal recovers. If you want to offset the balance, then by all means, take our newcomer with you."

The top half of Wren's face paled, and he crossed himself. He released the Wyvern's arm and turned his horse to leave, prompting his group to follow him. The group going east did likewise, and soon the Wyvern's group was left alone to confront his temper.

Her six fellow group members eyed her suspiciously, perhaps sensing the conversation was about her. When the Wyvern ignored their silent questions and rode on, the men avoided her. She remained behind them. This arrangement pleased her well enough, since she was still getting used to riding astride.

They rode in silence. The men seemed to sense their leader's continued poor mood. After a time, they became bolder and took up lively conversations that she was determined to ignore. She thought she saw the Wyvern glance back at her once, as though checking on her, but she couldn't be sure. Maybe it was wishful thinking.

The day progressed alongside the brutal ache of her thighs, and she longed for the group to take a break. She thought of calling to them to stop, but she had to maintain her guise as a man, and she doubted asking for rest would raise her estimation in these men's eyes. It was around dinnertime when the Wyvern called for a halt.

He was in good spirits now, having made progress on the ride. She sensed his underlying worry for Maggie, but he hid it well. He held back in the tight set of his jaw when he joked with his men.

She attempted to dismount but nearly fell when a hand steadied her. At first, she thought it was the Wyvern, but the eyes that met hers were an amber brown. He introduced himself as Lycan. The name itself sent a warning through her chest, and she stepped back from his grasp. He laughed as she stumbled, the sound resembling that of a bark. An appropriate name.

"You're new. A bit young to be riding with us. Where did he dig you up from?" He gave another barking laugh that became a wet cough.

She lowered her head and tried to ignore him and his prying gaze. She didn't think she could disguise her voice effectively enough, but he stepped closer to her, towering over her slight frame.

He raised his hand as if to cuff her. "Answer me. You wouldn't be the first newcomer I've broken in."

She flinched as his hand arced toward her head. The Wyvern caught Lycan's hand and shoved it back at him. An intelligent man would have backed down from the Wyvern's sharp stare. Lycan was not that man.

Lycan stood his ground. "Thought I would harden your cub."

"You will do nothing of the sort. I've lost good men to your interferences. Leave him be and go about your duties." A clear dismissal if Lynette had ever heard one, but Lycan didn't seem to care or understand.

"This one needs it more than others. Look, he doesn't have any weapons. Did you pull him out of the nursery? He would make a good plaything."

The Wyvern closed his eyes tightly, an act of self-control. If Lynette had a weapon, she would no doubt have used it already. Lycan was disgusting. Was he just one of the same from this sorry group? She would be surrounded by them for days, weeks if the search was unsuccessful. How did the Wyvern stomach this life?

"Lycan." The Wyvern's voice was all cool control. "You will go about your duties, or I will see your head on my wall."

Lycan stiffened, and with one last glare toward her, he stalked away. They were alone now, blocked from view by Athena and out of earshot of the group. She glanced up at his hazel eyes watching her. Maybe she'd been safer with Lycan.

A flash of metal sent her colliding with Athena in her retreat.

He sighed and extended his arm, presenting a smallsword to her, hilt first. She gripped the handle and found it surprisingly lightweight. She took a practice swing with the blade, and he shook his head at her.

"It's mostly for thrusting. See the blade?"

Indeed, the sword didn't have much of an edge to it, though she reasoned it could be sharpened enough for slashing if she had a mind to it. He untied a sash and scabbard from his waist and motioned for her to take them. She stared down at them, unsure what to do. She set the sword aside and fumbled with the sash. After watching her failed attempts, he took pity on her.

His scarf tickled along her neck as he arranged the sash around her waist, and the scabbard dangled along her side. She tilted her head mere inches to watch him work, and her face came within a heartbeat of his. He glanced up from his task and caught her gaze. Her heart skipped through her veins. They stood staring, daring the other to look away.

At last, he cleared his throat and stepped back, restoring the sense to her brain. This man was dangerous. He was just as bad or worse than the men she'd previously confronted. One she had ended up killing, and her sister had taken care of the other. She knew they'd both deserved it, but that didn't keep the guilt from looming over her. She didn't need another body to her name— that was, assuming she survived this encounter at all.

•⸻ ✕ ⸻•

CHAPTER EIGHT

T HE WYVERN SENT scouts ahead to check the rival group's whereabouts while the rest of them took a quick meal of bread and hard cheese. She sensed the gaze of each of them as she sat off to the side, perched under a tree. At least it was somewhat dry. The area the Wyvern had chosen for their meal was one of the only bits of land that wasn't deep in mud.

She waited for their interest in her to tire, which came when a reedy man recounted the story of his exploits with a barmaid. His account sounded like a gross exaggeration, but it kept them entertained and gave her the chance she needed to relieve herself. She slipped away, watching her footing as she trekked around swampy clusters of grass.

Once she thought she was out of view of the men, she found a group of shrubs to satisfy her modesty. Her eyes closed at the relief she found, having held her bladder for the better part of the day. She sighed, rearranged her disguise, and refastened her sword. The telltale signs of an animal rustled through the shrub behind her.

A cold sweat raced down her back. Did England have wolves? Wolf attacks weren't unheard of back in the colonies, but she couldn't picture such a threat here. Maybe a boar? She froze in place and waited for the animal to pass.

A hand went over her mouth, and she yelped into the moist

flesh positioned under her scarf. Another hand pressed her against a man's solid frame. She squirmed in his grasp, using her elbows to rain blows behind her.

The man grunted, and he slammed her against the gnarled trunk of a tree. Frantic energy scrambled up her body, and she sank her teeth into his hand. He punched her in the side, attempting to dislodge her bite, but instead, she gripped tighter and tasted blood.

He yelped but refused to remove his hand. His other one roamed over her body and stopped to throw off her sash and sword. He tugged at her pants, and she kicked out behind her. Her aim fell short.

Then came barking laughter.

She was dreaming. She would wake up in Briarwyck, and this would all be a nightmare that her confused memories had created. Soon Delia would wake her up and offer her one of her concoctions to calm her down.

She didn't wake up, and the throbbing in her arm told her she wasn't dreaming.

A hand slid down between her legs and stopped. Lycan released her and took a step back. She dropped to the ground and rolled off to the side. He was struck in place, staring down at her. He erupted in laughter. The sound contrasted with the hollow silence across the land.

He was doubled over, eyes shut in mirth when she impaled him with her sword. He stumbled backward from her, grasping the wound in his hands. She spit at him and planted her boot in his chest. He tumbled back behind the underbrush, and a splash followed his disappearance.

He struggled in a swampy pond surrounded by moss. He sputtered as his hands tried to find purchase on the tufts of grass growing from the water. She tilted her head and glared down at him.

He spit up a fountain of brown water. "Please."

"Can't you swim? A big man like you can rape a woman but

can't swim?"

"I can swim, bitch. This is a bog."

She folded her arms. "Such language."

He managed to get his head fully over the water, and he coughed and gasped for the air he was allowed. "I didn't know you were a woman."

"Just how does that make it any better? I should leave you here."

Voices called to them now. The Wyvern came up beside her and assessed the situation while his men stood back. Their movements were subdued as they realized what had transpired. Her hair and scarf had come down, and her soggy shirt was pressed into her skin. She had little chance of them not seeing her for what she was.

The Wyvern narrowed his eyes at Lycan and turned back to her. "It seems you have taken care of the situation. I wish you'd left me a punch or two. What would you like to do with him? Leave him here? We can fetch him out if you'd like to push him in again. I regret missing it the first time."

She smiled, revealing her teeth. "Oh, we may want to let the earth reclaim him."

"My father will have you hanged. Get me out. Now." Lycan splashed around as though he would thrash the water for trapping him.

She squinted down at Lycan. "What is he saying?"

The Wyvern waved his hand toward Lycan in dismissal. "The usual nobleman drivel. Think nothing of it."

"Nobleman? Lycan?" He must be mistaken. The man was as much a gentleman as a rabid dog.

The Wyvern's eyes widened at her in surprise. "Of course. Many of my men hail from the finer halls. How do you think anyone makes any money around here?"

She studied his expression for humor, but his face was solemn. "Oh, I don't know. Maybe farming. Rent. Trade, for God's sake."

He shook his head. "That's no way to make money."

"Damn it, Max. Get me out of here," Lycan said.

The Wyvern stiffened. "You know you brought this on yourself. If I had a mind to, I would have left you in a bog years ago."

"Why didn't you?" she asked him over her shoulder as she stepped closer to the bog.

"He's been useful to us. Never been much of a problem until you came into the group. I think you may carry a curse. There has been one disaster after another since I met you. I should have had Wren here to balance you out."

She scoffed. "Are you going to stand there or help me?"

"It's drier back here."

She inched closer, testing the ground as she went. When she had gotten as far as she dared, she streamed her sash toward Lycan, but it was too short. She glanced back at the Wyvern, and he studied her with a raised brow. The other men didn't offer any help for their companion.

She beckoned the Wyvern with a curl of her finger. His brows furrowed, but he moved to help, grabbing a fallen branch on the way.

"Lycan, you're wasting valuable riding time with your actions. I don't know why she wants you out of this bog. Since you decided to attack my Harpy, I suggest you apologize." The Wyvern hovered the branch out of Lycan's reach.

Lynette snatched the branch out of his hand and offered it to Lycan. His Harpy? As far as she was concerned, she wasn't his anything. This was no way to get a sincere apology out of anyone, and that was the only kind she would accept. Lycan was a deplorable piece of human filth, but she wasn't going to be the one to kill him. Not today anyway.

Once Lycan had hold of the branch, the Wyvern took it back from her. He pulled Lycan slowly toward them. The man dropped to the solid earth and looked up at Lynette with the wide eyes of a child.

"Thank you." Lycan closed his eyes against the tears that now rolled down his cheeks.

She bent down to examine the area around his side where she had stabbed him. He flinched from her touch, but the bleeding had stopped already. Perhaps the bog had been more of a blessing for him than anything. Whatever it was, the man smelled like the refuse of the city in the middle of summer.

"Well, Lycan, your smell has improved at least. I don't suppose you plan to attack me again?" Her boot nudged his leg.

He shook his head. The man must have given up. He mumbled what sounded like a prayer of thanks and kept his eyes shut as he drifted into silence.

The Wyvern advanced on Lycan. "You know, I don't normally kill my men, but you have made me reconsider that policy."

Lycan grunted in reply.

"Get up, or we'll leave you here. The scouts are back, and it's past time we leave." He turned to his men. "Outback, he'll need to be patched up. Throw him on a horse and be done with it."

A man with graying hair poked his head out from behind the group. He nodded and moved to assist Lycan.

"The rest of you, if you so much as glance at Harpy, I'll personally throw you in the bog. This time, she won't be helping anyone out." He directed a warning look at her. His gaze lingered over each of them as they gave their agreement. He dismissed them with a wave and signaled a retreat to the horses. She replaced her sword while following after them. He waited as she caught up and stayed her with his hand.

"You are with us one day, and already I'm out a man."

She shrugged. "How was I supposed to know one of your men likes young boys? Isn't that your job?"

"True. The subject has never come up before. Probably because I'm not used to having young boys or women in my camp. It's unfortunate because, as far as I know, the rest of them prefer women. You'll need to ride up front with me. You may also want to straighten your disguise for later. There's no way to predict what the other smugglers will do when they see your tight ass."

She lowered her brows. "What about my ass?"

His eyes crinkled up as his gaze wandered to the area in question. "It's a shame much of the view is lost to the saddle."

"You do know I just stabbed a man."

He patted the sword swinging from his belt. "Try it, love."

Her lips curled up a fraction. "You have to sleep sooner or later. Don't be surprised if you wake up missing certain body parts."

He choked on a laugh, coughing as he moved off to rejoin his men. "Remind me to get you a bigger blade, little Harpy," he called back to her.

The road up front was no different from in back, except now she had the lingering feeling that everyone was watching her rear. The Wyvern was preoccupied with his plans as they neared Plymouth while avoiding sinkholes and flooded areas. The trails they used were infrequently traveled, but the scouts had reassured them the way was clear.

At last, a lone pale house greeted them. By all appearances, it had been empty for years. Paint peeled off the wooden exterior, and the windows were clouded with dirt, preventing a view of the interior. Yet the men slowed their horses and fell into silence. The Wyvern dismounted and checked his weapons before approaching the front door. Half the group broke off, surrounding the building.

Lynette followed a few steps behind the Wyvern, too curious to exercise caution. He knocked with the back of his fist. He tapped his other set of fingers absently over the hilt of his sword.

A rustling came from inside.

"Wyvern?" the occupant shouted.

"Aye."

"Door's open."

The Wyvern muttered something to himself and stepped to the side of the door. She raised a brow at this, but he only gestured for her to do likewise. He twisted the handle from the side and pushed it open with his booted foot.

An explosion rocked the house.

Her throat tightened around the smoke, and she huddled into the Wyvern's back. She pulled herself away but not before he winked over his shoulder at her. She glared back at him. Of course he would find amusement at her distress.

He drew his sword, and an echo of swords being drawn went off behind them. She hesitated and did so as well. She didn't want to fight, but at least she could defend herself.

In one fluid motion, the Wyvern rushed the doorway. His men pooled in beside him, while she brought up the rear. A man sat at a table. His face was a wrinkled mess of panic.

"That was foolish." The blade of the Wyvern's sword rested against the man's throat.

At the table, the old man swallowed as if to escape the threat to his life with the movement. "Please, the gun discharged."

"Yes, of course. Your gun discharged before I was in view. An unfortunate circumstance. Would you like me to help you reload it so you can have another go?"

The men laughed and settled themselves around the table.

The man frowned at them. "I can load my own, thank you."

"Indeed, I know. You can stage kidnappings and smuggle good French brandy as well."

The man sniffed. "I don't know what you're talking about."

"I know who you are, Jasper. I've known for years. How do you think I was able to intercept so many of your transports? My compliments on the brandy. It's fine stuff."

"You've cost me a fortune. What do you want?"

"My good fellow, you get right to the point." The Wyvern chuckled as he let the blade draw blood. "Someone very dear to me is missing, and I mean to have her back."

"I don't have your whore." Jasper sneered, revealing crooked yellow teeth.

The Wyvern held his calm, but his men reacted as though they read the fury behind his scarf. They raised pistols and swords toward the offender. Jasper cowered into himself, favoring the

Wyvern with narrowed eyes.

"Aw, but I think you know where she may be. If death isn't incentive enough, let me throw in a bit of coin as well."

"You can take your coin and get out of my house."

The Wyvern cocked his head, examining Jasper as one might a horse. He reached into a pocket in his overcoat, brought out a purse, and upended it on the table. Coins were strewn across the surface. The man blinked down at the money as though unsure of his own eyes.

"Where do you come upon such money? There must be at least five hundred pounds here." Jasper's voice transformed to a dry croak.

"Never mind that. Take the coins and your life. Tell me where the girl is."

Jasper's gaze went from the Wyvern to the coins and back again as though he was hesitating. The Wyvern sighed and drew out another purse. Jasper's eyes widened at the sight as the Wyvern dumped it over the table.

"Fine, but you haven't heard it from me," Jasper said. "Old Jack came by not an hour ago. Said he just got back from a run up north."

"And who was he working for?"

Jasper rubbed his week-old beard.

The Wyvern cleared his throat.

"Old Jack took the job from another smuggler, new guy. Hubert? Henderson? I can't remember his name. Seems it was an animal name. Hare? Any case, Old Jack went off down to Plymouth afterward."

"Hawke?"

"Aye. Hawke, that's the one."

"Did he take the girl down to Plymouth?"

Jasper shook his head. "He parted ways with the others before he visited here. He didn't say where they were going but complained about not wanting to go through Exmoor."

The Wyvern snorted. "His wife lives around Exmoor."

"Aye."

"Any other things you'd like to add? If I find out you've been holding back on me, I'll send Harpy here to slit your throat. He's small but quick as a viper."

Lynette stayed silent. She folded her arms and glared at both of them. What made him think she would let him send her anywhere?

Jasper stared at her with wide eyes and shook his head.

"Good." The Wyvern patted Jasper on the back. "We'll need some brandy for the road. Can't make this a wasted trip."

Jasper started to protest, but the men were already searching the one-room house. The area was sparse, the table and chair being the majority of the furniture. A small bed lined the far wall. She doubted he lived there at all. Outback found a loose board in the floor and gave a cry of success. He passed out bottles of brandy as they surrounded him. The Wyvern gave Jasper another pat as though to congratulate the man they were robbing.

"Come, Harpy. Let the man count his coins." The Wyvern headed out the door.

The horses were as they'd left them, obediently awaiting their return. Lynette spoke to the Wyvern. "How did you come up with that much money to throw about?"

"What money?"

"The money you poured all over the table."

"I didn't pour any money on any table."

Her brows formed an inverted *v*, and she placed her hands on her hips. "Fine, what did you pour on the table?"

"Coins."

"But not money?" She made a sound at the back of her throat. "I don't understand."

"Never waste good money when you have fake money. Also, never give up your money—fake or otherwise—when you can use someone else's."

Her hands dropped. "You gave him fake coins that don't belong to you?"

He scoffed. "They were real coins, just fake money. And, sweet, you'll find I don't remember half of what belongs to me. It's neither here nor there." He ignored the look of slack-jawed outrage from her and mounted Hermes. He whistled, which appeared to signal the men it was time to depart.

Lynette was still shaking her head as she did as he commanded, not sparing a thought for why she was doing it.

CHAPTER NINE

THE SUN HAD just vanished over the horizon when the Wyvern ordered them to set up camp. She suspected he wanted to get as far away from Jasper as possible before resting. To her relief, nobody bothered to assign her a task. She had been afraid they would make her do the cooking once they found out she was female. A good thing, since she knew next to nothing about cooking, let alone campfire cooking.

Instead, the Wyvern was the one preparing their food while the rest of the men made camp. One of the scouts had caught a hare earlier in the day, and it was cooking over the campfire. The Wyvern had rubbed it with herbs from a pouch he kept in his saddlebags. The meat smelled of rosemary and smoke, and her stomach growled in anticipation.

The men were in high spirits with the addition of fresh meat and fine brandy. They added leftover bread to round out their meal and gathered loosely around the fire. One of them offered her brandy, and not wanting to be rude, she took a gulp.

She grimaced and tightened her eyes shut against the unfamiliar taste, and the group of men burst into peals of laughter.

The Wyvern drank little. Instead, he watched his men, amused in their merriment but not joining their drunken states. Although Lycan had ridden off from the group, the distressing memory of what had happened was enough for Lynette to keep near the Wyvern's side. Lycan had been dangerous sober, as were these men. She couldn't imagine what they were capable of drunk.

She caught the Wyvern's gaze. "Where will we go now, sir?"

"Is it 'sir' now? Not 'scoundrel'? Or 'blackguard'?"

She was trying to be civil. "Would you prefer that?"

"Hmm, you know, nobody has ever asked me before. I suppose any one of them would do. Adds a bit of danger to my reputation."

She studied him as he tended the fire. He poked absently at the wood. "Is that so important?" she asked. "What if I called you 'my lady'? Would people think you an elegant woman?"

He looked up, amusement dancing in his eyes. "On the contrary, I think people would find me ruthless and bloodthirsty. Noble ladies are some of the most dangerous creatures in existence."

She leaned toward him, arms resting on her elbows. "You still haven't answered my question."

"I was enjoying discussing what names you might call me, but I suppose we can explore that later." He waved his hand before him. "Exmoor is a vague expanse of land. I can't be sure where to find Hawke. Hopefully, Bull has had some leads. I plan to send some men ahead of us to both groups to exchange details. In the meantime, we'll head back north. Either way, we would need to be near Rycroft House or Exmoor."

"Who was that man Jasper?"

"My competition and predecessor. He should have retired by now. He's brilliant at smuggling but not so bright when it comes to money. By all rights, he should be rich by now." He sounded regretful.

"So you help him spend it?"

He laid a palm on his chest as though he was offended. "I put it to good use. He would just waste it."

She hesitated before asking the dreaded question she had been avoiding. "What about the Travers family? Might they know what happened to Maggie?"

He lowered his brows, and his voice deepened. "I doubt any of them would do the lifting work. If anything, they might have hired Hawke to take her. If it was them, we know where she'll be taken, but what we need to know is where she is now."

"I'm sorry. I know they're a sensitive topic, but I can't help but wonder, since they are my relatives too." She chose each word with care. "I could talk to them. You don't have to involve yourself."

His gaze wandered over to his uproarious men. "Listen, sweet, if it comes down to their guilt, it would be better if you were by my side."

"Do you mean to hold me against my will, then? Trade me for Maggie?"

His eyes shot back to her as he flinched back like she had slapped him across the face. "The thought hadn't occurred to me. I'm glad I know what you think of me though." He got to his feet, brushed off his pants, and wandered off beyond the camp.

She stared after him, uncertain whether she should follow and apologize or let him stew. He had done something similar when he had brought back Abigail, wanting to trade her for the family jewels. Lynette hadn't thought he would find offense in her suggestion. Just when she believed she understood him, he did something completely unexpected. She'd never thought it would bother her, but she wanted his good opinion. It didn't help she counted on him for her safety.

She arranged her blanket away from the men and lay back, staring into the expanse of stars. She wondered if Maggie was looking up at the same sky, terrified she would never see her home again. Would Lynette see her own home again? New York wasn't safe for her and not just because of the war. She was one step ahead of her violent past.

Yet New York no longer felt like home to her, but Briarwyck was little better. She didn't have the sense of safety that came with belonging. She envied Delia's unexpected happiness after the turmoil she had experienced. Even Abigail seemed to have found her own place in the world. Had fortune passed her over for more deserving subjects?

She woke with a jolt, the sun blinding her as she opened her eyes. An unfamiliar blanket rested over her. She peered around through squinted eyes at the ruined mess of the fire, and the vacant ground where the men had slept.

Her breath caught, and she sat up.

"Relax," the Wyvern's voice came from behind her.

She twisted around to face him. He stood not far off, brushing Hermes. He wore the same clothes as the day before, but his scarf rested around his neck. He hadn't shaved recently, stubble dusted along his chin and upper lip. The rough look suited him.

The effect woke a stirring deep in her belly.

"It's nearly noon. Why didn't you wake me?"

He shrugged. "You needed the rest, and we aren't in any hurry yet. We can't go anywhere without a clear destination. We'll start off in a bit. I sent half the group up ahead."

"To Wren and Bull?"

He nodded, distracted by the horse nuzzling him. He petted and murmured to the horse as though he was his firstborn. She found herself idly wondering what it would be like to be Hermes. Nobody had ever loved her like that. She mentally kicked herself for being jealous of a horse. His horse. The man despised her. How could she consider such a thing?

"Can I ask you something?" she ventured.

He let out a long breath, an attempt to show his displeasure, no doubt. "By all means. It hasn't stopped you before, though I may not answer you."

"It's nothing. I only wondered why you go by Wyvern. You choose the names, right?"

He smirked toward Hermes. "You think I'm self-absorbed enough to name myself after a dragon?"

"Yes."

He chuckled and fed Hermes something out of his hand.

She'd never seen such a spoiled horse. "You're right: I am."

"But why Wyvern?"

He leaned his head against the horse, then tilted his gaze toward her. "Why? Because Hermes was taken."

"Be serious. I already know you're in love with your horse."

"I'm dead serious. I should have named myself before my horse. Wyvern sounds better than Winged Serpent, Caduceus, or even Rooster. How else am I supposed to honor the patron of thieves?"

She frowned and then broke into uncontrollable giggles. "Oh, you are serious. That is too much. I think Rooster would have suited you nicely."

He straightened at that and moved to join her where she sat. "Have you found a better name for me, sweet? What exactly gives you that impression? Remember, I would know if we were that closely acquainted." He leaned toward her, awaiting her response.

Instead of showing offense, which was what he expected, she looked up at him through her eyelashes and smiled sweetly. "Well, Wyvern, roosters are rather...cocky. The Wyvern is a perfectly nice name, but it seems a bit grandiose. A more modest name like Rooster would draw far fewer assumptions into people's minds."

He raised a brow. "What assumptions, pray tell?"

Her grin broadened as she fought to keep in her laughter. "That you are trying to overcompensate for something."

His lips twitched between a frown and a grin. "That, my sweet, I have never been accused of."

She dropped her gaze to her lap and pretended to examine her hands. "Oh, I don't know. At least, not to your face. Of course, I cannot possibly imagine what goes on in men's minds, but women, now, women I know. I'm sure the ladies speak about you behind their fans and giggle. They say, 'He must be trying to make himself feel better, poor thing.'" She shook her head, feigning disgust. She glanced up to see his reaction, and her head nearly collided with his. He had been creeping closer the whole time. He didn't flinch, nor did he blink as he tracked her motions.

"What do you believe?" he said in an outtake of air, inches from her face.

Her gaze found his lips. She was unsure where she was going with this or what she was doing. "I prefer to form my own opinions."

His jaw slackened as though he was at a loss for words. She doubted he had expected her answer. Perhaps he was trying to intimidate her? She had the strangest urge to move the last few inches to take his lips with hers. He made the barest of movements toward her, but approaching footsteps sent them both scrambling backward.

The identical pair of men approaching watched them with knowing brown eyes and wide grins. The Wyvern scowled at them, and they attempted to school their faces. The twins were so alike she wondered how she hadn't noticed them before. Dirt caked their skin, which matched their tawny brown hair. They were shorter than the Wyvern by a couple of inches, but they shared the same strong, seafaring form.

"What?" The Wyvern ran a hand over his head.

"You asked to know when it was time," the braver one said.

"So I did." He straightened like a tired cat and stretched in one fluid movement. "Pack up, Harpy. Athena is ready."

He collected the rest of the cooking instruments before she rolled to her knees. Soreness encompassed every inch of her skin, though the pain in her arm was less, as it was each day when she wasn't abusing it. She moaned as her movement stretched the stiffness in her body from sleeping on the ground. The Wyvern froze as she let out another moan while she stood. He looked away from her, and a small smile tugged at her lips.

The four of them headed north. She rode side by side with the Wyvern and learned the so-called Wyvern names of the remaining men in their party. The Wyvern had fondly dubbed them Romulus and Remus after the twin brothers from Roman mythology. She laughed at him outright when he told her. Clearly the man had a theme.

"Does that mean they will commit fratricide?" She spoke through her smile.

"I often wonder. They're at each other's throats most of the time. We have a bet going to see who will kill the other."

She glanced over at him, brows raised. "You wouldn't. That's horrid."

He met her eyes, sporting a cheeky grin. "One day, we might just discover who is our real Romulus."

"Stop teasing me. You can't mean you'd let your men kill each other. You're barbaric." She trained her eyes on the road ahead and tried not to rise to his nonsense.

"You wound me, madam." He raised his voice and cried out, "These are not men but a pack of wolves."

Romulus and Remus let out triumphant cheers behind them. She shielded her mouth with her hand, trying to suppress the amusement the Wyvern had already noticed. It would be better if she stopped talking to him. Conversation would only lead to getting closer to him, and already that was becoming a problem. She didn't need the heartbreak again.

Not ever.

Instead, she busied herself watching the countryside in its vibrant green stillness. Although the fields were calm, there was a restlessness to the hills. The air itself promised an awakening she couldn't place. Time passed quickly once she joined the rush and flow of the landscape, and before she knew it, the sky beside them was awash in clouds of the brightest yellows and oranges. Her gaze lingered on the scene as the clouds transformed to the softest of violets and then a deep navy.

"Harpy, you're going to lead Athena astray." The Wyvern's voice was full of amusement.

"I can't help it. I wish I had my paints." She made an effort to face forward.

"You paint?" The disbelief coated his tone.

She straightened in her saddle. "I dabble. I can't seem to finish anything, but it passes the time. Briarwyck is a dull place when there isn't a murder."

"You sound like Maggie. She's always complaining about the dullness of Rycroft House. I'm sure she didn't mean she wanted this though."

The dying light receded from his slumped form atop Hermes. Her stomach clenched at seeing him so dejected.

"This isn't your fault, you know." She darted her eyes from the road, to him, and back, attempting to catch his gaze.

"You don't know that. I could have been more careful. Made a few fewer enemies."

"What would you have done? Locked her up as you did me? How well did that work for you? Maggie would have been far more rebellious than I have been. It would have destroyed her if she didn't kill you."

He snorted.

She continued in a firmer voice, "Stop feeling sorry for yourself. We'll get her back, and she'll return to lecturing you about what a fool you are."

A silence fell over their group. Had she gone too far? It wouldn't do if he moped. Maggie needed him to be strong. His men needed him to lead, and she needed him to see her home safely when this mess was over.

At last, he faced her, but she wished he hadn't. His face was stone, but his eyes sparked with anger.

"What of you, Harpy? What of the guilt for whatever you did to drive her off? Then you carelessly plant yourself in the middle of a group of dangerous men. What help would you have been to Maggie if Lycan had gotten his way? I'd tell you, but you wouldn't sleep at night again if I did. The world isn't all ball gowns and gossip, but I suppose I can't expect a cosseted chit like you to see that."

Wetness trickled down her cheeks before she realized she was crying. She registered his words, but all she saw was the arrogant face of Lieutenant Forrest forcing himself on her. The Wyvern had no idea how wrong he was.

The twins had ridden up on either side of them. One of them (Remus?) gestured for her to fall back with him. She would have preferred stopping, but she contented herself with slowing Athena instead. She held her face now, trying to conceal the sobs escaping through her fingers.

The Wyvern and Romulus fought ahead of them, but she didn't care to hear what they said. Her breathing calmed, her tears quieting enough for her to understand what Remus was saying.

"If you were one of his men, you'd be bleeding by now. Unless maybe you were Jackal or Wren." He watched her with concerned eyes.

"Why? Because I criticized him?"

"Not so much. He can take a great deal of criticism. It was the way you went about it. Maggie is the only one I have seen get away with bossing him around, and now you."

"I didn't get away with anything. He still attacked me." Her face was dry now, and she pulled her scarf up to hide the rest of the damage. There was nothing to be done about her eyes, which would be a mess.

"That was mild—a fallen man lashing out. I'm sure he didn't realize what the impact of his words would be. I can only guess he brought up an old wound. I won't venture to ask."

Her chest loosened. "Thank you."

The men in front of them slowed, forcing them to follow suit. Galloping hoofbeats became apparent, growing louder as they approached. The Wyvern called out to them, recognizing his men. They met moments later, with Wren joining up with him. She was still out of earshot, but Wren's face was downcast.

Wren glanced toward her, and his tone became lecturing. Romulus had joined the discussion, adding bits here and there. The Wyvern gave short, angry replies. At last, the Wyvern pushed past them with Hermes, escaping their attacks. If Remus was correct, the men were insane.

As though sensing her interest, Wren came to join her and studied her face.

"Aren't you back rather soon?" she asked him before he could comment on her eyes.

"The *Mary* was blocked in. We never made it out."

A whistle came from in front of them. The Wyvern had struck camp. Athena walked forward, and Wren kept pace with her.

"So that's it, then? What if they have Maggie on a ship?" Her voice sounded more outraged than she had intended.

"I've sent a smaller boat to patrol the coast, but it appears to be a waste. We got word from Bull's group on our way. They were ambushed and had to flee but not before they spotted Maggie."

CHAPTER TEN

"I DON'T UNDERSTAND. Why didn't they pursue?" Lynette asked Wren as they reined in their horses to join the rest of the camp for the night.

"They were outnumbered by then. Bull sent someone, I think Tempest, to follow at a distance. Fortune must have smiled on them." He dismounted and reached out to take Athena's reins.

She swung her legs down from the horse and groaned at the ache in her back and thighs. He steadied her as her legs failed, holding her by the waist. She found herself wishing he were someone else. A girlish dream.

She gazed up at Wren as his hands lingered. "How many of them are left?"

He put distance between them. "Four. They went on to Rycroft House to regroup. Perhaps Jackal will be healed enough to join us. Don't trouble yourself. They knew what they were getting into." He studied her, a curious light in his eyes. His mouth was partially open as though he wanted to ask a question. She wished he would put on his scarf. He was going to catch flies.

She edged away from him just as the Wyvern joined them.

"Wren, Remus is asking for you. Something about a bet. Which, by the way, I'm hurt I was left out of one." The Wyvern favored Wren with a scowl.

Wren grinned and slapped the Wyvern on his shoulder. "You

know why we don't include you. Same reason nobody wants to play cards with you. We're tired of losing."

Lynette perked up at the mention of cards. "Is someone carrying a deck of cards? I seem to have misplaced mine back when wolves robbed me. What did become of my things?"

The Wyvern blinked down at her as if he just realized she was there. "Your things are back at the house. I think most of us carry cards, though mine get little use these days. What do you want with cards? I doubt the men want to play whist."

She glared at him and crossed her arms. "You mean to tell me you had my things the entire time?"

He shrugged. "Naturally."

Wren watched them with an empty look as though he was waiting for something. She sensed him measuring her anger, which only refocused her ire against him instead. It wasn't that she was ungrateful for his help, but she didn't wish for protection at every moment.

She glared at Wren and responded to the Wyvern. "You'll give me back my things when we return. I also require the use of your cards, since you claim not to need them."

Wren's brows shot up his forehead.

The Wyvern chuckled and reached into a pocket on the inside of his overcoat. He offered the cards to her. Their bare hands met as they both gripped the deck, and she staggered back at the shock as soon as he released them. The cards carried the heat from his body. They were well cared for, unbent but well played. These would do.

"Now what will you do with them?" The Wyvern repeated his question.

"I'm a card reader."

He groaned, and she held the cards tightly to her chest. He fumbled for a chain around his neck and gripped whatever was dangling from it. He kissed it and put it back under his shirt.

Wren held in a laugh with tightened lips.

"Keep the cards. Just what I need, another fortune-telling

witch. Mrs. Johns must have seen it in you." The Wyvern moved off, but Lynette stopped him with a hand on his arm.

"Just what is so wrong with card reading?"

He craned his neck. "Nobody should know their future. See your death, and it will take you sooner."

"That's insane. I'm no witch. I simply find clarity in the game. Besides, only fools ask about their deaths."

He pointed at her chest with his free arm. "You see." He gazed over at Wren. "She understands what I have been trying to explain to you for years." He looked back at her. "I wouldn't play at telling fortunes, but I suppose I can respect the need for thought."

She moved her hand away, her skin tingling where she had touched him. It was like her hands had developed free will in their need to be close to him. Perhaps she should tie her hands behind her back, or at least keep her distance.

Wren muttered something under his breath in another language. He wandered off from them. She watched him go, wondering at the man's strange behavior. When she turned back to the Wyvern, he was grinning at her.

"What did he say?" She wasn't sure she wanted the answer.

"I have no idea. I only know a few words of Romani."

Her gaze trailed where Wren had gone, but he had disappeared. "You mean Wren is Romani?"

His tone became defensive. "Only from his grandmother's side. Mrs. Johns and Wren are some of the best people I know. More honest and loyal than most you will meet."

"I'm sorry. I didn't mean anything by it. I was just surprised. His hair is so red."

He chuckled and walked off toward the campfire. She followed him, curious at this newfound good mood. Perhaps the man was unhinged. The camp had grown to include Wren and two other men he had brought with him. They stayed unmasked, giving her the impression the current group was trustworthy, though apparently the Wyvern disagreed. He sat by the fire near her and watched the men as they devoured the chicken Wren had brought.

She ate as though starved, which freed her to take up the cards as soon as she could. She wiped her hands over her pants without more than a moment's consideration for what she was doing. It was long past time she did something she wanted. If the Wyvern didn't like it, then so be it. What did she care?

Before she could spread the cards, one of the men shouted. The Wyvern got to his feet and drew his sword. He got lost in the commotion and returned into view, dragging one of his men by the collar.

He threw the man to the ground and angled the sword at his gut. "Pace, I can take insults to me, but when you insult one of my men, you will pay for it."

"She isn't one of your men." Pace spit toward Lynette. He was one of Wren's men, a skinny, drowsy-faced fellow that was more limb than body.

Lynette stared on, openmouthed, as the Wyvern cut the fabric from the man's belly. She rushed toward them and pushed the sword away from Pace.

She gestured with her palm up to include the scene. "This isn't necessary. I can handle whatever it was he said."

The Wyvern set his narrowed eyes on her and moved the sword to rest on the man's chest.

Pace was still, glaring at Lynette with a twisted frown that contorted his face into one of contempt. "I said"—he pronounced each syllable—"that our noble leader is too tied up in his whore's legs to see reason. If it hadn't been for you, the Wyvern would have taken hell to Hawke."

Lynette yanked the sword out of the Wyvern's hand and thrust the blade into Pace's shoulder. He screamed, the sound echoing off the land and leaving a loaded silence behind. Nobody moved but the man on the ground, gripping his wound.

"I am no one's whore." She sensed more than saw everyone's eyes on her as she handed the sword back to the Wyvern and returned to her place by the fire. Let them think what they would, but she would not let them tear her down. Her hands shook as she set the cards aside.

Pace would survive. She knew his wound was minor, and she kept telling herself that. It wasn't so much stabbing him or the fact that he could have died that unnerved her. She understood stabbing him was wrong. She knew it with the weight of her guilt from killing Frederick Baker and contributing to Benjamin Forrest's death. What bothered her was the pleasure she had taken in thrusting the blade into the man's flesh. Had he deserved it? Most likely, but that didn't mean she'd needed to stab him.

Her past in New York had been a complicated one she did not need repeating. She remembered the satisfaction at seeing the rapist and murderer Mr. Baker fall to the ground after taking her poison. It had been necessary, inevitable. Yet in the end, it hadn't helped her sleep or her appetite. As for Mr. Forrest, he had threatened her life and nearly raped her before Delia had taken him down with her knife. Two stains on society that would no longer hurt anyone. Two stains on her soul that would mark her forever.

That night, the men avoided her. For good reason, no doubt. The Wyvern gave her a crooked smile and settled down between her and his men. Was he protecting her from them or them from her? Pace had kept his peace since she had wounded him, and he gave her a wide berth.

The next morning, the men continued to give her space but cast sidelong looks her way when they thought she wouldn't notice. The avoidance was nothing new, but the wariness was something else entirely. She kept her place next to the Wyvern while he chatted aimlessly with her or Wren.

They arrived at Rycroft House just as a drizzle escaped from the angry gray clouds. Bosworth was there to take the horses, but Lynette decided she would rather care for Athena herself. It was only proper she took the time for the borrowed horse, owing at least that much to Maggie.

The rain grew to a rapid downpour as she brushed Athena down. Lynette hadn't realized how much she was avoiding the house until she noticed she was alone. The heavy patter distracted from the silence and covered the sounds of footsteps advancing behind her.

She yelped when a hand closed on her shoulder, and she spun on her heel.

Rycroft stood a couple of paces away, merriment dancing in his eyes.

"Don't you know I could have hurt you?" She held a hand to her racing heart.

"More than most." He chuckled low. "I called out to you, but you didn't hear me over this storm. Mrs. Johns insists you come in to eat. You can leave Athena's care to Bosworth when he comes back out."

"I'm almost done. Besides, I'd like to see if this storm lets up."

He shook his head. "I don't think it's going to. Not soon, at any rate. You'd best run to the house, though I imagine it will soak you through."

His short dark hair dripped rain over his sodden overcoat and trousers, and water droplets shone off his boots in the pale light from beyond the clouds. A single drop slid down his face and settled at the corner of his mouth. He licked it off, and a smile tugged at his lips as he noticed her shift away.

"How is Pace?" She forced her attention back to Athena.

"Pace will heal and will likely follow Lycan off to better things. I'd appreciate it if you would stop skewering my men."

"Well, I would appreciate it if they would leave me be." She gave Athena one last pat and placed the grooming tools back where she had found them. She sensed Rycroft watching her and turned toward him.

"Perhaps you'd prefer staying behind this time." He shrugged as he joined her near the stable door.

"That isn't likely."

He sighed. "It's just as well. They are all terrified of you anyway. You needn't hide out here from them."

She squinted at the rain, toward the house. "I wasn't hiding."

"Right." He nodded solemnly.

She snapped her gaze to him with eyes narrowed on his amused face. "I wasn't." Her voice lowered. "Not from them anyway."

His brows climbed up. "Hiding from me, then?"

She swallowed back the lump in her throat. He was impossible. Couldn't he leave her be?

"I'm sorry, you know, for lashing out at you. Romulus says I need to have a gentler hand with women. Whatever that means. Maggie has never needed one, and I doubt you do either. He also said I need to apologize. So there it is."

"Did he also say what an ass you are?"

He leaned against the side of the stable door. "In so many words. He wouldn't say it outright. Few of them would. Now, may I ask what I am apologizing for?"

She considered bolting out into the rain but dismissed the urge. She still had hope the storm would calm. The insistent pattering held patches of silence, hinting at a possible end.

"No, you may not. Perhaps if you weren't such an ass, I would tell you." She used her sternest voice and folded her arms. It wasn't wise to provoke him, but it was either that or hit him.

His eyes lit with a spark she couldn't identify. He stepped toward her, and water rolled off his hair to land on her face. "I was wrong before. You don't need to be coddled. Whatever happened to you, I'm sorry. I had no right to judge you."

She nodded in acceptance and imitated her mother's haughty tone. "As long as you are aware of that. Imagine a scoundrel like you judging me?"

He fought a smile, lips twitching up as he lost the battle. He leaned closer to her, his gaze dancing along her face as though watching for any hint of disapproval or acceptance. She was frozen in place, pinned by those loathsome hazel eyes. She wanted this, even just for now. Her mind nagged at her, warning her this man was all wrong, but her body refused to listen as her breath caught in her throat.

He dipped down and pressed his lips to hers. The soft caress of his mouth contrasted with the coarseness of his unshaven skin. The sensation sent a thrill through her body, a rush that quickened her heart and heated her belly. She returned his kiss and tasted brandy with her tongue. A moan escaped his mouth. His hands met her hips, pulling her closer and soaking the front of her boys' shirt. She reached behind his neck, holding on as he embraced her.

Her heart slammed against her rib cage. The embrace was wet and heated in all the correct places, and his touch lit a match to keep her warm.

His fingers trailed up her spine, and she jumped back, breaking their embrace. What was she doing? This was how it had started with Forrest. A gentle kiss, a touch, and then there had been no refusing him. She had to end this now.

Rycroft ogled her shirt. The dampness had made her nipples visible through the fabric. She crossed her arms over her chest, earning a smile from him.

She shot him an icy look. "We can't do this. I can't do this."

His expression was serious. "I'm a scoundrel. We've covered that."

"A scoundrel, a blackguard, and a cad."

"No need to get ugly now."

She spread her hands, gesturing to him. "I don't know what you are used to, but I'm not some random woman who you throw over when you get bored. Besides, we are in the stables of all places."

"Of course."

"Not to mention what my family would say, what both our families would say. My word, what would I tell Delia?"

"Imagine."

She threw up her hands. "You are the worst kind of man to get involved with. I don't know what I was thinking."

"You weren't."

He stared again at her chest. She had uncovered herself, but she placed her hands on her hips this time and glowered at him.

"Rycroft. My face."

He glanced up to meet her gaze, his face lighting up with a wide smile. "Such a pretty face too." He reclaimed the steps between them and pulled her into his arms.

For a moment, she hesitated. For a moment, she allowed him to kiss the sensitive skin along her neck, paying special attention to the area where her neck met her shoulder. For a moment, she let his fingers tickle over her sides, and her insides somersaulted. For a moment, she let the heat inside her grow until she wanted him to take her in the stables.

She pulled away from him again and raised a hand between them. He seemed as though he wanted to protest, but he stayed silent and watched her with half-closed eyes. She tossed her head, an effort to ward him off and to dispel her desire.

Words wouldn't stop this. Only distance could give her a clear head. Without another thought, she rushed out into the storm, her feet leading her back to the house.

CHAPTER ELEVEN

B Y THE TIME she made it inside, she was soaked through. Her things from the carriage had been moved to her new room as requested. She understood they couldn't have fixed the window in her old room yet, but it did nothing to curtail her irritation.

She rubbed down her skin, drying herself while restoring warmth to the rain-chilled areas. A knock sounded on the door, and she peeked out at Mrs. Johns in the hall. She accepted the old woman's help dressing, grateful for the extra pair of hands. They said little unless gestures wouldn't do. She knew Mrs. Johns had a firm grasp of English and simply chose not to use it.

Mrs. Johns pulled out Lynette's blue gown from her chest and insisted she wear it. The dress was travel-worn but otherwise in good shape. She couldn't help but ask why, out of all the gowns she had, did she insist on the blue one.

Mrs. Johns considered her with a slight tilt to her lips. "Favorite."

Perhaps Lynette was doomed to live in Mary's favorites for the extent of her stay. She sighed and surrendered to Mrs. Johns's ministrations.

When she finally escaped the room, she was dressed better than she had been in months. Mrs. Johns had taken pains to match her clothes and jewelry, choosing a necklace and earring set with sapphires and pearls. Mrs. Johns did Lynette's hair in an elaborate braid that settled at the nape of her neck. The effort seemed a waste to her, but she marveled in the feel of changing from her boys' clothes. The storm still raged outside, and they weren't going anywhere anytime soon.

It was nearly dinner time, and Mrs. Johns led her to what appeared to be a drawing room. To her surprise, at least a dozen men lounged about the room. Most of them had bothered to freshen up before joining the group, and they cleaned up nicely. Perhaps Mrs. Johns's efforts were not wasted after all. When they noticed Lynette enter, they stood in a disorderly way, distracted by cards and drink.

Riley rushed to greet her and led her to an empty place near his chair. Her stomach growled at the sight of scones, her having missed the last meal. She itched to grab one but didn't want to appear ravenous. She almost laughed at her reasoning. These men had seen her stab someone.

Rycroft sipped a rare brandy at the edge of the room. He was watching her with a spark of interest in his gaze. He tilted his glass to her and returned his attention to his companion, Howell. The latter appeared improved. He showed no evidence of bandaging.

She jumped when she realized Riley stared at her. She cleared her throat. "How is Mr. Howell recovering?"

"Well enough," he replied. "I imagine he will join us once this storm leaves."

"What of Pace?"

He smiled crookedly. "Pace, or shall we say, Baron Summers, shall make a full recovery. He left shortly after we arrived."

"Baron? Oh God. You must be joking."

He chuckled. "Relax. He is a bit of a fiend, but he knows he won't get anything from Rycroft if he retaliates. Besides, he had a good sense of humor about the whole mess, though I wish he had kept his mouth shut. They are all animals when following the Wyvern."

She poured herself some tea from the table laden between them. "I hadn't noticed. What does he want from Rycroft?"

"What else? Money. Baron Summers is in debt, as are many in this country. Rycroft has found an opportunity for profit, an attractive motivator for loyalty. Not to mention, he's fair about sharing his wealth."

She paused midsip, considering his words. "What does Rycroft get out of all this? He doesn't seem in want of money."

Riley placed a scone on his plate with a mechanical air. "He isn't. Never has been. I think you'll have to ask him."

She blew out a puff of air. "I was hoping you would let me know. I can't believe half of what he tells me."

"It's a fool's errand to speculate on why he does anything. My guess is for sport or, more likely, for revenge. If you truly wish to know, ask him about our time at sea this past year." He was withdrawing from the conversation. She narrowed her eyes at him as he nibbled his scone. She wouldn't get any more out of him.

"What of you? Why do you do it?" She snatched up her own scone.

He coughed, choking on his food. "I don't know. I don't have use for money. It's more of a burden than anything. I suppose I haven't anything better to do than see what trouble he'll cause." He frowned, his gaze caught on something behind her. She twisted in her seat to a cabinet with glass doors and gazed back at him and to the cabinet. He watched the reflection of Rycroft in the glass.

Rycroft stretched catlike from his chair and walked toward them. Riley shook his head at the reflection, but Rycroft didn't seem to notice.

"Miss Wolcott, if I'd known you had that gown, I'd have given you your things sooner," Rycroft said by way of greeting.

She lowered her brows. "Or perhaps you could have given me my things for the mere fact they belong to me."

He chuckled. One of his men vacated a chair nearby, which

he pulled up beside her. His voice sobered. "Maggie said something similar."

A silence followed, anxiety for Maggie thick in the air.

She rubbed a hand over her dress. "When do you expect this storm to clear?"

His fingers tapped the arm of his chair. "I don't know. I'm wondering if maybe we should set out anyway."

"If we get trapped, it won't help Maggie any," Riley said.

"Agreed. At least Hawke is trapped in the same situation. He won't be going anywhere for some time."

Riley's frown deepened the lines in his face, making him appear older than his twenty or so years. "That is assuming he hasn't already."

"Hmm." Rycroft's mouth twisted up. "It couldn't hurt to send a couple of men out. How would you like to go?"

"You're trying to get rid of me. It won't work. Send Jason and John."

"Who are Jason and John?" Lynette scanned the room.

Rycroft gave her a wry smile. "The twins." He spoke to Riley. "Why would I be trying to get rid of you?"

Riley snorted. "You know full well why."

Rycroft favored him with a dazzling smile. "In that case, why don't you see what is keeping dinner?" he asked just as Mrs. Johns opened the drawing room door.

"It appears to be done." Riley returned his smile.

Lynette groaned and rubbed at her forehead. What were they about now?

Those gathered in the drawing room appeared to be waiting for something. Rycroft took her arm before she could find the words to protest and led her to the dining room. That settled the matter, and the rest of the room rustled behind them.

He motioned for Howell to take the table's head and sat next to him, placing Lynette at his side. Riley sat on her other side, and the rest of the men arranged themselves around them. There was room to spare at the table after everyone was seated—enough space for Maggie.

The meal was small, consisting of a delicious lamb stew and fresh bread. Mrs. Johns was a miracle. Lynette wondered absently if she could whisk her away to Briarwyck. The calm conversations of the drawing room faded with the addition of food and alcohol. The men became the uproarious animals she had witnessed on the trip.

Riley poured her some brandy, which she pushed away before considering it. Rycroft took note of this and asked Mrs. Johns for tea. Lynette thanked him when it arrived and caught his eyes as she sipped from her cup. His gaze seemed to embrace her as she consumed the warm liquid. Her thoughts shifted to the kiss in the stables, and her cheeks heated.

Rycroft ran a tongue over his lips and kept her gaze until Riley asked her something, and he shot a glare at the other man.

Once the meal was over, the men contented themselves with stolen spirits and tobacco. The smoke lingered over the table, resisting her attempts to sweep it away with her hand. Lynette started to rise, but Rycroft steadied her in her seat with a raised hand.

"I have something for you." He reached under the table for a long parcel.

Her eyes widened. She hesitated, wondering if it was something wildly inappropriate like the rest of this experience. Her fingers twitched to open it, and she tipped off the lid, revealing a long, curved blade nestled in an elaborate scabbard. She lifted it, finding it light. It was the most beautiful gift she had ever received.

She gazed up from the blade and shook her head. "I can't accept this."

"Oh, but you can. You need a proper blade if you're going to dispatch more of my men."

She scoffed. "I had no plans to. Besides, I thought I had a proper blade. Do I need to return it?"

"No, you can have them both. It's always better to carry

more than one weapon. I was going to order you a pistol, but it would have taken too much time. Now you can do more than stab."

She drew the blade, drawing the attention of the rest of the men at the table. The engravings on the steel matched the scabbard in intricate vines and soaring birds. Her smile was giddy, excitement racing along her spine as she thought of holding the blade against a man like Jasper or Lycan.

She reached out and rested the blade near Rycroft's neck. A half dozen men got to their feet, drawing swords. Rycroft's eyes lit in surprise and smoldered down to amusement. He waved at his men to sit.

"Tell me, Mr. Rycroft. Do you fear death?" Her wide smile revealed her teeth.

"Not from you, sweet. If you choose to slit my throat, I'll call it fair judgment and rest in peace from your wisdom."

"You mock me, sir." She raised the sword to just below his chin.

He choked on a laugh and kept his throat clear of the blade. "Nonsense."

He grasped the dull side of the blade and pulled her forward into his lap. In one fluid motion, he grabbed the handle from her. She gasped as she found her head resting on his chest, breathing in the scent of horse and brandy. He'd done that on purpose.

Her face burned. It wasn't that he had disarmed her, but he was so close in a room full of strangers. She pushed away from him and lowered her eyes. He offered the sword back to her, and she sensed his amusement.

"I'll teach you to use it once we get going," he said to the laughter of his men.

She kept her gaze averted. "Thank you." She replaced the sword in its scabbard.

He reached out and tilted her chin for her to meet his eyes. "You like it, then? Does it feel right?"

She couldn't help the smile that washed over her features. "I adore it. It's perfect," she said shyly.

He dropped his hand and allowed her to excuse herself back to her room. As she exited, Riley spoke behind her.

"Half the men will be missing their balls by the end of the week, yours included."

"Yes, don't forget to add yourself to that count." Laughter tinged Rycroft's words.

"Oh, I haven't. I wouldn't have aided her hand though."

She squeezed her eyes shut as the door closed behind her, hoping foolishly to drown out the voices.

When she returned to her room, a fresh set of boys' clothes waited for her. This time, a pair of properly fitting boots was included. She rubbed the soft leather of the Hessians and silently thanked whoever had located them. She drew the curtains aside to watch the storm as she lay back on her bed.

It wasn't until she heard the decisive click of the lock on her door that she realized she had fallen asleep. At first, she thought someone was entering the room, but she hadn't locked the door. The window was dark now. No sign of the rain came from outside.

She jumped to her feet and tested the door for confirmation. It was indeed locked. She glared at it, willing it open, and moved to the other door that led to Rycroft's room—also locked. She pounded on the door and screamed his name.

"I'm sorry, sweet. They convinced me to leave you behind."

She dropped her shoulders. "Please. You said you would teach me to use the sword. I even have better clothes. How can you leave me here?"

"I know. I promise you'll come next time. We shouldn't be gone more than a few days, a week tops. Don't try to climb out the window either. That drop will kill you."

She knew he was right. She had no intention of falling to the rocky ledge below, but she'd thought they were past this.

"What about Maggie? I know I can help."

"That is precisely the point they made to me. If you die, Maggie will never forgive me. Hell, my brothers will never forgive me. They will have my head mounted on the wall at Briarwyck."

"Damn Carrington and Hugh. Let me out. Maggie will understand." She pounded on the door once more.

A moment of silence followed. "Hush. Mrs. Johns needs her sleep."

"You're leaving now? In the middle of the night?"

"Yes, the storm has let up."

She scowled at the door. "Isn't it my choice if I die or not? I'm ready. These men will pay for what they are doing, and I won't let you leave me behind."

His sigh was audible through the door. "This isn't a negotiation. You are staying here."

Lynette stared at the door as though she could glare at him through the wood. "You really are going to leave me here. I can't believe it. I thought you were better than this. If you leave me here, I will never forgive you."

"Better for you to hate me than get yourself killed."

She was stunned into silence. Hadn't she shown on the last trip that she was capable of not dying? She sat back on her bed, fuming as she stared into the night outside her window. He must have left, because she no longer heard his footsteps or movement from the other room.

She took a deep breath and started to dress into her new boys' clothes. They were a good fit, and she appreciated the way the boots hugged her calves. It was no wonder men wore these instead of slippers. She fastened a red scarf around her neck. Her hair was a mess, and she didn't have the patience to deal with it.

She pulled her hair tight to the side and used her new sword to cut through the strands. Hair tumbled to the ground as she watched in openmouthed horror. She closed her eyes, counting to ten before completing the job. Her thin strands now brushed the tops of her shoulders. There were men with longer hair.

She finished the look with her cocked hat and swords. She rummaged through the hair accessories Mrs. Johns had left behind earlier that day. What Rycroft hadn't counted on was her ability to pick locks. She had learned the skill from Delia, who had little respect for a locked door. It had been unfortunate her previous room had not provided a better opportunity, having a one-sided lock. Her hands closed on two hairpins, and she went to work.

The lock took longer than she'd expected, and by the time she finished, she was afraid she had lost the men. She rushed down the stairs and out the door, hesitating to grab an oil lamp as she ran. The house seemed empty. Mrs. Johns must have been the only one left inside. Perhaps the older woman felt as insulted as her.

Lynette saddled Athena in minutes and led her out into the yard, where she searched for signs of hoofprints. The rain had washed away the old indents, and a large group of horses couldn't hide so easily in the mud. Oil lamp held high, she followed after them.

Athena picked her way skillfully over the road, and Lynette trusted the horse to see the path better than her. She thought about what she would do to Rycroft when she caught up with him. Of course, he claimed his men had convinced him, but he couldn't be convinced of something if he didn't already lean in that general direction. The sword must have been to appease her until he had locked her away. She suspected the clothes had been Mrs. Johns's doing.

She spotted lights ahead and pushed Athena toward them. Then came a shout.

Athena reared, and Lynette screamed with the horse.

A hand grasped her reins before she could get control of Athena. The horse jerked her head away, throwing Lynette this way and that. A sharp pain settled in her side. Her eyes were spared a moment from the wild movement to spot a long blade aimed at her and a face she did not recognize.

CHAPTER TWELVE

L YNETTE SQUINTED AT the man before her, trying to place him among the Wyvern gang. A shout came from up ahead, and riders galloped toward them. The man looked back over his shoulder to await their approach.

"What do you have there, Jerry?" a newcomer asked.

They weren't with the Wyvern. Where had they gotten off to? Who were these men?

"I intercepted this boy following us." Jerry watched her from the corners of his eyes. "Made a hell of a noise."

Her heart pinched in her chest when Lord Carrington came into view. His eyes grew wide with recognition as he realized who sat in front of him. He shook his head as though to erase her from his sight.

"You're much like your sister." Carrington ran his hand over his face. "I don't know what happened to you, but we're going back to Briarwyck."

Jerry scanned her features anew. "What? Who is it?"

Carrington considered the other man. "Mr. Jeremiah Rycroft, allow me to introduce you to Miss Lynette Wolcott."

Jeremiah stiffened. Just then, another rider came up beside Carrington. At once, she recognized Mr. Hugh Travers, Carrington's brother. He squinted at her as though he was trying to confirm what he saw.

"What are you doing here?" Lynette backed Athena up in the cramped space.

Carrington seemed to notice her wariness in the gesture. "Well, little sister, when I came to collect you after the flooding had gone down, you weren't at Rycroft House. An old woman directed me away, though I don't think she understood a word of what I said. I assumed the worst and assembled a search party." Mrs. Johns, loyal to the end.

Hugh tilted his head toward her. "We thought Max had kidnapped you and taken you off somewhere he could ransom you."

She waved this away with her hand. "You can see I'm well. I have things to attend to if you would kindly move."

"What sort of things? I promised Delia I would bring you home. She has been worried terribly over you. She almost came after you herself." Carrington's voice had grown low, angry.

Lynette closed her eyes. Of course she loved her sister, and she hated to worry her, but Delia could take care of herself. Maggie needed Lynette now. As much as Rycroft said otherwise, she knew she could make all the difference in bringing her back.

"This is none of your concern. In fact, you'll only make matters worse. I'll come to Briarwyck when everything is handled."

Jeremiah Rycroft studied her with upturned brows. He turned to Carrington and Hugh. "May I have a moment alone with Miss Wolcott? It's about a mutual acquaintance."

Carrington puffed out a lungful of air. "Fine." He gestured for Hugh to follow and directed his horse toward Rycroft House.

She and Mr. Rycroft both watched until the brothers were out of earshot. She caught his gaze. How had she missed the similarities between this man and his portrait? He had the same silver-gray eyes and dusting of freckles as Maggie. But the picture had revealed a head of auburn hair, while this man's hair was darker as though he stayed indoors.

"I should have recognized you," she said.

He grunted. "I'm afraid I cannot say the same. What has my idiot brother done? Has something happened to Maggie?"

She squinted at him. "Your idiot brother is out searching for her. She was taken earlier in the week. I thought he had sent word to your father?"

"Oh God. If something happened to her, I'll kill the bastard. It's likely he did send word, but I've not seen my father in a month. I'm sorry you got tangled up in this. Please say nothing to the Travers family." The statement sounded like a dismissal. He faced his horse back to the muddied path.

"Mr. Rycroft," she called after him. He stopped but didn't turn. "This wasn't his fault. He has done everything he can to bring her home."

His back stiffened as she addressed him. "That remains to be seen. Max is a no-good degenerate. It would be best if you forgot the matter, Miss Wolcott." He led his horse after the Wyvern gang.

If her brother were as rude as Jeremiah, she'd slap him over the head. She wouldn't be dismissed like this. Athena shot out after him as Lynette knew she would. Carrington and Hugh shouted as they followed. Maggie needed her. She wasn't about to let these men stop her.

Jeremiah noticed her pursuit and hurried his horse further. The four of them raced along the path until the horses panted and sweat. It wasn't long before they saw movement. She heard a familiar sharp whistle. Men blocked the trail ahead, and their horses slowed. In her peripheral, the men surrounded them. Another whistle sounded, and the men drew their weapons.

The Wyvern stalked out from behind the group. He wore his red scarf as he advanced on foot to her horse.

"What is the meaning of this?" Carrington asked. The fear in his voice was unlike anything she had heard from him.

The Wyvern tilted his head at Carrington, his eyes full of amusement. Jeremiah folded his arms over his chest, peering down on his brother. Hugh followed Carrington's lead, looking uncertainly around at the group of men threatening them.

She rolled her eyes. "Is this really necessary?"

The Wyvern raised a hand to her, offering to help her off Athena.

"Don't touch her." Carrington attempted to hasten his horse toward her, but the Wyvern's men blocked him off.

By way of answer, the Wyvern hoisted her off her horse. A look of mischief played across his face as he led her beyond his men. Carrington and Hugh shouted after her and yelled threats and insults at those that thwarted them. Jeremiah was curiously silent.

The Wyvern brought her out of earshot but in easy view of the men. The area of light from the lamps made distance somewhat limited. Whether he was trying to appease or irritate Carrington by remaining in view, she didn't know.

"I told you to stay behind." His scarf muffled his voice.

She swung at him, slamming her fist into his jaw. He stumbled backward, and some of his men rushed toward them. He froze them in their path with a glare. The men fell silent, watchful.

He rubbed at his jaw from under the scarf, watching her with slit eyes. "I suppose I deserved that."

She put her hands on her hips.

He gripped the hilt of his sword. "Why did you bring them here? You invite a world of complications."

"I had little choice in the matter. This wouldn't have happened if you hadn't left me behind. By the way, your brother is an arrogant ass."

She sensed his grin under the scarf. "Which one?" he asked.

She scoffed. "All the ones I've met but Jeremiah in particular."

He nodded. "That is all well and good, but why did you follow me? How did you get out? Don't tell me Mrs. Johns let you out."

"Do you really think I'm going to tell you? You'll just lock me away again. I'm here for Maggie, not you."

A twig snapped near them. Someone approached, making themselves known. The Wyvern sighed as Wren came into view.

"What is it?" The Wyvern favored Wren with a level stare.

"Everyone is getting restless. Do you think it wise to hold Viscount Carrington hostage? He's the last person we should be making enemies with."

"Don't you think I know that?" The Wyvern's hand clenched white on the hilt.

Wren raised his hands as if to ward the other man off. "Send her back with them."

"He'll do nothing of the sort." Lynette thrust her ire on Wren. "I won't be sent anywhere. I'm not some parcel to hand off."

"Try telling your brother-in-law that." Wren rounded on her, coming within inches of her face. She saw the danger there in his eyes. It was like a spark waiting to ignite. Something cold pressed against her collar, and she stilled as he held a knife to her throat.

The silence around them was like a rush. The air spoke of blood and betrayal. Commotion spread among the men, but it was like sound was sucked from around them.

"Wren, drop the blade." The Wyvern's voice was a growl.

"She brought them to us. Have her take them away."

The Wyvern nodded, but she didn't dare move. Her eyes fixed on Wren, unblinking. Wren stashed the knife away, and her hand slapped her throat. He dropped his gaze, and she sensed the shame in his gesture.

"I'm sorry, but you're like poison to us. To him." Wren's posture slouched, and a defeated cast clouded his eyes.

The Wyvern's eyes appeared worn, joyless. A far cry from the man he'd been ten minutes ago. She wanted to cry, to lash out at these men. Instead, she pled.

"I can stay out of the way."

The Wyvern shook his head and gestured toward the men behind them. "What would we do with them? They won't leave without you, and we can't bring them along." He made a valid point. She had no idea how they would lose them or avoid their questions. Carrington was curious by nature, and it wouldn't be long before he figured things out. It would be better to keep some distance between them.

"I'll agree to take them back," Lynette said. "Return to the men and let them know. We've wasted enough time with this."

Wren hesitated, watching the Wyvern for confirmation, and the Wyvern nodded. Once he was gone, she rounded on the Wyvern.

"If you think this is over, you're very much mistaken. You owe me. If you so much as think of locking me in a room again, I'll feed you your balls."

His eyes widened, and he burst into laughter but stopped when she glared at him. He raised his hands in surrender.

"You think I'm poison now. Foxglove is a close personal friend of mine, and you wouldn't be the first person he killed with me. If Maggie suffers in any way because I was not there, I will kill you. I'll say nothing of your menagerie or Maggie's circumstances, but I get the feeling you'll need to explain things to Carrington and Hugh eventually. They're too close to this. It's their father too, after all."

He considered her with unblinking, unmoving eyes. Before she could retreat back to Athena or utter a word of protest, he'd closed the distance between them. His back to the group, he used one hand to bring her close and pulled down his scarf with the other.

His lips were insistent, possessive. His tongue explored her as though he would consume her. She wiggled her arms between them and pushed against his chest. A mixture of shouting and cheering came from behind them that was drowned out by the airlessness inhabiting her head.

She returned his kiss and angled her body to give him better access. All thoughts were suspended as she tasted his breath on hers, a hint of coffee lingering on his tongue. The tingling in her belly intensified in a wave she had never experienced. She moaned into his lips. He pulled back and stared down at her with glazed eyes. He leaned his forehead against hers and tilted his chin to kiss her nose. She reached up and tugged the scarf to cover his delicious mouth.

They stepped away from each other with no small amount of regret. Lynette was the first to walk back to the group. She sensed the appreciative stares of the men but ignored them as she pulled herself onto Athena. She looked between Carrington's and Hugh's confused expressions.

She smirked. "Shall we go?"

Carrington gave a short nod, seeming to have lost his voice.

"I'm staying," Jeremiah said to the Wyvern as he approached. The Wyvern nodded at him in agreement.

Lynette pointed Athena back the way they had come. She eyed the men in their way and frowned at them. "Move, or I will trample you."

The Wyvern chuckled behind her. "Do as the lady says. I don't doubt she will take at least one of you out." With that, the men parted. Carrington and Hugh stayed silent, wisely deciding not to ask questions about their release without harm.

She led them forward. Carrington rode up beside her, carrying a lamp. He attempted to gain her attention. She sighed and glanced his way.

"What am I supposed to tell your sister? That you have been hanging around the most notorious man in England and that he has ruined you for all fashionable society?"

She sniffed and leaned her horse forward. "I don't care what you tell her. I believe she will agree with me when I say fashionable society can hang itself."

"How did this happen? Where is Rycroft?"

Lynette laughed, wiping tears from her eyes as they streamed down her cheeks. The man was his brother, and he hadn't even recognized him. It was no wonder he had gotten away with being the Wyvern for so long. The people who knew were loyal to the core, and those who did not never guessed his identity. It was all too amusing. She wasn't going to be the one to tell Carrington.

Carrington glared at her, which only renewed her laughter.

He held out a hand, signaling for her to stop. She ignored him, letting Athena set her own pace. They carried on like this in silence. He had given up on getting an explanation out of her, and she had her mind set on retrieving her things from Rycroft House.

Lights emitted from the house as it came into view. Her heart pounded at the sight of the now familiar building. A dark weight passed over her. Would this be the last time she set foot in Rycroft House? Carrington shouted something behind her, but she ignored him, wanting to enjoy the last few moments she had.

Maggie belonged here. If the Wyvern failed to bring her back safe, would it ever be the same? It was a vacant place without her, a hollow place with empty people. The Wyvern's failure would tear him apart, and Lynette would not be here to help repair the damage. It would be up to his family and the odd collection of men he seemed to collect like stray cats.

Athena jerked, rearing back. Lynette lost hold of the reins and flew off the side, to the ground. The horse darted away, and she regained her feet. The darkness closed around her. Carrington's lamp was gone, put out by some unknown force. She no longer heard him or Hugh.

She held her hands to her mouth to still her breathing. Wherever they were, she needed to get to Rycroft House. There would be more light there, more help.

A dark form moved to her right, sending her off guard as she teetered to the side. She drew her sword, and she said a prayer to the Wyvern for giving her the means to defend herself.

Another shadow loomed across her vision.

She thrust her sword toward it, meeting flesh. A hand gripped her sword arm from behind and wheeled her about. A gasp escaped her lips, followed by an earsplitting scream as the blade was knocked to the dirt.

Hands explored her struggling body and found her mouth. She bit into the hand and let out another deafening scream. The effort earned her a sharp blow to the head. The ground came up to meet her, and she slammed her knees in a sudden burst of pain. She crawled on all fours, refusing to give up her retreat to Rycroft House. Laughter erupted behind her, and she fancied it sounded much like a dog. The blow to her head must have been worse than she'd thought. Her head pounded behind her eyes, prompting her to close her lids as she crawled.

"Where do you think you're going?" His voice was familiar, but her muddled head refused to identify it.

A whimper traveled from deep in her throat. She was alone. Something had happened to Carrington and Hugh. The Wyvern and his gang were too far away to get there.

Her hand searched the sash around her side, but her other sword was gone. He moved closer and leaned in. She could smell a hint of whiskey and roast beef. She held back a gag as her stomach threatened to heave.

He jerked her up by the shirt, and she made a last effort to save herself from her end. She kicked out, slamming her foot into his groin. He doubled over, giving her the opportunity she needed.

She screamed. The sound ripped from her throat in an explosion of sound. It quieted all movement, reverberating over the hills and grassy fields. The sound faded as she toppled over again. Her throat burned with the effort, but she raised her chin to scream again in her desperation.

The cry never came. Lycan tackled her to the ground and forced her mouth shut with her own scarf. Not a whimper or whisper would escape the binding. Her hands and feet were secured, and she was tossed over the side of a horse to meet whatever fate she knew she deserved.

CHAPTER THIRTEEN

L YNETTE LEARNED EARLY on that struggling was cause for beating. Her back and ribs ached from being kicked with the hard toe of Lycan's boot. The horse's jostling did not help her rest, forcing her to experience every stain to her dignity and every second of foreboding.

She counted three of them, though there could easily be more. They never let her see them as she rode blindfolded and facedown across the horse's back. Their journey seemed mindless, a blind rush to an unknown destination.

She couldn't fathom why they had taken her. There was nothing to suggest they had kidnapped Carrington or Hugh. Lycan's hatred for her must be greater than she and the Wyvern had expected. What fool would kidnap her from Viscount Carrington and a gang of violent thieves? He must want something. Something other than her. If it was money, there were easier ways for him to get that. Perhaps revenge?

The more she thought about it, the more it made sense. She pushed her poisonous thoughts aside and focused on trying to doze off. There was no point in her reasoning this out or trying to find where she was. The country was unfamiliar to her, and she might as well be in Africa.

The jostling stopped long enough for her to be handed off to another horse. The rider took the opportunity to rub his hands along her body, causing her stomach to lurch into her throat. She squirmed away, but it was no use. She couldn't say whether this was better or worse than Lycan's beatings. When she pictured Rycroft's caresses, she decided this rider was worse. He perverted those moments she had shared with Rycroft.

The dawn peeked through her blindfold, and she hoped the light also meant an end to her torture. No such luck. They stopped for a rest, leaving her dangling on her perch. Their muffled voices made merry over their meal. Her stomach rumbled at the neglect, but they either didn't care or didn't remember she needed food too. She wiggled about on the horse, earning a slap to her backside for her efforts.

By this time, her back sent a dull pain up and down her body. Her head was a mess of useless weight, and she no longer believed rescue was imminent. Wherever she was headed, she would die there. Nobody would know what had happened to her.

They resumed their journey, and Lynette found herself pitying the horses. At least she would have company when she surrendered to death. The horse underneath her sweat through her clothes and struggled as the trail descended. A wash of cool spray spread over her, and salt tingled in the air. They had reached the coast.

A new fear surfaced inside her, clenching at her stomach with an iron grip. The last of her hope was dispersed by the possibility of being thrown onto a ship. She wanted to cry, to let the tears wash her away with the tide. There was no satisfaction in these men seeing her broken, and she steeled herself against the urge.

The horses came to a halt. Then she was lifted off the horse and carried like a sack of grain. The man carrying her caressed her thigh, causing her heart to slam into her throat. Her lack of resistance prompted him further, and he brought his other hand to close around her neck, steadying her in place as he explored her body with rough hands.

The memory she had fought so hard to suppress came to join them. After so many months of healing, she thought she had outlived this. A flash of Forrest's hands groping her in the dark as she squirmed to get away. The resounding slap of his hand and the resulting burning in her cheek when she threw off his attentions. His viselike hands closing off the last bit of her air while she struggled to remain conscious.

Her breath caught in her throat as though Forrest was there now and not rotting away in his grave. She thrashed against the hands, her muffled protests trapped behind the scarf. She heard one of the men call, and her handler froze in his steps.

"Stop sampling the wares, Gibbons," another man growled at him.

The man carrying her grunted but did as he was told. He hoisted her off his shoulder with another grunt and placed her on a soft surface that she soon identified as sand. She dropped her head back, relieved to finally lie flat. She let her thoughts float above her, but before she could escape to her dreams, a feminine shriek and a man's yelp roused her.

She faced the source as though she could see through the blindfold.

"Let me go!" Maggie shouted. A wave of relief at her friend's voice washed over Lynette. Maggie was alive, and she was still on land. Yet that also meant the Wyvern hadn't found her. She had held out hope that maybe her absence had been enough to turn the search in Maggie's favor.

"Oh my God, Lynette," Maggie said. Hands gripped at her head, and her blindfold was tugged away with strands of her hair. She flinched, squinting her eyes against the sun. Then she blinked through a sheet of sweat at the haloed figure of Maggie.

Concern etched her silver-gray eyes as Lynette's gag went to join her blindfold. She sucked in the salty breeze, closing her eyes as the fresh air swam through her. Maggie was working at her bindings, getting as far as freeing her hands before a shout stopped her from untying Lynette's ankles.

Maggie was shaking. "How did you get here?"

Lynette tested her voice and ended up coughing. She cleared

her throat. "They took me from outside Rycroft House. Where did they find you? Why haven't they moved you?"

"I left Athena for just a moment to stretch my legs. Did Max find her?"

Lynette nodded, flexing her newly freed hands.

"I don't know why it has taken them so long. I was supposed to go on a ship the first night. I suspect they spotted patrols looking for smugglers. Other than that..." She shrugged. "It isn't like they confide in me, but at least they stopped tying me up," Maggie said, leaning in to hug Lynette. "You're here now though. As much as I would love the company, I'd rather you hadn't been taken."

"Your brother has half the country looking for you."

Maggie sighed. "Yes, his band of merry men. It is a rare man who resists following him into certain peril. Did you know Howell tried to kill him when they first met?"

"You're joking. Howell is the best-tempered man of them all."

"Yes, I know. Howell was imprisoned on a ship Max was—um—borrowing. Of course, most men would have attacked him or run. Howell thought my brother meant to sell him after taking the ship."

Lynette's brows rose. "What happened?"

"Max made him his second and set the ship on fire."

Lynette gave a dry laugh.

"I know. Men are queer. My brother is especially strange. He would rather burn slave ships than sell them for profit. Says it prevents them from finding new human cargo. Mind you, he doesn't burn any remaining passengers, which is where Howell came in. He'd prefer to sell tobacco and brandy instead of ships though."

When Lynette didn't respond, Maggie continued, "Now that you are here with me, Max can send the other half of the country for you." Maggie grinned.

"Oh, I doubt that. Though I'm sure Carrington will send his

own force. He was with me when I was taken."

Maggie stiffened.

"The worst has already happened. If Lord Aberlane has kidnapped us, then it can't get any worse, but if his sons know, then we have a better chance," Lynette reasoned.

Maggie shook her head. "I don't know who is behind all this. Hawke is in charge here, but he isn't the one who wanted me."

They both scanned the beach, watching as the half dozen men chatted among themselves. They seemed confident, needing only a couple of men to attend their charges. One of the men off to the side appeared to be the leader. He was picking at his nails with a knife, and a cocked hat rested on his sun-bleached hair. Hawke.

"I know what you're thinking, and I already tried. I lost both my shoes," Maggie said, gesturing to her feet. The swelling and cuts along the skin struggled to heal and bled from want of care. "You'd be surprised how much glass you can step on before being caught. I wouldn't try it again though. Perhaps if we could free your feet, you could save yourself."

Lynette gripped Maggie's hand in hers. "I'm not leaving you here. Besides, they have horses, and I'm injured. I don't think I could walk a straight line right now, let alone run."

They stilled, awaiting whatever it was the men had planned. If they had wanted Lynette and Maggie dead, they would have already killed them. For now, they rested. Maggie lay beside her, wrapping her arms around Lynette like she was a doll. Lynette took comfort in the embrace and tried not to think of what lay ahead.

One of the men rode off down the coast as though searching. He came back shortly after, shouting for the rest of the men. They made her and Maggie follow them on foot, leaving Lynette to hobble after them. Maggie tried to help her, but she ended up falling more than walking. Hawke brought his horse around to watch her progress, but instead of untying her ankles, he rebound her hands and attached the bindings to his saddle. She would either run or be dragged.

In the end, she let the horse drag her. Maggie stayed beside her the best she could but nothing could be done for the nicks and bruises she picked up from the sandy shore. The ground was soft for the most part. It was the bumps and stray pieces of glass from strewn bottles that plagued her.

"A boat up ahead," Maggie informed her.

She didn't know whether to be relieved or terrified. At least she would be able to rest. How she had wanted to sleep through this journey. If they weren't going to provide sustenance for her, the least they could do was let her sleep through it. She reasoned it was to disorient her, but it was more likely they simply didn't care. Clearly it mattered less what shape she was in than Maggie.

She thought they had finally reached the boat when the horses stopped, and she tumbled to the side, taking great gulps of air. Maggie rushed to her and worked the bindings on Lynette's hands. The strain on the rope had tightened the knot and would have to be cut. Maggie had better luck with the rope on Lynette's ankles, releasing her feet to the rush of blood from her heart.

"What are you doing?" she asked Maggie, her mind dazed from her trip.

"Shh," Maggie said. "Don't draw attention to yourself."

"But what is happening?"

Maggie laid a hand over her mouth and crouched down low, covering Lynette from view.

Horses sounded in the distance, and she closed her eyes to concentrate on their progress. She knew there were more than two but couldn't figure past that. The ring of steel let her know her captors had drawn their swords. If this wasn't a rescue, at least those approaching were the enemies of these men.

There was splashing in the water and a shout to bring them onboard. They both stilled as a shadow crept over them.

"Get to your feet!" someone yelled.

Maggie held on to Lynette's arm but was made to stand. The weight on Maggie's wounded feet seemed to cause her pain, but she bore it with her chin held high. Maggie helped her stand, though the rope tugged at her in the process.

The man came to fiddle with the rope binding her, grunting when he saw the mess it was in. He took a knife from his boot and sawed at the rope.

Maggie's eyes were wide as she looked back and forth along the coast. Her teeth appeared tight in her jaw. Lynette blinked at the commotion, but her eyes refused to focus. Their captors were fighting someone, but other than that, her mind wouldn't cooperate.

"Just the one!" the man on the water yelled. "Leave the other. There isn't time."

The man sawing at her bindings dropped her hands and took hold of Maggie. Maggie's grip loosened, and Lynette scrambled to hold on to her friend. This she understood. They would not retake her friend. Maggie's grip became equally tight on her, and Lynette called for help.

He kicked at her like she was a dog fighting for scraps. When that failed to release Maggie, he brought his knife up to stab her.

Maggie knocked the knife away but at the expense of her grip. The struggle jostled Lynette, and her hands slipped back to hang by their bindings.

"Run!" she yelled to Maggie. "Leave me here."

It was too late. The man carried Maggie out into the water.

Lynette pulled frantically at the rope, now hanging by half its width. Maggie struggled, screaming to be released. She wasn't going without a fight.

The commotion had grown louder, closer, causing the horse holding Lynette's rope to back up. She was dragged away. Her body tossed along the sand as the horse escaped the turmoil behind it.

The horse leaped forward, throwing her high in the air. The rope from her bindings snapped, and she screamed as it hurtled her along the beach. Her body hit a mound of sand, just off the hard underbrush. She slid down the surface and stopped.

Her eyes stared up to the sky as she listened for the fighting behind her, but there was nothing. How far had the horse dragged her? She closed her eyes and rolled to her stomach. She tested her feet, and when she stood, her joints and muscles protested at the movement.

The boots had held up well without allowing any scraps through to her legs. Her clothes were a mess of rips, but they stayed in place. Tiny cuts sent blood through her shirt, and a wound to her scalp trickled some down her face. Her arms were similarly scraped up but were kept elevated from much of the damage. Her worst wounds were to her addled brain and her pride.

She shielded her eyes, looking up and down the coast for any sign of life. She thought she saw the boat retreating from the shore, a black shape moving out to sea. At least now she knew where she'd been dragged from.

A tear escaped to join the blood down her cheek. She wiped it away with irritation. They'd taken Maggie. She'd had Maggie with her, and she hadn't been able to hold on. If only Maggie had let the man stab Lynette. She could have withstood it if it meant her friend wouldn't be taken again.

She stepped into the water, letting the waves wash away the dirt on her boots. Surprisingly, the boots kept the water out. She leaned down, allowing the water to sting along her cuts. She smeared the gash on her head, wincing at the pain.

A shout pierced the silence. A rider advanced on her.

She scrambled out of the water, thrusting her feet forward as she ran. She aimed for the rocky outcrop up ahead. If she could reach it, the rider would have to dismount to chase her, but she lost her footing to the uneven sand. She glanced over her shoulder and dropped the rest of the way to the beach.

It was Hermes.

The sight made her tears fall freely. She rolled back to her feet as Rycroft jumped off his horse. He was running before he hit the beach. His body slammed into hers as he embraced her. She winced at the pain that echoed along her body, pulling away from his grasp.

He scanned her body, looking for injuries. "Are you all right? Is anything broken?"

She shook her head, answering both questions. She let him see the tears fall as her lip wobbled.

"Maggie?" she asked.

"Maggie will be fine. She's made of strong stuff. Wren got to her just in time."

She let out a breath she hadn't realized she'd been holding. "And Hawke?"

Rycroft shook his head. "Got away. We still don't know why he took you or Maggie."

Her fists clenched at her sides, she brought one to cover her sobs. He moved as though to comfort her, but she lifted a hand to shield herself. She took deep breaths, willing Forrest out of her mind. He had surfaced again. When the kidnappers had violated her body, it had brought him back. Forrest couldn't hurt her now. She wouldn't let him control her. She'd thought this part of her past was over. It had been almost a year ago, and yet she felt as though she was still dirty from Forrest's touch.

Rycroft watched her, his brow wavering. Hurt rimmed his eyes. She didn't know what her feelings were for him, but he had become a friend to her. She couldn't explain away that look in his eyes. Her heart still pounded from her mistreatment. She needed to breathe.

"Rycroft," she began. "I... I don't know."

He nodded, though she knew he was still trying to understand. He whistled for Hermes, and the horse moved up beside them. To his credit, he realized she didn't want to be touched right now. He gestured to his horse, and she tried to pull herself up. She fell back. She hesitated a moment and put her hand out for his.

His touch didn't cause any discomfort. She let out a long breath of relief and waited for Rycroft to take the spot behind her, but he stayed on the ground. With the reins in hand, he led his horse down the beach, letting her have the peace he thought she needed, but the peace she wanted was the one he offered at her side.

CHAPTER FOURTEEN

LYNETTE SAT FORWARD as Rycroft led Hermes back toward the others. She needed to remind herself this man wasn't her friend. He was the villain in her story. A battle waged in her mind. Doubt tugged at her thoughts. She didn't know what to believe anymore.

He glanced back at her and returned his attention to the walk. "I'm sorry we weren't here sooner. We almost didn't make it."

Her gaze grew unfocused. "Were we hard to find?"

"Not so much. It was embarrassing how easy it was to find your trail. Ironically, your kidnapping made Maggie's rescue possible. Carrington and Hugh held us back. They refused to believe I didn't kidnap you. It turns out you were right. I had to explain everything to them before they would budge."

Her attention darted to him, but he remained facing forward. "You mean they're here now? You told them about the Wyvern?"

"Yes. At least, Carrington is here. Hugh rode off earlier to confront our father. That damned Greymore is here too. I'd appreciate it if you didn't mention the mix-up with his carriage."

She scoffed. "Mix-up? Is that what you call a robbery?"

"You know what I mean."

"What of your kidnapping me? They weren't entirely wrong. Would you prefer I stay silent about your locking me up?"

He stiffened his shoulders. "Do what you will."

She wanted to shake him, to attack him for no other purpose than to see his response. The quiet unnerved her, but she couldn't think what she could say or do that would restore civility. She wanted him to know the pain that was crawling just under her skin. Yet she couldn't utter the words to make him understand, because they didn't exist.

When she and Rycroft approached the others, they were waiting for her return. Maggie waved at her from the ground where Greymore was patching her feet. He was being the flirt he was, batting his eyes at his patient. Lynette smirked at that. She hoped it wouldn't go to Maggie's head.

Carrington strode up to Rycroft, who stood in his path to Lynette. "I appreciate that you brought her back, but I can't deny you're the reason she's in this mess to begin with."

To her surprise, Rycroft stepped aside, still holding the reins. Carrington walked past him to Lynette.

"Are you hurt?"

She shook her head. No more hurt than when she'd been shot anyway. What hurt her now was not something Carrington could fix. He gave her a quick nod and offered her his hand.

Before she could refuse, Rycroft interceded. "We are short on horses. She can ride Hermes with Maggie."

She eyed him with raised brows. Hermes was dear to him; sending his horse off with anyone was unlikely at best.

"What will you do?" she asked him.

He shrugged. "I'll figure something out." He handed the reins to her and walked over to Maggie. Carrington left to mount his own horse, and Greymore stalked off when he saw Rycroft advancing, prompting a smile from Lynette.

Rycroft helped Maggie stand, whispering to her as they went. She nodded in response to him, her eyes on Lynette. She frowned back at Maggie. If they were going to discuss her, at least they could have the decency not to be so obvious about it. She shook the thought away. She could think ill of him but not her.

Maggie joined her atop Hermes, shooing Rycroft away with

her hand. "Don't give me that look. It isn't my fault you're hungry."

Lynette laughed, unable to help herself. "You're right. I'm famished."

Maggie handed her half a sandwich, followed by a flask of alcohol.

She coughed on the liquid but took another gulp. "I don't know what this vile liquid is, but I'm too thirsty to care."

Maggie laughed to herself and took the bottle back, taking a gulp. "I'm not sure what it is supposed to be, but one of the men brewed it. I suppose it's better than nothing." Maggie sniffed the flask, twisting up her face at the taste.

She and Maggie were forced to the group's center as though they were given an armed guard, which wasn't far from the truth. Rycroft and Carrington led the way. She giggled to herself. They were sharing a horse. She wondered who proposed such a notion and whether the men would survive the trip back.

"The Travers don't seem like such bad men," Maggie said, noticing the object of Lynette's attention.

"I thought not, but apparently I don't know the family well enough. I'm not sure I'm the best judge of character anyway."

"Nonsense. Are you going to be all right, dear?"

Lynette squeezed Maggie's hands clasped in front of her. "I should be asking you that. You were captive for much longer than I was."

Maggie shook her head. "They also treated me better. The only time one of the men fancied me, he lost an eye to Hawke. They kept their distance after that. I don't know if they were careless or spiteful with you, but there is no excuse."

She sighed, closing her eyes. "I don't think they were especially cruel to me. I have had worse, much worse. That's the whole trouble."

Maggie fell silent, which was a rare state for her. Maybe Lynette shouldn't unburden herself to Maggie. Her friend had enough problems to deal with, and Lynette would be just another one.

At last, Maggie squeezed her in a hug, making her feel more cherished than she had in some time. "Whoever hurt you, I hope they realize what a terrible thing they did," Maggie said in a whisper.

"He's dead. I don't think he would have cared if he were alive."

"That's too bad. I was hoping to kill him myself or, more likely, send Max to kill him."

Lynette gasped, turning back to Maggie's smiling face. "That's rather bloodthirsty of you. I didn't know you had it in you."

Maggie's grin widened. "I think any man who abuses women deserves to hang. Any man who abuses my friends deserves much worse. Please tell me he at least suffered."

Lynette couldn't help but grin at her friend's uncharacteristic attitude. "No, it was fast."

"Good, then. Is this what you were afraid to tell me? Do you not recall who my brother is?"

Lynette gave her a pained look in response.

Maggie continued in a serious tone, "You know I love my brother, and we share no blood between us. I'm not going to judge you for ridding the world of men who prey on women. As far as I'm concerned, if they are going to attack us, then we have no other option but to retaliate."

"What of the law?" she asked.

"You know as well as I do that the law doesn't protect women well enough. Wives are beaten because it is the husband's right. Women are ruined to society for the same acts for which men are congratulated. Tell me, what would have happened if those men had not died?"

She bit her lip, gazing down at Hermes. "They would have gotten away with it. I would have died a spinster. I still might."

Maggie chuckled, and Lynette raised a brow. "Now enough of this. Do you feel any better?"

She did feel lighter, reassured. In all the months since she had been holding on to her guilt, she hadn't once gotten the chance to tell anyone. Delia had been so torn up at the same time that Lynette hadn't been able to share it with her. As much as she was grateful to Maggie, she knew talking to her would not erase the feeling in the pit of her stomach.

They made good timing, now that they could make a straight path back to Rycroft House, along the coast. When their destination was in view, many of the group complained of the need for a decent meal and a bed. Rycroft offered everyone a room, though Maggie joked they'd have to straighten them but a meal wouldn't be a problem. Mrs. Johns always cooked for an army, maybe because Rycroft often returned with one.

Such was the case when they arrived. Mrs. Johns was preparing a roast with root vegetables and yeasty rolls. She threw on some chickens when she spotted them coming. Those who had chosen to join them numbered a dozen, but there was more than enough food. After a short rest, they settled around the long table with Max seated next to Maggie and Howell. Riley and Jeremiah Rycroft sat to the side of Howell. Lynette sat by Maggie with Carrington and Greymore on her other side. The rest of the men filled the table with barely enough walking room.

"When do you mean to set out?" Max was asking Carrington.

"I'd like to go tonight, but I'm afraid Miss Wolcott needs to rest. If Hugh sends word after we leave, I'll notify you of what he's learned. My wife will hang me if I don't get back soon."

"Lord Carrington," Maggie said, "wouldn't it be easier if you let Lynette rest here for a time? I'm sure the trip wouldn't be good for her, and your wife can get news without delay."

Carrington met Maggie's gaze, and Lynette wondered at the odd circumstances that had brought these people together. Maggie had lived in dread of the Travers family her whole life, and now they were sitting amicably at a meal. Perhaps the past could be forgotten.

"Miss de Lacey, I mean no offense, but I worry leaving her

here would be a bad idea," Carrington responded, his gaze falling on Max.

Max nodded in agreement, but Maggie would have nothing of it. "Really, she would be safer here at Rycroft House than on the road. There will be no ambush here with locked doors."

Maggie referred to when Carrington and Hugh had been taken for fools, leaving Lynette alone to be captured. Carrington's jaw set tight.

Greymore came to the rescue, applying his charm to Carrington. "It isn't a bad idea. I can stay here with Miss Wolcott while she is recovering. Besides, Max owes me, and I intend to get my payment." He poured himself more brandy, glaring at Rycroft with meaning.

Carrington sighed, shaking his head. "I don't like it. I promised to bring her back, but I can't argue with the need for it. Greymore, I want word if anyone discovers who hired Hawke. I still don't believe my father is involved, but I can't rule it out from what you've all been telling me. Miss de Lacey, you have my word that no harm will come to you from my family. We simply won't accept that from my father."

"How can you be so sure she will be safe from them?" Max asked, his voice low.

"Because, dear brother, I don't care who our father thinks he is. I would turn him in for kidnapping. There's no reason a woman should be abducted from British soil. I intend to see this through."

Max snorted. "That will be the day."

"Max, that's enough," Maggie said, glaring at him with a look of warning.

Carrington leaned back, watching Max with narrowed eyes. "I don't care what you think of my family or me. My sister-in-law has suffered on account of you, and blood or no blood, I should call you out."

Max stood, hand resting on the sword hanging at his side. Carrington stood with him, his hand on a pistol.

"Stop. This is madness," Lynette said, finding her feet. She pointed to Carrington. "You don't need to make my decisions for me. If Maggie thinks I should stay here, then I will do so. If you mean to blame Mr. Rycroft for my kidnapping, then you might as well blame yourself as well." She pointed at Max. "If you think I'll just walk away from taking down Hawke and whoever hired him, then you are badly mistaken."

Carrington stared at her and dropped back to his chair, taking a new interest in the chicken on his plate. Max was grinning at her—that was, until she cut him a sharp glare. He sobered up and sat back down. She took her seat, but her appetite was gone.

She addressed Maggie. "Dear, I have a headache. I think I'd like to lie down."

Maggie made to stand, but Lynette shook her head.

"It's nothing a little peace won't fix. You go ahead and eat," Lynette said, rising again from her chair.

"I'll bring tea up to you later," Maggie said as Lynette left the room.

She stopped in the hall to gather herself, taking deep breaths. She didn't know how she had managed at that table as long as she had. Never mind the ill-mannered behavior all around. They'd spoken as though she hadn't been right there. She would decide when she was ready to go back to Briarwyck. Delia, of all people, would understand what her kidnapping had cost her.

Her life could no longer go on the path it had. She had to see this through, had to fight against her past. As much as Maggie said otherwise, Lynette knew what had happened would leave scars on both of them. They couldn't let those men think they would get away with this. Maggie was right. Too many times, men faced no consequences for ruining people's lives. Women couldn't wait around to be saved all the time.

She shuffled back to her room, wondering if maybe her things had finally been moved to her old room. Her feet tripped along the carpet, reminding her just how tired she was. It was fortunate she hadn't stayed at dinner. She would have fallen on her plate.

She made the top of the stairs when someone came up behind her. She angled her head at Rycroft following.

She hesitated. She didn't know if she should be alone with him again. Carrington certainly thought she should avoid him. In the end, she let him catch up to her while she tried to remind herself they had been alone plenty of times now and what she was feeling was from her experience, not from him.

"I thought you'd never stop," he said as he gained the last step. "I wanted to return your swords to you. We found them in the yard."

He led her back to his room, where she waited for him outside the door. He came out a moment later, carrying the swords and her sash.

"I have always found it a comfort to have a blade nearby," he said.

She stopped at the threshold to her room and gave him a wavering smile.

"If you would like me to sleep somewhere else, there are plenty of rooms. No need for me to be so close," he said.

She faced him then. Concern had returned to the corners of his eyes. She let out a breath. "That isn't necessary. Besides, this is your house. If anything, I should move."

He shook his head. "What can I do? Have I done something? Said something?"

A masculine voice echoed through the stairway, down the hall. "Rycroft?"

"Damn it, Greymore, give me a minute!" he yelled back.

"Paying your dues?" she asked with a raised brow.

"Indeed. I'll be doing a lot of groveling for the time being." He gave her a pained look.

"There's one thing you can do for me."

He perked up, tilting his head in question. "Name it."

"Train me. Let me help take down these men."

For a moment, she thought he would refuse. He shifted from foot to foot before settling against one wall. He was puzzling out his answer, she mused. How many ways were there to say no?

He gave her a quick nod, a movement that seemed to escape from him rather than come from him.

She held out her hand, and he looked between it and her eyes. The unanswered question lingered on his lips as he brought them to her hand. He turned it over, kissing her palm. The touch was so unlike what she was used to that the ripple of pleasure was genuine. She caught her breath as he continued his attentions on her wrist. She sensed the hesitancy in his movements as he caressed a hand up her forearm.

She moved her arm away with as much delicacy as she could manage. She couldn't be caught like this. He stepped away but didn't try to hide the hurt or the resentment at her reaction.

He cleared his throat. "If you need anything else, let me know," he said in an even voice. He sounded cold, serious. When she didn't answer, he spun on his heel, leaving her in the doorway to stare after him.

CHAPTER FIFTEEN

WHY HAD LYNETTE thought this man would be any different? She must have been lying to herself when they'd kissed. Had she gone mad? This was Rycroft she was thinking about. The man who had taken the Travers jewels. He was a dangerous man with loose morals and looser attentions. England was probably filled with his conquests. If it weren't for Maggie, Lynette would leave with Carrington at the first opportunity.

She locked the door to her room with a comforting click and went to the door connecting her room to Rycroft's. It didn't appear to lock on her side. She would need to discuss that with him. Maybe she could convince one of the men to fix the window in her old room. He wouldn't dare come through after Maggie's lecture, would he?

Her reputation should no longer concern her. She had been unchaperoned in this house long enough and consorting with a band of thieves. She would have no reputation to speak of at this point. It was unlikely any of the men in the colonies would know about her exploits here anyway, which was where she would be expected to find a husband. A future she would rather not think about. She had never had any intention of marrying, especially now that Delia was wed. There was far less pressure on her to give her parents grandchildren. Why let a man own her when she could be the doting aunt and eccentric spinster?

The door between her room and Rycroft's opened to a world of defenselessness whether he intended anything or not. She couldn't have that possibility hanging over her. He'd made his interest in her clear, but what she didn't know was what he intended to do about it.

A kiss seemed innocent enough, but it created other possibilities she was unprepared to consider. One day she would venture down that path, but for now, she would rather there be a locked door between her and temptation.

She dropped the swords on one side of the bed. They would rest next to her as she slept tonight. Rycroft was right about one thing: having a blade next to her was comforting. She hadn't been given much time to wash up before, and now she sorely wanted a bath. The newcomers were putting such a strain on Mrs. Johns that Lynette would be rude to request the labor. But it couldn't hurt to ask.

She pulled the bell.

She idled away at the window, watching the distant, murky waves. It wasn't long before a light tap sounded at her door, but where she expected Mrs. Johns, Mr. Howell stood.

"I'm sorry. I thought Mrs. Johns would come," she said through the open door.

He grinned at her. "She's attending Miss de Lacey. Did you need anything?"

She sighed. "I need some water. A bath would be nice, but I don't think I have the energy for it. Perhaps a basin of water?"

"I'll just steal some from Rycroft's room. Give me a moment."

He moved to Rycroft's door and twisted the knob, finding it unlocked. Imagine the man was sure enough of himself that he didn't lock his door. A moment passed before Howell reappeared with a wash basin filled with cool water and a clean cloth.

"Won't he need that?" she asked as he handed them to her. She set it down inside the room.

"What do I care? I'm not his servant." His wide grin produced a giggle from deep in her chest. "Did you need anything else?"

She shook her head.

"Good. I want to sleep. I'm supposed to train you in the morning. You better get some rest too."

"You're training me? What about Rycroft? I didn't realize we'd start so soon."

He lowered his chin, gazing at her with upturned eyes. "Mr. Self-Important is riding off early to ask after Hawke. He requested I start your training. We can go easy if you'd like, but the road you're going down won't be. There may be times you have to fight when you'd rather crawl under your bed."

"Not that I'm ungrateful, but why you?"

"Because, Miss Wolcott, I'm the only one he can trust not to…" He cleared his throat. "Take advantage of the situation. It's not that I have anything against you, but I am faithful to my wife."

Her jaw dropped open. "You're married?"

"Indeed, and I mean to return to her with a clear mind. That is, once I find her. She was removed from the ship I was left on."

"I'm so sorry. That's heartbreaking. You don't have any idea where she is?"

He shifted uncomfortably, and she thought he would change the subject. "We went looking for her while we were at sea. She could be anywhere by now. I have a better chance of finding her once this war calms down."

"Yes. I'd imagine. Do tell me if I can be of any help."

Howell's posture was slumped when he made to exit. She had gotten the impression he was a cheerful man, but underneath his ready smile, he'd revealed a sadness she hadn't picked up on.

"Good night, Miss Wolcott," he said as he retreated down the hall.

The day had been full of revelations, and the morning turned out to be following a similar trend when she learned what Howell considered going easy. His definition was far remote from her own. He started by ordering her to run laps along the yard. As her governess had informed her, ladies didn't run. Lynette proved her wrong—that was, if one could call what she was doing running.

She hoped nobody was watching while she made a calamity out of the word *run*. She must have looked like a broken-down horse or a fleeing dog. Her legs fell in front of her, but she knew nothing else as they carried her on every leaden step. When she finally finished her laps, she was panting, dropping to the ground in front of Howell.

"You look as though you've never run before," he said.

She glowered at him through pants.

"Get up," he said, nudging her with a wooden staff.

She groaned, pushing her burning legs to comply. He used the staff to move her right leg forward and her left leg back, guiding her into a comfortable stance.

"Bend your knees a little more." He nodded as she did so. "Good. Now hold that position. I will be back in half an hour."

He walked off before she could protest. Her breath was still short from her run. The muscles in her legs twitched and tingled as she tried to hold her stance. She thought she would topple over at times, but she corrected herself, hoping Howell wasn't watching from somewhere.

She was questioning her judgment of asking for training. When was she supposed to actually learn something? She would happily swing a sword at Howell right now. Rycroft too, for putting her through this. Their idea of training must be similar if Howell was starting her off. Her thighs were protesting as gravel crunched behind her. She thought with relief that it was Howell, but instead, Riley came up to stand in front of her.

"You look like you need a break," he said, looking her over. "If you want to sit down, I won't tell anyone."

"How do I know you aren't tricking me? I'll bet Howell has planned all sorts of torture if I'm not standing here when he gets back."

He tsked. "Howell is just doing what Rycroft asked. I fancy

our dear leader has left you to suffer while he's having fun groping a tavern whore. Should have taken me with him."

She tried to ignore the blow to her gut as she narrowed her eyes at him. "If you're bored, why don't you go bother someone else?"

"Oh, I would, but I'm supposed to remain here, and my choices are limited. I don't do well in one place for long though. I thought I'd be rewarded for saving Maggie. Instead, he tells me I drink too much and need to stay behind. I think he just didn't want competition for women."

She kept her peace, deciding he must be baiting her. Why he was trying to unnerve her, she didn't know.

He pulled out a flask and offered it to her. She shook her head, and he upended the container to his lips. He wiped his mouth on his hand.

"Are you bothering my student?" Howell's voice came from behind her.

"Hardly. I'm keeping her company while you dawdle. The poor girl just got back from being kidnapped, and you are already forcing her to work."

Howell stopped next to Riley. "This was her choice. Nobody is forcing her to do anything. Are you still drinking? You're supposed to dry out while they're gone."

Riley puffed out an exasperated breath. "Not you too. I don't drink too much."

Howell lowered his brows. "I know you don't drink too much, but you've been drunk for three days. Nobody wants a drunk around, which is why you were left behind. I'm sure Miss Wolcott doesn't want your company either. Get your grandmother to make you some coffee." He turned his back on Riley, looking over Lynette.

He corrected her stance with the staff again and nodded before walking off.

She groaned at his back, and Riley let out a low laugh.

"I hate to tell you he'll leave you like that for hours. Probably until midday. Good luck to you." He rose the flask in a toast. "Let me know if you'd rather drown yourself in whiskey."

She seriously considered his suggestion as he left her there. She was given time to think as the sun grew hotter over her sore limbs. Too much time to think. Instead of it changing her mind, though, it hardened her resolve. Rycroft must have expected her to quit. That's what this was all about. He didn't want her along when he found Hawke. She was a burden, a distraction from the cause. She wasn't about to prove him right.

By the time Howell returned, her muscles were rigid and her back straight. She refused to have it otherwise. He looked at her with wide eyes, beckoning her into the house. They were headed to the dining room, but she had no appetite when they sat down to eat. She picked at her food, eating bits here and there, scarcely aware of what she ate.

Once she was through, Howell led her back outside and directed her to make the same stance. She took it with a newfound determination. He only shook his head and walked off. She didn't know how long she was left there and didn't care to ask. She had found a sort of peace in the stillness, a sense of belonging that ate away the time into nothing.

As the sun tilted toward the horizon, the beat of horses approached. Rycroft must have spotted her as he came. He made his way directly to her after leaving his horse at the stables. He had Howell's staff in his hand.

"Tired?" he asked through a frown.

"No," she lied.

He swept the staff through the air in a curving arc that tricked her eyes away from his target, her legs. She flew backward, landing with a whoosh of air from her lungs. He stood over her with a boyish grin on his face. She would have slapped him if she could have reached his face.

"Come back out in the morning and get back into your stance," he said.

She groaned. "Do you delight in torturing me?"

He laughed, kindling her anger.

She continued and rose to her elbow. "You mean to leave me behind to stand all day while you cavort with whores and do the real fighting? Taking me along didn't bother you before."

His back faced her when he stiffened. He turned around, his brows pinched together. "Who told you that?"

"Riley. I thought you were asking after Hawke."

He bared his teeth at her. "Of course he did," he said through his them. "In case you don't remember, your coming along was the reason you were kidnapped."

She pushed herself up with her hands, staring at him from a sitting position. "Then Riley was lying?"

He drew himself up. "I didn't say that."

She blinked up at him, wanting him to deny it. Of course after she had refused him, he would seek out other women. She had no right to her jealousy, but it was there all the same. Her gaze dropped as he remained silent.

"Get up. Food is getting cold," he said, leaving her on the ground. She supposed he didn't want her rejection after the last time they'd touched. Still, she wouldn't have minded a hand up.

She sighed, staring off to the sun as it kissed the horizon, sending cascades of shimmering orange light into the clouds. The dirt and grass beneath her were soft enough that she didn't feel the urge to move. She thought she had held up well today, but there was no acknowledgment from Howell or Rycroft. She would have at least expected Rycroft to show some sense of disappointment that she had performed well on his obstacle. Instead, he had seemed uninterested, as though he'd been performing a task on his to-do list.

The moon had come out to greet her off to the west. She mused that it was almost full, perhaps another few days until it would be. Maybe it was better that she stayed behind. Surely Rycroft's men turned into wolves when the moon was full. She wouldn't put it past them.

"Are you dead?"

She angled her head back at Greymore striding up to her. "Perhaps."

"Dead or not, I'm supposed to keep you intact until you go back to Briarwyck." He folded his arms over his chest.

"I didn't ask you to. By all means, leave," she said, gazing back at the sprinkling of stars.

"Why are you doing this?"

"I happen to enjoy looking at the stars."

He shook his head. "That isn't what I meant. Why are you staying here when you can be at home, helping Lady Carrington?"

She let the rest of her body drop to the ground as she considered his question. "I'm not sure. It's something I need to do. This is my decision. Too many choices have been made for me. Too much of my life has been dictated by my mother's decisions in New York or Delia's life here. For once, I feel like I'm free, though I'm sure Carrington thinks he was given a choice."

"I haven't known you long, but from what I have seen, you have been given a great deal of choice."

"No. Aside from moving to Cornwall, I haven't had much of any decision over my life. You see how well that turned out. As soon as I leave, I'm taken away to Devonshire."

"Is that why you are refusing to come inside? You want the choice of eating?"

She scoffed. "That is ridiculous. I'm not avoiding eating."

He grunted. "From my experience, nobody avoids eating if they can help it. You're avoiding your problems, as I'm sure you are aware. It seems to be a particular talent of yours."

She scowled at him. The nerve of the man, implying she was a brat. Greymore was almost as conceited as Rycroft. All good looks and little consideration for others. She wondered how Carrington could stand him being around his wife with his classical features, touchable auburn hair, and kind blue eyes. He was an Adonis. Maybe she could convince Rycroft to throw him out.

She rolled to her feet. Her body groaned as it protested her standing. She brushed off her pants with her hands, glaring at him as she worked. "I do not avoid my problems. Don't think that knowing Delia or Abigail means you know something about me. You are fortunate I don't have my swords."

He gave a low laugh, nodding. "Quite true."

This was that damned British humor she could do without. Instead of wasting her time, she hurried off to the house, not looking back as Greymore followed behind. Let him think what he would. She wasn't going to give him any more attention than she had to. Let them all do what they would and leave her out of it. She'd rise to their expectations and surpass them.

But it wouldn't do if she didn't eat. She would have to go through this whole process again tomorrow, but this time, at least she knew what to expect, a day of being ignored while her body was worn down. Or so she assumed.

CHAPTER SIXTEEN

THE NEXT DAY turned out not to be the painful boredom of yesterday. It was worse.

After Lynette had taken up her position, Rycroft decided to accelerate her training or what he considered accelerating. He added her new sword to her stance, making her hold it out before her in a ready position. She would have preferred to swing it at him, but every time she moved to do just that, he thumped her with that infernal staff.

He seemed to instinctively know when she would grow tired and put down her guard, coming around the house to inspect her progress. When he did grace her with his presence, he seemed to be anxious, his gaze jumping from side to side as though he was looking for signs of attack. The gesture sent a chill along her skin. After all, she was being left out here.

"Would you stop making me feel like I'll be attacked at any minute?"

His lip quirked up. "Why? It's good practice."

"I know you aren't doing it to benefit me. What are you waiting for? Will the kidnappers return?"

"Perhaps, though I'm looking for any sign of messengers. Your hand is wavering," he said, pushing her arm up with the staff none too gently.

"Ow. Must you do that?" She suppressed the urge to rub her

arm. "What messengers?"

"I have Jason and John looking for Hawke. It's likely Travers might also send word, but I doubt it. Howell set off to the *Mary* this morning. I'm offering a reward for information as well. Take your pick."

"If it bothers you so much to be left behind, why are you still here?"

He grunted, forcing her leg back into place. "I want to make sure Rycroft House is secure before I leave. Not to mention I have no idea where to go."

She chose to ignore the pain that traveled up her leg from the staff. Every new bruise he gave her she imagined returning with the sword. Not exactly a fair exchange, but she didn't care.

"Do you need to stop?" he asked, watching with a faint smile. She knew he wanted her to quit, not just for a break or lunch, but to quit their training.

She sniffed. "I'll stop when I'm dead."

His face fell. "There's no shame in accepting defeat. Nobody would blame you for wanting to quit."

She narrowed her eyes at him, saying nothing.

The staff swept in the air, a blinding arc of movement that landed at the backs of her knees. Her legs wobbled, dropping her knee to the ground. She huffed, glowering up at him with all the anger she had cultivated over the past two days. She couldn't believe he'd done it again. At least she had only lost her footing this time.

"Your stance is off."

She didn't know what possessed her or whether she meant to act. A roar escaped her throat as she pounced him, taking his chest with her shoulder. He made a surprised sound, half gasp and half groan, flipping onto his back on the marshy earth.

She had cast her sword aside rather than impale him with it. She couldn't say whether she meant to hurt him or not. His eyes were wide, and she realized she was sprawled on top of him. Rather than scramble off, she stilled.

His lips spread into a toothy grin as his hands gripped her hips, positioning her to straddle him. His desire pressed against their breeches, sending a tingling heat through her belly. The position gave her a sense of power over him, a thrilling urge to possess his body the way he had come to possess her thoughts. She rubbed against the bulge in his pants, a half smile playing on her lips.

He made a strangled sound from the back of his throat and allowed his hands to roam over her bottom, kneading and pressing her into him.

Her breath caught in her throat as a wave of pleasure was sent bursting through her core, out to the tips of her toes. She wanted this, needed it like she needed water or air. Hang her past. This villain already held a part of her and kept it safe to his chest.

He studied her face with half-closed eyes. "As much as I like watching you strut around in those tight pants, couldn't you have worn a skirt today?"

She blinked, his words bringing her back to herself. A flush of warmth journeyed up her neck, into her face. She glanced off to the side, avoiding his gaze. "Is that all you want? A bedmate?"

He snorted. "What else is there? We both know this can't go anywhere."

"Charming."

She rolled herself off him to stand, then slapped the dirt from her clothes. He cushioned his hands behind his head, watching her forceful, angry movements.

"What did you expect from me? Marriage?" He crossed his ankle over his other leg. "I'm sorry, love, but if that's what you're looking for, then you're fooling yourself."

Her hands froze over her legs as she glanced over to his relaxed posture. "Stop calling me that. I don't expect anything from you. Ever." She retrieved her sword from the ground, pointing it at him. "This isn't working. I don't want to train with you anymore."

He shrugged into the ground. "There is nobody else."

"Fine."

"Meet me here after lunch. We'll try something different. You've been standing long enough."

She puffed out a laugh but nodded and left him to watch her retreat back to the house. Anger and hurt mingled in her chest. A scream rested in the back of her throat, but she pushed it down, concealing its weight in her stomach. She kept a steady pace until she rounded the house. Out of sight of Rycroft, she ran to the entrance. There was no sound or indication he was following her, but just the same, she wanted a head start. She needed to be out of his captivating presence. He was like one of those beasts that lured one in before snatching one with his razor-like teeth.

A venom that gave pleasure while it killed.

She had wanted him again. Her body was a mystery she couldn't hope to answer nor predict. If she let this go any further, she was likely surrendering to spinsterhood, which was already the path with which she was flirting. Perhaps the idea of being Rycroft's bedmate wasn't such a bad one. When would she get the chance again if she refused to marry?

Coming upon the entryway, she slowed as she heard low voices. She considered turning back but remembered Rycroft would come up from behind her any minute. With a quick intake of breath, she entered the house.

She caught a glimpse of Maggie retreating up the stairs. Mrs. Johns was standing next to Riley. Her arms were folded as her body angled between him and Greymore. She was lecturing Riley in their shared tongue as Greymore looked on with tightened lips.

"No," Riley answered his grandmother in English.

She said something else, her tone an angry whisper.

"I can, but I'm not going to like it."

Mrs. Johns nodded at him, then turned her frown on Greymore before leaving them.

"What was that about?" Lynette asked as Mrs. Johns moved toward the kitchens.

Riley narrowed his eyes at Greymore. "Nothing I can't handle."

Greymore waved a dismissive hand at the man. "It is of no consequence. A misunderstanding, nothing more. How is your training going?"

She cocked her head. "What training?"

He let out a low laugh. "I see your point. We can go anytime you want. I assure you, I've put up with enough nonsense here. Better yet, I will smash some teeth in if you prefer it?"

In one blinding moment, Riley drew a knife from nowhere. "You should go, Miss Wolcott. Don't want you witnessing this," Riley said as he inched closer to Greymore. "In fact, take the carriage back to Briarwyck. I'll take care of him."

Without hesitation, she put herself between them, raising her hands to shield herself. "Didn't Mrs. Johns just tell you not to do this?"

Riley kept his eyes on Greymore as he spoke to her. "She's not in here now, but this filth is." He angled his knife at Greymore.

"But I'm here," Rycroft said as she caught a glimpse of him at the corner of her eye.

"Stay out of this, Max," Riley growled.

Rycroft placed himself in front of Riley, shielding her from him. "Unlikely. Greymore here is our guest, and I'd hate to see our lovely Miss Wolcott injured while you try to slaughter him."

"I won't miss."

Rycroft shook his head. "I know, but that doesn't mean Greymore or Miss Wolcott won't get injured while you're bathing in blood. May I ask what this is all about?"

Riley squinted, making the red rims of his eyes more apparent. "He was giving Miss de Lacey unwanted attention."

Lynette scoffed. "Greymore gives everyone in a skirt attention."

Rycroft grinned back at her from over his shoulder. "Maybe it is a good thing you aren't wearing skirts." He faced Riley. "Maggie can stand up for herself. I'm sure she doesn't need your interference."

"For God's sake, he's drunk. I was merely talking to her in passing," Greymore interjected.

Rycroft sighed. "Riley, get some rest. I'll take you with me as soon as word arrives, but I can't have you along if you've been drinking. Mrs. Johns would have my head if you got trampled by a horse." He shivered. "That woman terrifies me."

Lynette released a nervous giggle as Riley replaced the knife into his sleeve.

"This wouldn't have happened if you had taken me to the tavern. I have needs too, you know?" Riley said in a high-pitched whine.

Rycroft stilled like a cat ready to strike. "No, I don't know."

"I need to get out of this house. Find release."

Rycroft made a guttural sound. "Mrs. Johns does fine. She's never once shown a desire to leave the house."

"He means he wants a whore, Rycroft," Greymore said, his voice a lazy drawl.

"I know that," Rycroft snapped. "Miss Wolcott is right there, you know."

Greymore chuckled. "She's heard worse. Hell, she's been through worse from what I understand."

Riley burst into drunken laughter. They watched him in confusion as he leaned over, grabbing his stomach in his fit. He stopped to wipe a stray tear and looked among their faces. "You misunderstand, Greymore. He doesn't want Miss Wolcott hearing he was with whores."

Her heart beat in her ears, and her stomach soured.

Everyone fell silent while Riley continued his laughter into the dining room. Lynette gritted her teeth together against the response she wanted to shout at them. Let the man have his whores.

Greymore followed Riley into lunch, leaving her alone with Rycroft.

He made a slow turn toward her, brows raised as he assessed

her mood. "It wasn't like that. We went to the tavern to talk to the owner. Some of my men used the facilities, but I stayed at the bar, talking to the regulars."

She nodded once, pushing past him to the dining room. "As I said, I don't expect anything of you. Just don't expect anything from me." She didn't bother to look back at him, though she knew the words would sting. Good.

The meal was uneventful. Riley mumbled over his coffee while the rest of them stared off. To her surprise, Jeremiah Rycroft joined them, spending the majority of the time talking to his brother and Greymore. Maggie never came back down for the meal. Lynette spent most of the time silent, speaking up only to answer direct questions. She picked at the simple meats and cheeses with bread as long as she could stand it and made a dignified exit.

She found Maggie in her room, changing into a delicious riding habit of pale pink. Lynette glanced down at her own loose linen shirt and breeches with some regret.

Maggie noticed her frown and giggled. "I have another if you would like to borrow it, though if I were you, I would be grateful for the pants. At least you don't have to ride sidesaddle."

Lynette raised her brows. "You're going riding, then? I thought Rycroft insisted on accompanying you."

Maggie giggled again. "We all are, silly. That is, Max, you, Greymore, and I. Jeremiah was invited, but he tends to prefer reading in the library." Maggie narrowed her eyes as she studied Lynette. "I've meant to ask you, What did you do to your hair?"

Lynette's jaw slackened. She had been wearing her hair up, hiding the loss of length since she had cut it, but occasionally, thin wisps of hair would escape. "It was getting in the way. You're the only one who has noticed."

"Oh, I doubt that. That mane of yours was so long I often thought you could clothe yourself in it. You'd have to be blind not to notice." Maggie startled as though she was surprised by her own words. "I didn't mean that to sound rude. Don't worry, dear.

It will grow back."

"I'm not sure I want it to." Lynette sighed, shaking her head. "What happened back there with Greymore and Riley?"

Maggie fetched her riding gloves from the bed. "They're both fools. I can't say I understood half of what they were arguing about, but I am sheltered, not stupid. They are fighting over me. Not that I have shown either of them any interest—quite the opposite, actually."

It was Lynette's turn to giggle. "I'd be careful of Greymore. He breaks hearts before a woman can realize he owns hers. I didn't know Riley had it in him."

"Riley has been in love with me for years. We all grew up together, you know." Maggie waved away the conversation in dismissal, walking to the door. "Come. I have yet to see what horse my brother has conjured for you. He has the most astonishing luck finding horses."

Lynette followed her out the door. "Certainly you mean he has the nimblest hands at finding horses?"

Maggie snorted as they made their way down the hall. "Indeed. I believe you hit the heart of the matter. He assured me he bought this one. Really, he is the most superstitious man. A bit obsessed with fairy tales, if you ask me."

Lynette let out a slow breath. She wasn't one to judge, knowing she was almost as watchful of omens. Just yesterday, during training, she had caught herself counting magpies. There had been seven, which made perfect sense to her. The song still echoed through her mind: *One for sorrow, two for mirth, three for a wedding, four for a death, five for silver, six for gold, seven for a secret not to be told.* She could think of any number of secrets the magpies might indicate.

She thought better of revealing this to her friend. Instead, she asked, "What's that he wears around his neck? I thought maybe it was a medal of a saint, but that doesn't seem like him."

Maggie stopped at the top of the stairs to consider her. "I'm surprised you've seen it. You're right. That doesn't sound like him. It's a locket, a miniature of his mother. My father had one made for each of us to honor her memory. Max is the only one who wears it around his neck. I'm afraid it is another superstitious quirk of his. He doesn't like the idea of putting the necklace down as though putting down the trinket would let his mother down. I know; it makes little sense." Maggie shook her head as she descended the stairs.

Rycroft's actions made perfect sense to her. It wasn't so much putting down the trinket but the act of discarding it that would blur the memory of his mother. He was trying to remember, attempting to stop the toll of time on the fragments remaining of her. To put down the locket would be to forget, to abandon. For once, she understood Rycroft and what drove him. Loyalty.

CHAPTER SEVENTEEN

THEY WERE THE last ones to arrive at the stables. Greymore and Rycroft had already saddled the horses. Greymore had his flame-colored Ember ready to go. Hermes and Athena were both pawing at the ground while Rycroft was attending to a third animal. The mare was a sleek dark-chocolate bay, the light-brown leather saddle contrasted with her dark coat. At a distance, she would appear black.

The men looked up at their approach, both smiling in the rare sunny weather. It was a day for riding if she had ever seen one. For a moment, her mind went to Delia, who would mourn the fine day from her bed. Lynette shook the thought away. She would be back in time.

"Imagine, ladies, I've found something in common with Greymore. If I had known he had a passion for horses, I might have moved our little mix-up to include Ember," Rycroft said, shaking his head. "A pity he found the animal before me." He sighed. "Such a waste."

Greymore smiled at his horse. "Don't think I wouldn't have found her. I would know Ember from any other horse. She'd have to be confined to your stables. There would be little chance I would find her here."

"Yes, but I imagine Miss Wolcott would have recognized her from Briarwyck, or my brothers might have taken notice. Are you sure you don't want to sell? Or maybe a game of cards?"

Greymore chuckled. "Making a deal with you is like making a wish in the old stories. You get what you thought you wanted, but then you realize you are now twice as bad off as you were. No, thank you."

"A pity." He faced Lynette. "Love, what do you think of her?" he asked, indicating the horse.

She decided to ignore his continued familiarity. Perhaps he called every woman that. "A beauty. What's her name?"

"That has yet to be decided. I thought maybe you could help me come up with one. You'll have to ride her before making any rash decisions. I was thinking Persephone."

Lynette shook her head. "If I am going to have a say in this, I'm not going to go along with your strange naming patterns. Mix it up a bit, Rycroft."

He crossed his arms in front of his chest. "Persephone is a perfectly good name. A fitting one for her rider."

"I don't mean to interrupt, but there is only so much nice weather. I'm afraid we are pushing our luck with this one," Greymore said, mounting Ember.

Maggie followed his lead, joining him on Athena. They exited the stables, waiting in the yard for them. Rycroft seemed to expect some sort of cue from Lynette. She wished she was as adept at mounting horses as Maggie. It didn't help that this horse was unfamiliar.

She held out her hand to Rycroft for assistance. He gave her an encouraging smile as he took it, helping her up.

"Does this mean no more standing in the yard?" she asked with a small smile.

He scoffed. "Of course not. You're a small woman. I decided it would be better if you learned to flee first. You need to improve your horsemanship to do that. Plus, a fast horse couldn't hurt. This horse should give you a good lead. She's from a family of racehorses."

"Then why is it that she isn't racing?"

"Because I bought her," he said as though that explained everything. He leaped upon Hermes in one quick movement and beckoned Lynette out to the yard.

The mare she rode was as easy to ride as Athena, except she was skittish at times. Rycroft reassured Lynette she would get used to the horse over time, which was why she needed practice. She tried not to take offense, but she knew he was right. She had never been good at sports, though she prided herself on her riding astride being better than her sidesaddle. That wasn't saying much, but she had her dignity to protect.

Maggie and Greymore took the lead, turning their horses down a well-traveled path that Maggie was accustomed to. Rycroft politely walked his horse beside Lynette's, occasionally giving unwanted advice on riding. She made her horse nervous, but it didn't help that he had to point it out.

They were already trailing behind. The pair in front of them waited up ahead, but Rycroft waved them on. Maggie leaped Athena forward, causing Ember to rush after her.

"Aren't you concerned about leaving Maggie alone?" Lynette asked.

"No, she will be fine. She was taken unaware before. Plus, she has Greymore with her. Both of them are armed, and I know where they are going."

She urged her horse on, hoping she wasn't embarrassing herself too much. He nodded in approval. A childish grin spread across her face. She could do this. A little speed at a time should do it. Perhaps she wouldn't fall to her death that way. Athena was a more manageable horse to ride, but that didn't mean she couldn't master this one.

They were headed into a wooded area now. Maggie and Greymore had vanished from the path. She narrowed her eyes at the dirt trail as though it was to blame for her crawling pace. Her hands twitched in impatience, and she quickened the horse once again. This time, the motion sent the horse into a bolt of speed.

Her heart and stomach crammed into her throat. She cried

out as they sped forward. The reins were forced out of her hands. Rycroft shouted after her, but Hermes struggled to keep up.

A small branch smacked across her face as the mare made her own path through the trees. She closed her eyes against the sting, lowering her body to avoid further injury. It seemed the whole equine world was out to kill her.

Lynette curled into herself and clenched her teeth. She tried to soothe the horse, whispering and then shouting for it to stop. Still, they crashed through the forest in a mad dash to nowhere. This was exactly the way she pictured she would die.

Rycroft shouted beside her.

She squinted. He rode up to grasp the fallen reins. He brought the horse under control with calm patience that she could only dream of. Her body shook as he brought both horses to a halt. Her hands were clenched in the poor mare's shiny black mane. It was no wonder the horse was trying to kill her. She let out a breath and uncurled her hands.

Rycroft had dismounted, offering her a hand down. She scrambled off the horse, falling more than jumping into his arms.

"I'm going to kill that horse," Lynette said, righting her posture.

Rycroft stiffened, staring off into the trees.

"What is it?" she asked.

"Hush," he said, laying a hand over her mouth. He cocked his head a moment and tugged her by the hand, through the trees. He brought the horses along to a heavily wooded area and tied them off before he started to run.

If she hadn't been running the past two days, she would have protested at his pace. The exercise didn't soften the exertion, but she knew what to expect. Her breath became pants as they tunneled through branches and jumped over fallen logs. She tripped countless times only to have him hoist her to her feet.

He climbed over the trunk of a massive fallen oak and tugged her down behind it. She lay next to the trunk. Rycroft covered her body with his as he listened for whatever he had heard. His hand went back to her mouth as he attempted to quiet her. She sucked in a breath, letting short spurts of air escape. Her chest was threatening to heave for lost air.

Then she heard them.

Men's voices. At least three of them. They were trampling through the woods, not bothering to disguise their noise. The men must not be aware of her and Rycroft. She almost sighed with relief but for the hand at her mouth. These men must mean trouble, or Rycroft wouldn't have gone to such pains to hide them.

A barking laugh echoed through the trees.

Rycroft angled his gaze sideways as if he could see through the trunk. Lynette pressed herself deeper into the ground, the bed of earth more comforting than she would have thought. If only she could burrow away from here. She'd thought Lycan would be long gone by now, having left with Hawke. If Lycan was here, then more of the kidnappers were with him.

"Are you sure they went this way?" one of them called. They must have thought their prey was deaf.

"There was only one other path," a second man said.

"Let's turn back. They probably went the other way. I'm taking that Arabian mount when we catch them. You can split my share. That horse is a treasure," the first man said.

Rycroft's eyes met hers. The Arabian mount could only be Ember. They were after Maggie, not Lynette or Rycroft. She hoped Maggie and Greymore were far away by now, but Rycroft was right. They could take care of themselves.

The men retreated, their rustling growing more distant. After an eternity passed, Rycroft removed his hand from her mouth, but he stilled her when she tried to move.

"This could be a trick. Stay still," he whispered next to her ear. His warm breath tickled her skin, and she shifted under him to relieve the sensation.

He frowned at her, willing her to stop moving. The weight of his body rested on hers. He had been right in his assessment of her size. His body covered her from head to toe with more of him to spare. Instead of feeling heavy, though, he was a comforting cocoon of hard muscle.

She wrestled her hand free from being pinned to her side, and she brought it to her nose to scratch. Her eyes closed, and her mouth dropped open in a silent moan of relief. She blinked up at Rycroft, whose frown had deepened. The men must have been long gone by now. He was paranoid.

She let her fingers trace along his waistcoat buttons, tugging them out of their holes. She glanced up to see his eyes narrowed at her progress. What else was she supposed to do? She was bored, and her hands got nervous. He allowed her to continue this way, his head cocked to listen until she got to the bottom button on his shirt. He snatched her wrist so she couldn't go any further.

His shirt gaped open above her, revealing a triangle of muscled chest with a dashing mix of hair and scars. Her gaze jumped back to his annoyed glare, and she turned a sweet smile on him. She angled her neck up to lick along his collarbone. He had an exotic, salty taste, like a foreign dish that seemed familiar and new.

He brought his hand to cover her mouth again only to have her lick that too. His hand refused to budge, and he closed his eyes as she moved her mouth to his fingers, sucking each of them as she ran her tongue along their lengths. He was showing admirable restraint against her attentions, revealing no other emotion than his stony disapproval. She knew better. His erection was pressed against her lower belly.

When it seemed he could take no more, he rolled to the side, releasing her from the ground. He stalked away like an angry child, toward the horses, showing his disapproval with each dramatic step. She giggled and walked after him, a spring in her step. Once they reached the horses, he rounded on her.

"You could have gotten us killed," he said through his teeth while buttoning his shirt.

She put her hands on her hips. "They were long gone. Besides, I was quiet."

"You're driving me mad. Get on the damned horse. We need to get back."

She accepted his hand up and took the reins from him. "Do you think Maggie and Greymore have returned?"

He nodded as he mounted Hermes. "I have no doubt of it. The path Maggie takes is a loop. There is no way they caught up to them."

The mare followed Hermes through the trees. Lynette let her horse guide the way as Hermes gained speed. She should have trusted the horse if only to save her own neck. They were racing on now, having gained the clearing. There was nobody in sight as the stables came into view.

"Rycroft, how did they know we were there?" she asked as her mount drew beside him.

"I don't know, but I intend to find out. Say nothing of what happened today. I need to figure out who betrayed me." He whistled, and Hermes picked up speed, taking the mare with him.

They spotted Maggie and Greymore standing just outside of the stables and reined in next to them. Maggie's arms were folded as she watched their approach.

"What took you so long?" Maggie asked in her stern, motherly tone.

"We ran into some old friends. You might remember them from your little journey," Rycroft said.

Maggie's arms and jaw dropped. "Are you all right?" Her eyes went to Lynette. "You look like you've had a scuffle."

Rycroft choked at her words. "We had to hide out until they were gone. Seems they were chasing you. Seen anything?"

Maggie and Greymore exchanged glances, then shook their heads in unison. "There was nobody behind us, including you," Greymore said, his tone accusing.

"Good. Go inside. Tell nobody what happened." Rycroft dismounted and pulled the reins from Lynette's hands. He guided the mare and Hermes into the stable without bothering to help her down.

Maggie and Greymore left without another word, though Greymore glanced back to them until the stables obstructed her view. Carrington could not have chosen a worse man to protect her. He didn't seem to care at all for her virtue. Perhaps he thought she no longer had any. She could have died today, and the man was safely back here with Maggie. Not that she regretted his protecting her friend.

Rycroft left her mounted as he went to stable Hermes. She considered jumping down but thought better of it. When she remembered her fall out the window, her blood chilled. Upon returning, he pulled his new mare back into her stall and met Lynette's eyes.

"Are you going to help me down?" she asked, her words uncertain.

"I haven't decided. Let me seethe a bit longer."

She tsked. "Please? I'll be good." She pouted her lower lip at him.

His mouth grew into a wide, mischievous grin. "Oh, I doubt that, but why would I want you to be?" He came to her side, arms outstretched for her.

She twisted in the saddle, placing her hands on his shoulders. He gripped her waist and pulled her from the horse. He froze as their bodies touched, holding her angled above him. Her chest was just above his eyes. He let her slide along his body, every inch of her thrilling at his touch. How did he make her feel this way? Had her body accepted him before she had?

He stopped her descent inches from the ground. Their faces were level, a short movement away. Hungry want shone from his eyes, and she knew they mirrored her own.

"Say it," he breathed. She tasted his exhale like warm honey.

"Kiss me."

He brought her in closer, taking her lips in a gentle caress. He inched back, and her breath caught as he studied her expression.

Sparks like fire danced in his gaze. His mouth teased hers with slow pecks along her lips. A burst of need pooled into her belly.

She pulled his face in closer and ran her fingers through his hair. She nipped at his plump lips, causing him to laugh, a deep rumble in his chest. He lifted her higher, grasping her bottom with both hands, prompting her to circle him with her legs.

He rained kisses along her jaw and neck, stopping only to suck and tease the sensitive skin along the side of it. A moan trickled out of her mouth. He paused, watching her growing need with a knowing smile.

"Why did you stop?" she asked, breathlessly.

"We're in a stable."

She blinked. "Is that going to stop you?"

He growled at her from the back of his throat. He adjusted his grip on her and brought her to an empty stall. She yelped as he laid her down on the fresh hay.

"This better be clean," she warned, but already she was pulling him down by his waistcoat.

His attentions had become more heated, the man letting his raw need show in his frantic kisses. His head moved to her chest, where he stroked her nipple with his tongue through her men's shirt.

"Oh," she cried in surprise. A current ran from her breast to the sensitive area between her legs.

He lifted her shirt, untucking it from her pants. "So beautiful," he mumbled and took her other breast into his mouth. He teased and pinched the other nipple with his hand.

Her gasp was followed by a sharp cry that echoed off the walls. She arched her back to give him better access as he devoured her. Her hands tugged at his hair to tell him what her lips could not. Why had she ever flinched at his touch? His mouth alone was enough to send her over the edge.

The flesh between her legs began to throb, and she squeezed her legs together to satisfy it. He caught the reaction and pushed apart her legs with his knee, which he used to stroke her.

Her eyes widened. What he was doing was wicked, as naughty as his suckling her breasts.

"What are you doing to me?" she said through throaty pants. Her nails fastened into his shoulders to hold on.

He met her gaze, his mouth still absorbed in its scandalous pursuits. She screamed as he watched her ride his leg through their clothes. A euphoric wave crashed over her, causing her head to drop back into the hay. Her chest heaved as he raised his head.

"You're a virgin," he accused, brows knitted in confusion.

She closed her eyes, trying to shut out his words.

"You are, aren't you?"

She nodded once.

"Damn." His weight lifted off her as he steadied himself on his arms. She reached out to him, holding him in place while her legs pulled him back down.

He sighed. "I don't bed virgins."

She snorted. "You were doing just fine before."

He pushed himself up to peck her on the nose. "Why are you so eager to ruin yourself? I'm not worth it."

"You mean you don't want me. What is so wrong with being a virgin? Do you prefer whores?"

He shook his head. "You know that isn't what I meant. I want nothing more than to take you here and now until your screams alarm everyone in the next two counties." Indeed, his hardness was pressed against her to emphasize his point. "And for your information, I don't ever pay for sex."

"Then what is the problem?"

He pressed his lips against hers, rekindling the longing in her body. She ran her legs along his bottom as he gave her sweet, slow kisses.

"You know I want you," he whispered.

"Then I'm yours," she said, her lashes dusting along her cheeks.

A lazy grin played at his mouth as she nuzzled his face. She kissed the corner of his lips, coaxing him to continue. She traced her tongue along his bottom lip. He moaned, pressing his hips further into her. A moment passed where she thought he would give in to her demands.

Then his body stiffened over her, and behind him, a throat cleared.

CHAPTER EIGHTEEN

RYCROFT BRACED HIS arms around Lynette, attempting to maintain her modesty. She froze into him, hoping his body was sufficient coverage for her top half.

"What is it?" he asked the newcomer.

The man cleared his throat again. "The twins have arrived. They wanted to speak with you." She recognized Riley's voice.

"Did it occur to you to wait before interrupting?" she snapped.

Rycroft chuckled, bending down to give her a brief kiss with his smiling lips.

"About that..." Riley cleared his throat yet again.

"Do you have a cold or something?" Rycroft asked in a distracted voice.

"I'm sorry, Max, but Greymore is on his way here. He was starting to get suspicious when you didn't return to the house."

"Who cares?" Lynette asked, staring up at Rycroft with a teasing smile.

Rycroft craned his neck to peer at Riley. "Damn it. Go distract him for a minute. Let us straighten up."

Riley must have left when Rycroft rolled off her. He checked his buttons and hair. Then he studied her. One side of his mouth quirked up as he admired her disheveled state.

She stuck her tongue out at him. "Are you really going to let him dictate your actions? Where is the notorious bandit?"

He offered her a hand up, and she took it. "Why do you have such poor timing with your desires?"

She buttoned up her shirt as fast as her fingers would move. "I don't have poor timing. You have ill luck."

He made a choked sound. "No, I don't. Never mind. I'll go out there and help with the distraction. Start grooming the bay. Unless you have a better idea?"

She smirked at him. "Oh, I have a lot of ideas. Unfortunately, you appear to be afraid of a single viscount."

"It isn't him I worry about. It's my brothers, Maggie, and whoever you have over the pond." He ran his hand through his hair as he turned to leave.

For a man that led a small army, he was a coward.

She finished straightening her shirt and hair and did as he suggested. The horse stayed calm as she approached and seemed to welcome the grooming. She could learn to like this horse if she could get over their wild ride into the forest. In a way, the detour had been beneficial too. Not just the enjoyment she got from hiding with Rycroft but also being a distraction for Maggie.

The sounds of arguing approached the stall. She didn't see what they had to shout over. For once, she understood what Delia had been going through back in New York. At least she didn't have to worry about her family intervening. Freedom suited her. Perhaps she would take to wearing breeches regularly.

Rycroft appeared at the stall door, backing up to the entrance. He blocked her view of the men following him.

"Where is she?" She heard a familiar voice ask. Her jaw dropped, and her hand stilled its brushing. It couldn't be. No, she was imagining things. She shook her head to clear the thought away.

"Miss Wolcott, this man says he's your brother," Rycroft said, turning to face her as he moved to reveal the people behind him.

Sure enough, her brother, Jeffrey, stood behind him. His white-blond hair was ruffled, and his brown eyes were narrowed in an unfriendly glare, but it was him. He towered over Rycroft as he did everyone, and Rycroft took a wary step back as he saw the look of recognition on her face.

"Jeffrey, what are you doing here?" she asked in a quiet voice.

He scowled at her. "I could ask you the same. You should be at Briarwyck, where I came to see you. What has happened to you? You're wearing pants. Did you cut your hair?" He studied her with wide eyes. "Please tell me you didn't cut your hair."

She folded her arms. "What if I did?"

He rubbed at his forehead as though he was in pain. "Mother is going to kill you. Hell, I'll have to kill Carrington. Go change your clothes. We're leaving."

She held her ground. "I will not."

He blinked at her in confusion. "Are you wearing a sword?"

She twirled full circle to show off her swords.

He covered his eyes. "Those pants are far too revealing. I knew your sister would be a bad influence on you. You should have stayed in New York."

Rycroft tried to hold back a laugh behind his hand but failed, drawing Jeffrey's attention to him.

Jeffrey pointed at Rycroft. "You. What have you done to my darling sister? She was a baby when she left. Do I have to call you out as well? I should have brought my dueling pistols." He grabbed Lynette by the arm, half dragging and half carrying her into the yard.

"Netty, I don't know what happened. I'm not sure I care to know what happened, but we are leaving now. Your sister is close to her due date, and you'll most likely miss your friend's wedding. Our parents are back at Briarwyck."

She let him drag her back toward the house, too shocked and ashamed to say anything. Rycroft watched them as he followed behind with Riley and Greymore. She gave them a sheepish grin. Rycroft and Greymore looked chastened, while Riley was shaking his head.

"Jeffrey, stop," she pleaded as they went through the entrance. "Please, let me say something."

He released a long sigh but stopped in the entryway. They were drawing a crowd. The three men caught up to them, and Carrington and the twins were already there. Rycroft stood off to the side of her, a sword's length away from Jeffrey.

"Jeffrey," she said in her calmest voice, "it's already late in the day. At least wait until morning before you drag me off."

"She has a point, Mr. Wolcott," Maggie said from behind Carrington. She stepped out to join them. "Please don't take Lynette into danger. We just got back from the kidnapping."

"Kidnapping?" The color drained from Jeffrey's face. He studied the faces around, looking for answers.

Carrington swore, then shot a look at Maggie.

"Don't look at her like that," Lynette said to Carrington. "Why didn't you tell Jeffrey what happened?"

Jeffrey pinched the bridge of his nose. "I thought Delia was difficult. I told myself you would be a breeze. Of course Lord Carrington can protect a mousy little girl. Really, how hard can it be to keep up with this slip of a female? How much trouble can one person get into in the middle of the country? Apparently a lot." He held out his hand to Riley. "Can I borrow your sword? I prefer my pistols, but sadly, I didn't predict this."

Riley grinned wolfishly at him and handed over his sword.

Rycroft grunted. "Traitor."

"You can't be serious. Delia will kill you if you lift a hand to her husband," Lynette said.

"Aren't you afraid Carrington will harm your brother?" Maggie asked as she came up beside Lynette.

Lynette scoffed. "Carrington knows better than to kill my brother. His wife would slaughter him."

Carrington chuckled. "She is correct. My wife would slit my throat if I so much as bruised him." He paused. His face grew serious. "Our fighting days are over, brother. I apologize for not telling you. Some things in that story are not mine to reveal. Lynette came out fine, as did Miss de Lacey. We are searching for the kidnappers now, which is why Hugh was absent from Briarwyck.

"Sir," one of the twins interrupted, addressing Rycroft.

He nodded to him to continue.

"We spotted their camp not far from here. Hawke and Lycan are among them. It seems they're persistent in their efforts."

Rycroft lowered his brows. "Were you seen?"

The second twin folded his arms, narrowing his eyes at their leader.

"Right. I won't insult you," Rycroft said. "We will have to take them unaware." He spoke to Jeffrey. "You and Miss Wolcott are safe here, but if you leave before the threat is passed, I can't guarantee your safety."

Jeffrey stepped forward, meeting Rycroft toe-to-toe. He glared down at him. "Who are you again?"

Rycroft returned the stare. His hand rested on the butt of his sword. "I'm the one who saved your sister. More than once, might I add."

Jeffrey assessed him, reading his eyes the way hounds sized each other up. "Fine. We'll stay for now. You remind me of Carrington and Hugh, which is good enough. For now."

Carrington and Rycroft burst into laughter.

Jeffrey frowned at them in confusion. "What's so humorous?"

Carrington grinned at his brother-in-law and came around to put his arm across the man's big shoulders. "Mr. Jeffrey Wolcott, this is Maxwell Rycroft. He is my half brother."

"How...?" Jeffrey trailed off as Carrington led him away.

"I will explain later. For now, I believe that wonderful house-keeper has finished our meal," Carrington said, glancing over at Rycroft in a pleading way.

Rycroft turned his lip up at him. "Indeed. Lead the way. Brother."

Carrington had disarmed Jeffrey without the man realizing it. Carrington handed the blade back to Riley as he followed them to the dining room. The twins followed as well, with Greymore by their side.

Lynette lingered behind with Maggie and Rycroft.

"You didn't tell me you have a brother," Maggie said.

"You also didn't mention the man is a giant who will likely eat me if I move a finger wrong," Rycroft added.

Lynette looked between the siblings. She seemed to remember mentioning her brother to them, but maybe she'd spoken of Carrington. She made a mental note to thank her brother-in-law for keeping Jeffrey and Rycroft from killing each other.

"I'm sorry. I had no idea he would visit." She let out a long groan. "My parents are here too. Can't I just hide here?"

"Why wouldn't you want to see your parents?" Maggie asked.

"If you stay here, we'll have to stock up on food. They will lay siege to the house," Rycroft joked. He wasn't wrong.

"I don't mind my father, but my mother is overbearing. She probably packed a husband for me in her trunk."

Maggie giggled but covered her mouth when her eyes caught the shadow over Rycroft's face. She looked between them before murmuring her excuses as she went off to the dining room. They peered after her as she left.

"You think your mother is going to wed you off?" Rycroft asked, avoiding her gaze.

She shrugged. "I don't know. It was what she was doing in New York."

"About before," he said, rubbing his neck. "It didn't happen. You can consider your mind guilt-free." He fidgeted in place, more nervous than she had ever seen him.

"Max, I don't want to leave."

His gaze jumped to hers at the use of his given name. "I don't know what to tell you."

"Ask me to stay. Make some kind of excuse. Push me out a window if you have to. Briarwyck is as much a prison as New York was." Her lip quivered as she held back the tears.

He shook his head. "You know I can't do that."

"Can't or won't?" A tear raced down her face.

His hand rose, and he brushed her tear away with his thumb. His touch lingered as he cupped her chin. "Don't ask this of me. I don't have what you want."

She rubbed her cheek into his palm. "You are enough."

He pulled his hand from her. She felt stung, like a jolt to her nerves ran through the surface of her skin. He would let her go, abandon her the same way Forrest had meant to. No, he had to be better than this. She couldn't believe it of him. Could she?

"Come," he said, nodding toward the dining room.

She didn't mean to follow him, but somehow she found herself sitting at the dining table between Maggie and Jeffrey. Maggie squeezed her hand under the table, and Lynette gave her a weak smile. She avoided Jeffrey's eyes, trying to hide her mood. It was like falling into her old role of mousy sister. Nobody asked after her, and she was left to her own inner torment. Nobody except Maggie.

Rycroft was seated next to Carrington, who sat next to Jeffrey. She sensed Rycroft's eyes on her from time to time, but she kept her gaze down at her plate. She ate but didn't notice or see what she was eating. At first, Maggie whispered comforting things to her, then she attempted to make her laugh, but Lynette didn't react. At last, her friend simply held her unused hand in silence.

When the meal concluded, Maggie stood, taking Lynette with her. The men seemed startled by the abruptness of their departure, but Maggie didn't seem to notice. She pulled Lynette into the hall and up the stairs. They went into Maggie's room, where she set Lynette down on her bed.

"What did he do?"

She gazed into Maggie's stern face. "Who?"

Maggie scoffed. "You know who. My idiot brother. Do I need to go knock some sense into him?"

Lynette dropped her head. "Don't do that. This is my fault."

"How could this possibly be your fault?" Maggie began pacing the room. Anger accented each step.

"I demand too much. My mother always said so. It doesn't matter. He doesn't care two figs for me. I will be back at Briarwyck soon, and I can look forward to needlework and painting."

"You're mistaken," Maggie said, uncertainty coloring her words.

"I'm not," Lynette said, her voice firm.

Maggie pulled Lynette into a deep hug. "Please visit me. For as long you are in England, you're welcome here. Don't hesitate to come to me at the first chance you get. I've never had a sister, but if I did, I would want her to be like you."

Lynette returned the hug, taking comfort in the embrace. "And you should come to Briarwyck as well. At least, when this is all over. I intend to try to stay in England." Her limbs were growing heavy, and she pulled back from Maggie. "I had better bathe before I'm too tired. I've probably got dirt and hay all over me."

Maggie chuckled. "Oh, you do, but I don't think anyone noticed. Your brother was too caught up in your men's clothes, and everyone else was too afraid of your brother to look at you. I'm sure Max saw it. If Mary was still around, she would have insisted you bathe before coming into the dining room. I blame Max's band of ruffians for the informality here." She made a sound of disapproval, something between a sigh and grunt. "Now let me get your bath settled. The tub to your room is in Max's chambers. So you can bathe in here instead. You wait right here, and I'll get everything ready."

"You must be exhausted too. Why don't you let Mrs. Johns handle everything?"

Her friend put her hands on her hips in the way she had done with Rycroft. "I've only had a pleasant ride in the country. You had the scare of your life and likely a tumble in the hay." Maggie's lips curled up.

Lynette covered her face, attempting to hide the damning thoughts written across her face. She heard no judgment in

Maggie's words, only a friendly teasing. At least she wouldn't have to attempt the subject in the future. In a way, it was nice to have someone who shared her secrets. Her own sister couldn't be a better option.

As Maggie made preparations for the bath, Lynette thought back over the day behind her. She had no regrets and would have done everything the same if given a choice. The wild ride through the forest hadn't been pleasant, but the outcome had been. She must be a wanton to have desired Rycroft there in the stables. Perhaps that was why he had thought she wasn't a virgin. Surely no normal woman would want her first time to be in a bed of hay?

True to her word, Maggie ordered the bath prepared, and in half the time it would have taken at Briarwyck with paid servants. She bossed Rycroft's highwaymen into heating and hauling the water up the stairs from the kitchen. Yet the men never complained about the task. Instead, they worked gladly to please Maggie. Lynette fancied half of them were in love with her friend.

The bath itself was divine. Perfumed water swirled around her as she lathered the rose soap Maggie had provided. She hadn't had a soak so relaxing since she'd been back at Briarwyck, and even then, they hadn't had such quality soap or water this warm. When she reluctantly got out, Maggie was there to help her towel down.

"I forgot to get your night rail, but then I remembered what you have for a night rail," Maggie teased. "So I brought you one of mine."

Lynette set the white garment over her head and studied the fit in Maggie's mirror. The neckline slid off her shoulders, but she suspected it was designed to. The edges were trimmed in a pretty lace pattern. She had never slept in anything nicer. She tilted her body to the light and realized the fabric was almost translucent.

She slumped her shoulders. "Maggie, I can't wear this back to my room. If my brother saw me, I'd be escorted by my ear to a nunnery."

"Oh, sweety, it's dark in the hall. Besides, your room is only a few doors off."

Lynette accepted this reasoning because she adored the beautiful garment and didn't want to give it up. She picked up her slippers in one hand and dashed off for her room, pausing only when she came to the door. Her hand jerked the knob, but it wouldn't give. She stared down at it with pinched brows and tried again. Her door was locked.

She was about to rush back to Maggie's room to beg her to get a key when a voice broke the silence of the hall.

CHAPTER NINETEEN

"**W**HAT SEEMS TO be the trouble?" Rycroft's voice was low with a hint of concern.

Lynette whirled around to face him, not remembering in her haste that she would be revealing much of her body beneath the thin fabric. Rycroft's eyes widened as he caught sight of her in the low light of the lamp he carried. She cursed her ill luck, crossing her arms over her chest.

"Did you lock my door?" she asked, fury darkening her voice.

His eyes jumped between her face and her body. "Why would I do that? Maggie took the keys again. I can't even lock my own door, which means people keep taking things."

She remembered Howell walking right into Rycroft's room to get the wash basin from before.

"Damn," she said, stomping her bare foot on the floor.

It all came to her in a rush. Maggie taking the keys. Maggie offering to help her to a luxurious bath. Maggie taking away her clothes only to give her this revealing, sorry excuse for a nightgown. Maggie encouraging her to go back to her room. Maggie locking her out of her room.

"Is something wrong?" Rycroft asked. His brain must have left when he'd seen her. "Maggie said you needed my help."

Maggie setting them up.

Lynette clenched her teeth, examining her options. She wanted to run, but where would she go? Not to Maggie. There was only one other way back to her room, and it was not an option she wanted to explore.

"Maggie must have locked me out," she explained to Rycroft.

"Why would she do that?" His eyes drew a line down her body. "Do you always sleep in that?" His voice was husky, almost a whisper.

She shook her head. "Just let me back in my room. We can deal with Maggie later."

He beckoned her to his bedroom door. She peered inside, hesitating to enter the domain of the beast. The Wyvern's den. She would have laughed if she weren't so uneasy.

She walked inside, her steps light as though she would fall through the floor. The master bedroom was done in dark green and chocolaty leather. It was the reverse mirror image of her room but featuring a giant fireplace with ornate medieval dragons carved into the stone.

"This seems a bit much," she said, indicating the fireplace.

"I like to keep warm," he said from just over her shoulder.

He had snuck up behind her, making her heart catch in her throat. She peeked over her shoulder at him. The crooked smile on his face warned her to run to the door or push him away. She did neither.

His breath tingled along her cheek as they stood facing the fireplace and the door that meant an escape to her room. Her pulse drummed in her throat, much as prey waiting on its predator, sensing danger but not knowing where or when it would strike. The space between them was charged with anticipation.

When his hands slid along her hips, caressing the fabric into her skin, her senses were nearly overwhelmed. She didn't freeze or draw away. His calm patience had won him her trust. His touch was sensual, drawing her back against him. His lips wandered a path lightly along the side of her neck.

A moan broke through her throat.

One of his hands had found its way to her breast. He teased her nipple through the fabric, rubbing it with his thumb. She arched back into his body, feeling the hard press of him, smelling the hay and dirt still clinging to his skin. The scent only served to arouse her further, bringing back the memory of his body over hers.

He pushed his hips more firmly to her backside. His erection pressed against her tailbone. His hand continued its torment of her breast, rubbing and kneading the hungry skin. With his other hand, he tugged up the bottom of her nightgown, caressing her hip. His touch moved to her stomach, where it ventured down into the hair between her legs.

She gave a gasp-like cry as his thumb rubbed the sensitive area. She attempted to face him, to reach back and touch him, but he had her firmly fixed. She surrendered to his attentions as her mind became cloudy with desire.

He kissed and nipped her neck, murmuring unintelligible words into her skin. The hand at her breast continued to stroke, but his focus was between her legs. His thumb traced a circular path, making her frantic and overheated.

She squirmed into him, earning a low chuckle.

His fingers dipped inside her, causing her to jerk back into him, where he steadied her against his hand. He guided her with his hips. Her heart was thudding wildly while the pressure built deep inside her, desperately seeking release. Her breaths came in quick pants as the tension reached explosive heights.

He bit the tender flesh of her neck as he drove inside her, forcing her over the edge. She convulsed against him, letting the waves carry her where they would. He held her as her limbs became liquid against him.

His arms scooped her up against his chest, and he carried her limp body over to his bed. She nestled into the soft down blanket under her and blinked up in surprise.

"Don't you want me to go back to my room?" she asked through her mental haze.

One side of his lips curved up. "Maggie locked that door too."
"You checked?"
"I don't have to. I know my sister."
Lynette nodded lazily. "It's just as well. I don't particularly want to sleep." She pointed to his waistcoat. "Take that off."
His face broke into a wide grin, but he complied. He ripped the fabric in his haste to remove it. She wrinkled her nose at the shirt beneath it, which he quickly discarded as well. She gestured toward his lower half when he finished. He didn't hesitate as she thought he would, discarding boots and breeches before pausing when he reached his small clothes, but he removed them as well when she glared at his oversight.

His muscles were toned from frequent use—the result of his riding, sailing, and fighting, no doubt. Two prominent scars caught her attention. A long white line ran along his left shoulder, and a short, thick, raised line the size of her pinky decorated his side. The scars mixed with hair brushed along his chest, which sprinkled over his stomach to lead down to the dark hair framing his erection.

He was still grinning at her when she met his gaze. "Have you had your fill yet?"
"No, you vain thing, come here. Did you know some people see with their hands? I'm one of them."
He choked on a laugh. "You mean blind people?"
"Shut up."
He moved to stand at the foot of the bed, and she beckoned him closer. He bent over the bed and crawled atop her. She let out a gasp, which transformed into a giggle as he held himself above her on hands and knees. His hand strayed to the bottom of the last bit of clothing between them, bunching the gown above her waist.

He nibbled the corner of his mouth, his eyes pleading with her. She reached up to him for a kiss, hoping to silence whatever idiotic things he was going to say. It worked for a time. Their needs took control, demanding completion.

Rycroft rose above her in some sort of heroic gesture. "Love, are you sure you want this? You know we can't marry. I'm too much of a scoundrel to settle down."

Lynette shut her eyes, willing him to be silent. "What makes you think I want to marry you? I'd be miserable as a wife. I want you." She let out a steadying breath. "I need you to ease what happened to me in New York. Make me feel good, not as a wife but a lover, a woman."

His fingers ran down her cheek. She nudged her face into his hand, kissing his palm. He nuzzled her to face him, taking her lips in a gentle caress. He used his leg to part hers, settling himself between them on his knees. His thumb glided over the overheated skin between them, feeding the throb with her rushed heartbeat.

"I'm sorry, love. This is going to hurt."

She nodded, angling her hips to welcome him.

He nudged at her entrance, letting out a throaty moan as he pushed forward. She stretched to accommodate him, but the pain was minimal with his slow progress. She thrust her hips to meet him, taking him by surprise. A sharp discomfort met her effort. He rocked back, his eyes full of concern.

Lynette greeted his gaze with a half smile and wrapped her legs around him. His face melted in relief. He drove inside her again, causing a wave of pleasure that shot to her toes. He did it again, and she rocked with him. She tilted her head into the pillow as wave after wave of sensation spiraled through her.

Their eyes locked as the pressure built. He laid his chest on top of her, merging their bodies. Then he met her lips with sweet devotion, his expression like a warm caress. She laced her fingers through his just as their breath merged.

His breaths were heavy, his movements jerked. A growl escaped his teeth, and he thrust once more before her world exploded in light.

She shook beneath him, clasping her arms and legs tighter around his body. They both fell still except for the hurried movements of their chests. Their eyes continued their worshipful stares as they lay together in contented silence.

Lynette ran her legs across his. Being with him seemed right, and she was at peace. She hadn't known how naked she could be, not just her body but her mind. It was as though he had laid out every secret, every thought, and examined them. He'd unburdened her. The relief was palpable. She never wanted to let go.

Rycroft rolled off her, stretching out at her side. He looked like a drunken cat. A content drunken cat. He shut his eyes as he dozed.

"Max?"

His eye cracked open. "Hmm?"

"Is the adjoining door really locked?"

He shook his head as he stifled a yawn with his hand.

"Why would you tell me otherwise?" Her brows furrowed.

"Didn't want you to leave," he mumbled.

She poked his chest with her finger, and his eyes fluttered open. "So Maggie didn't just trap me here?"

His lips curled up. "She prefers the illusion of choice."

A strangled sound escaped her, but she closed her eyes and curled onto her side, facing away from him. The bed shook, and his arm came around her as he nestled up to her. Their exhausted bodies left little room for complaint. She sighed, letting the protective embrace lull her to sleep.

They were awakened by a loud rap on the door followed by a gust of air from the hallway and the choked sound the intruder made when he entered.

"Can't I find any peace in my own house?" Rycroft groaned from beside her.

Lynette scrambled to cover herself with the bedding beneath her, but it seemed a futile task given the damage was already done. Howell stood in the doorway, looking away into the hall. At least he was attempting to be courteous. She doubted any of the other men would have done the same.

"Hello, Howell. I see you're back from your trip," Lynette

said once she had regained her senses.

Howell was making little coughing sounds, holding in his laughter. "Indeed, Miss Wolcott. Good morning to you. Max, I didn't want to wake you, but it's time to go. Riley filled me in."

Rycroft sat, pulling on his clothes. He'd made it to his breeches when Lynette bolted to her room, leaving the door ajar as she donned her men's clothes.

"What are you doing, love?" Rycroft asked from the door as he threw on his shirt.

"You said I could come with you, and there is no way I'm going to miss my revenge." She was already pulling on her boots, not having to worry about as many buttons as Rycroft. They hadn't yet found a waistcoat that would fit her.

"Sweet, you aren't ready yet. I haven't even gotten to teaching you to use your sword." He stepped further into the room as though proximity would make his point more convincing.

"How is this any different from before?"

"It just is. We know there's danger this time."

A glimpse in the mirror revealed flushed cheeks and messy hair. She ran a comb through the tangles as he came up from behind. She ignored him as she straightened her appearance. Did one summon a hairdresser before going into battle? She would just have to wear her cocked hat.

"I'm going. This isn't negotiable," she said, voice stern.

He wrapped his arms around her waist, impeding her progress. She squeaked in protest, slapping at his hands. He took the punishment and kissed along her neck to distract her.

"Don't think this will change my mind, horrible man," she said, grinning at his reflection.

He took a final nip at her ear and sighed. "All right, but I have conditions."

"No conditions. You aren't my mother, and you certainly aren't my husband. Not that I would obey you if you were." She freed herself from his grip and found her hat and gloves.

His brows were bent in a worried expression. "Please, I can't let you get yourself killed. It would crush Maggie." He must have seen the hurt in her eyes at his omission. "I would be out a bed partner too."

She stared down at her gloves as she slipped them on. "You think this is going to happen again? It certainly won't if you leave me here."

A wicked spark shone in his eyes. "I'm not done with you yet."

She turned to him, rolling her eyes. "I'll ride away if things get too bad. You'll find I have a particular preference for staying alive. Besides, I don't think I'm done with you either. A bit difficult to explore that if I'm dead, wouldn't you agree?"

His tongue traced his lips as he closed the distance between them. "I wish we had a few more minutes."

"Max, now," Howell called from the other room.

Rycroft glared toward the adjoining door and pulled her into an enveloping kiss. His lips told her his longing and promises but filled her with his regret and sorrow at the possibility of death separating them. He released her lips, resting his forehead on hers as he closed his eyes and breathed in.

Lynette pecked him and ran a hand over his chest. "We'll be fine. Just think, we can be home in time for dinner, and Jeffrey won't even know I was gone."

He groaned. "That brother of yours."

She didn't bother to defend Jeffrey. Of course, she loved Jeffrey, but he had a way of being around when he wasn't wanted and being scarce when he was needed. As much as she placed a positive air on the morning, she had a nagging feeling in her chest that something was about to go horribly wrong.

He took her hand in his, giving it a gentle squeeze. "Be careful. Revenge isn't worth dying for."

She squeezed his hand back. "That goes for you too. Maggie would kill me if I let them hurt you." She grinned at his answering laugh. "I mean it, Max."

"I mean it too, Max," Howell said from the doorway. "We

need to go. The horses are all ready."

"The bay too?" Lynette asked, voice full of hope.

Howell beamed at her. "Of course. I wouldn't forget our lady's horse."

"You see, Max. He understands these things."

Rycroft muttered something under his breath. "What did you decide to name your horse anyway?"

Her eyes widened as she met his stare. "My horse?"

He nodded impatiently. "Could she really be anyone else's?"

"I can pay you back when I get more of my funds from Briarwyck," she said. "What do I owe you? I'm afraid I've never bought a horse before."

He brought her hand to his lips, silencing her with the gesture. "No, Harpy. She's a gift."

She watched in confusion as Rycroft grabbed his things and checked to make sure she was armed. He pulled her after him as they followed Howell into the hall, sending her tripping in dumb shock.

"Glue," she said as they made the top of the stairs.

"What's that?" Rycroft asked, glancing back at her.

"Her name is Glue. I figure it will warn her against bad behavior."

Rycroft and Howell erupted in laughter, their mirth echoing down the stairs.

A smile tugged at her lips, but it didn't form. Lynette still had that teasing of doubt in her stomach, telling her they wouldn't get out of this unscathed. The threat against herself and Maggie was not something they could ignore. Nor could they let the law handle it. There was too much to explain that would lead to someone's hanging or transportation. Their circumstances weren't ideal, but it was what they had to work with.

A shudder crawled up her spine as if footsteps advanced over her grave. Somebody was going to die.

CHAPTER TWENTY

T HE SUN WAS still down when they mounted their horses. The morning was clear with a bright moon that would take them most of their journey. Peace had settled over the land, one they would soon be breaking. Even the birds were silent as they descended onto the coast in a trot.

The Wyvern assured Lynette the camp wasn't far from there, but at the rate their mounts were going, it seemed an eternity. Traveling with such a large group was troublesome, and the Wyvern had settled for splitting into two groups, each consisting of ten men. One group, headed by Wren, would go overland, while the other group would take the coast, led by the Wyvern with Lynette at his side.

To Lynette's mind, they traveled with an army. She doubted their enemies would escape them once their camp was surrounded. Still, they rode on without the benefit of conversation or song. The only sound was hoofbeats, but even that was a thunderous roar to her ears. They would be heard long before they reached the camp.

Her fears were settled when the Wyvern had them leave their horses as they got too close to the camp. Without their horses, progress slowed to a crawl. Her fear of capture was replaced by impatience and anxiety to be done with the matter. Her body shook with every fresh step until she wanted to scream and flee from the task.

A pale-blue sky crept up behind them. Still, they trudged on.

She had become jumpy since leaving Glue behind. The mare's quick senses were enough for her before, but now every twig snap and every low cough startled her. So when the Wyvern stopped suddenly, raising a hand to halt them, she nearly fell over herself. He glared at her to remain still.

She gritted her teeth, giving him a bashful smile. She tried to mimic the stealth of the men behind her. Remus (or was it Romulus?) gave her an encouraging grin, but it was unlikely she was succeeding. She steadied her hand on her new sword as she scanned the area in front of them.

The Wyvern had his head cocked, listening to the sounds of the morning. When one of the men coughed, the Wyvern looked back at him with an icy stare. The man grew pale, his eyes pleading his apology. He seemed like he would impale himself on his sword if the Wyvern asked. What had he done to inspire such loyalty in these men? Money didn't make men act this way. In the past, she would have assumed they feared him, but seeing him around them, she knew the fear was only out of their desire to please him.

A faint bird call sounded. The Wyvern whistled back and gestured for them to follow him forward. They ascended a hill leading up to an outcrop of rocks separated by a path, sliding along the sandy trail as they advanced. Lynette was so engrossed in keeping her footing she didn't register the creeping sensation along her skin until it was almost too late.

She was inches behind the Wyvern as they reached the outcrop, when a shout came from their group. The Wyvern pushed her aside as the crack of a pistol sounded.

Lynette cried out, hitting the sand with bruising force. Her eyes jumped from man to man, searching for the source.

Smoke rose with the new dawn.

The Wyvern lay along the path. A figure stood over him with the sun silhouetting him, obstructing his features.

"Get away from him!" she shouted, scrambling to her feet. She drew her sword, rushing at the man. The dread came to a standstill, a heavy throbbing in her stomach. *Not him. Please, not him.*

The man raised his hands as if in surrender. "I'm unarmed. It wasn't me."

She took in the empty hands and then studied the other men. Half of them had run off in pursuit of someone rushing down the hill. She brought her attention back to the man as he knelt next to the Wyvern, the sun no longer at his back. It was Jackal, but where had he come from? He had been with the other group.

"Is he...?" Her knuckles grew white on her sword.

His hands moved over the Wyvern, checking his injuries.

"No. He's unconscious but bleeding. I need to take him back to Rycroft House. We should assess his head injury." He removed the Wyvern's sash and tied it tight around his injured leg.

"We need horses now," she yelled as the group scrambled about. "Who was it? Did you see?"

Jackal sighed, his eyes tightly shut. "We were betrayed from the first. Lycan knew where we would go. He was waiting for us."

"I don't understand. Where were you? How did you know?"

He shook his head. "There isn't time." He looked back down the hill. "Romulus, grab Hermes and Wind for me." His brows rose as he regarded her. "You need to go too. Get Glue and ride as hard as you can."

She scowled at him. "No. Tell me, now." Her glower encompassed the group as she sought out the long-awaited mounts.

He looked up to the sky, mumbling something to himself. "I suspected something was wrong as soon as we set out. Wren kept looking around as though he was being watched. He hadn't dried out enough, or that is what I kept telling myself. We were behind your group when I saw the destination and realized it was a trap. The Wyvern should have seen it, or he might have seen it and taken the chance anyway. Fool thinks he's invincible."

"Wren told Lycan where to find us?"

"No, he told Lycan where to find you. In their misguided way, they're still loyal to the Wyvern."

She squeezed her eyes shut. The Wyvern lay like death on the ground. His chest moved, which would be reassuring if not for the blood soaking the sand. Her knees hit the earth next to him.

She ran her fingers along his cheek. His eyes blinked open at her.

"Max, if you think for one moment I'm going to let you save me..." Her voice caught in her throat.

His lips formed a wistful smile.

"Don't you dare die," she managed. "Revenge isn't worth dying for."

"But love, you're worth dying for."

She choked on her tears, watching his eyes fall closed. She wiped at her face with frustrated movements.

"Where are those horses?" Her blurry eyes found Jackal. "You will help him?"

Jackal grunted. "I'll do my best. Mrs. Johns and Maggie will be of some help."

At the mention of Mrs. Johns, Lynette paled. "Why did Wren do it? Does he hate me too? His grandmother seems to approve of me."

"I think it goes deeper than that, but I suspect you'll have to ask him yourself if we ever find him. I'm sorry, Miss Wolcott. We should have figured it out sooner. He has been with the Wyvern from the beginning."

Bull and Bear came into view, dragging a still form between them. They had wide grins etched deep into their faces.

They looked to Jackal, but he shook his head. "I don't know what to do with him. Figure it out among yourselves."

"Bring him here," Harpy demanded, gaining her feet.

They studied her thoughtfully before delivering as one the man who had tried to kill her. Lycan, or whatever his real name was, lay crumpled in a heap at her boots. His face was smashed, and blood dripped from his nose and a cut at his temple. She nudged him with her toe, attempting to wake him.

"Oh, Lycan," she called in a singsong voice.

The man groaned, one eye slit open to squint up at her. Hatred shot through her from his stare. If the man hadn't been injured, she might have been offended.

"Silly man," she cooed. "Did you really think we would let you get away after shooting the Wyvern?"

"Whore. It was supposed to be you."

"My, you have a dirty mouth." She tsked. "You should wish you had shot me because what I'm going to do to you is far worse than anything the Wyvern had planned."

A low laugh rumbled from the injured leader.

"Do you see what you did? You woke him up," she said to Lycan, landing a kick to his stomach.

He yelped, recoiling to shield the new injury.

Harpy craned her neck to peer back at the Wyvern. "Sweet, do you have any requests before I do away with him? I can't promise I'll carry them out if they're too soft."

He chuckled. "Do what you will, love." His voice sobered as he propped himself up to stare at the man who'd used to be one of his own. "Lycan—or should I say Daniel—I can forgive you for shooting me. Hell, my own brothers want to shoot me. I can't forgive you for shooting one of my men. You're out of my hands now. I don't envy your fate. Harpy is going to rip you apart."

"She isn't one of your men. Don't confuse this whore with one of us!" Daniel yelled, his voice nasal.

"Yes, but I'm *his* whore." Harpy smiled around her bared teeth. She ran Daniel's shoulder into the ground with her heel.

At last, Romulus approached with the two horses. Harpy signaled with a brush of her hand to move Daniel out of the way. Bull grabbed him by the ankle and dragged him off to the side to make way for the horses. The Wyvern was able to assist Jackal in getting him to his feet.

Harpy gave a small smile. "You're bleeding all over that poor horse of yours. Get moving."

"Indeed. Stay safe, love." He winked at her as he urged Hermes forward. "Jackal. Bear." They descended the hill, setting a dangerous pace toward Rycroft House.

The men were looking about uncertainly, shifting from foot to foot and fidgeting with their weapons. Harpy realized they were waiting for her to do something.

She cleared her throat and raised her voice above them. "I haven't known you for long, but we all have a common purpose. We need to find Wren and Hawke. This traitor you captured will serve us well. When we find them, we'll bring them to justice for the Wyvern and Maggie." She scanned the crowd, assessing their reactions. "If any of you have a problem with me or have had a change of heart, now would be a good time to leave."

All the men glanced around, watching for their neighbors' response to her words. Nobody moved to leave. The traitors had already left. Fifteen of their group now remained. They returned their attention to her, one at a time. Anticipation flooded the air as they waited to see what she would do.

She nodded to them, trying to conceal her relief that they hadn't all deserted her. It wouldn't have mattered. She would still have gone after Wren and Hawke, even if it had meant going alone. An outright attack was one thing, but betrayal from one's friends was something else entirely. Hawke was just another enemy making his money on someone's misery. What Wren had done would hurt the Wyvern deeply. These men must also feel his betrayal. He was one of their own.

"Bring that maggot here," she said to Bull.

He complied without hesitation, dragging Daniel in front of the group as though he was nothing more than a child. Daniel didn't protest, letting Bull treat him like a sack of grain. When he noticed Harpy, he tried to stand but was pressed to the ground by Bull's boot. His foot must have felt like a boulder on Daniel's chest.

"I should have let you die in the bog," she said.

He squirmed under all that weight. Good. He didn't answer her and avoided her stare. Instead, he chose to use his energy to push at Bull, a pitiful display to watch.

"I'm going to give you a choice. Tell us where they are, and you will live. If you don't, I will cut you up piece by piece. Perhaps you will change your mind before you bleed to death." She brought out her sword, running her fingers down the flat edge of the steel.

He grunted in response, renewing his assault on Bull's leg.

Bull gave the struggling man a lazy frown as he might a pestering fly.

Harpy sighed and settled her blade against one of his hands, which struggled to move Bull away. When he didn't respond, she sliced the sharp edge along his thumb, rendering a deep gash. His thumb was only saved when he jerked back from the blade.

He yelped, gripping his hands together. His amber-brown eyes snapped to her face with renewed fury.

"This doesn't have to be hard." She lowered her blade to the front of his pants. "I do have quite an imagination, but I'm sure you would rather not find out."

His eyes widened, and his face blanched. "Fine. They don't mean anything to me. Hawke has a cave where they have their dealings. You'll find both of them there. We were supposed to meet back there. If we were able."

Harpy puffed out a gust of air. "Really? Where is this cave?"

"The old shipwreck. It's just up the coast and deep into the cliff. You'll find it if you're looking."

Harpy glanced at the group of men. "Do any of you know what he's blathering about?"

Several of the heads bobbed.

"That was entirely too easy. Do you feel better about yourself now, Daniel?"

Daniel regarded her with a half frown, his eyes full of dumb hope. "Can I go now?"

She tapped her lip with her finger, studying the landscape around her. Four magpies perched along the rocks bordering the path. "Do you recall that I was lenient to you last time? I tend to believe in second chances. Third chances? Not so much."

"You said you would let me live," he protested, starting up his struggle against Bull's boot again.

She studied him thoughtfully. "I did. I mean to leave you alive. What happens to you afterward is up to the Fates."

"What? You can't be serious. Release me. You're as mad as the Wyvern."

She shrugged. "It is what it is. Would one of you clever men happen to have some rope? I'd prefer chains, but rope will do."

A few of the men had rope in their saddlebags, having come to expect its use in the Wyvern's company. Harpy instructed Bull, Romulus, and Remus to tie Daniel to a large rock, the very rock he had hidden behind when they'd approached. When they were done, Daniel was a bent mess of rope. If he ever freed himself, he'd be sore for days.

"You're going to leave me here? Alone?" He struggled, showing his bare inch of give on the rope.

"Don't be rude. Of course you won't be alone." She waved to the four magpies watching their movements. One of them cocked its head in greeting before making a sound like a cackle. The sound sent a tingle down her spine, and she gave the bird a faint smile and joined the men.

Some men had brought Glue and the rest of the horses they had left behind, while they had tied up Daniel. She paused a moment before pulling herself up into the saddle. She managed to gain her seat without looking too clumsy.

Daniel was wailing behind them, an ear-bursting sound that echoed through her head.

"Would someone gag him? We don't want to make it too easy."

A young man with shining dark-brown hair jumped off his horse to follow her orders. She watched his swift movements with admiration and turned her horse forward. She could get used to this.

"Masks up." She tugged her own scarf into place. There were a few chuckles, but all of them did as she asked. None of them knew what they would be riding into, and it would be better if they were prepared.

"Lead on," she told the twins, slowing her horse enough to allow them to gain the front. She thought of them as the unofficial scouts of the Wyvern's men, and if they were going to lead the group astray, they would have done it already.

A wave of anxiety fluttered in Harpy's stomach, but she pushed it deep down until she couldn't be bothered by it. She would lead these men to finish this business with Hawke, and she would see Wren brought down for his betrayal.

"I don't care what you do with Hawke," she said to the men around her. "Capture or kill him. It doesn't matter. The man who gets to him first can decide. Just make sure he pays. But when we find Wren, keep him alive. He answers to the Wyvern alone."

CHAPTER TWENTY-ONE

T HE TWINS SET off at a gallop down the coast, swinging their
horses back to go around the outcrop holding Daniel. The
horses took the pace well, even thriving at the speeds. She
remembered what the Wyvern had said about Hermes being part
of the group. The same could be said about these horses. It was as
though they wanted Hawke and Wren as much as the men did, as
much as Harpy. Even Glue lived up to their expectations of her.
Perhaps she sensed the urgency of the matter.

A current of anticipation lingered above the group. She
sensed they were imagining being the ones to take down Hawke,
to clip his wings, to speak. She saw it in Remus's white-knuckle
grip on his reins and in Outback's rigid jaw. She heard it in their
grumbling, heated voices and raspy curses. Betrayal had a way of
making one feel hopeless. They needed this outlet more than she
did.

Harpy would give them that much, but she had to make sure
Wren was still breathing when they brought him back to Rycroft
House. He had too much to answer for to die on that coast. She
still held out hope Jackal was mistaken. In the short time she had
known Wren, he hadn't given her enough reason to doubt him or
to believe he hated her. Of course, he had been drunk more than
not the past few days, making it difficult to judge his character.
But to send Harpy to her death? It seemed extreme considering

she barely knew him.

The sun had climbed to its peak, illuminating an old ship-wreck just off the coast, nestled in a group of towering rocks shooting out of the water. It had been there for some time, becoming a landmark of its own.

Romulus increased his pace, leaving them behind as he searched the cliff face. Some distance down the beach, he brought up his horse and waved for them to catch up. Remus sent his horse bolting forward, and the rest of them followed his lead. Glue was hungry for the chase and soon surpassed Remus's mount.

The thunder of hooves echoed off the cliffs for miles. The figure of a man had come out from somewhere in the cliff face, pivoting back as he saw them approaching.

Harpy emitted a whooping battle cry. The men joined her in an echo of voices. The singing of steel matched their call as swords were drawn, preparing for what lay beyond the cliff face. Men were beginning to gather on the beach, readying to defend their hideout. Romulus pulled up short of their group and fired his pistol.

A resounding crack signaled the beginning of the battle.

The Wyvern's gang fell on their rivals in an unwavering slaughter. The men on foot were no match for the horses beating down on them. Many of them were trampled by the well-trained mounts. They had been ill prepared to defend themselves, but rather than flee for their lives, they stood their ground, inviting death or mercy.

Horses screamed with the dying men as more of them were forced to fight on foot. Remus's horse suffered a fatal headshot from a pistol. Remus was thrown down, barely missing the felled horse as he rolled away. She urged Glue to his side, bringing him up behind her.

Remus reloaded his pistol as she brandished her sword at the remaining men. What she lacked in skill, she made up for with speed and determination. Glue danced around blades and obstructions as though she was trained for battle. Perhaps her moniker had fostered a need for self-preservation.

A whirlwind of metal came short of Harpy's thigh, cutting across her calf through her boot. She screamed with the discharge of Remus's pistol, which caught the attacker straight in the forehead. When the smoke from the gun cleared, Remus stared down at her leg.

"Are you all right?" he asked, drawing his sword to fend off attackers as she recovered.

"Hopefully. My boots are ruined though. What horrible man would destroy a woman's shoes?"

He laughed under his breath as he swung at a man brandishing a bloody long sword. "A dead man?"

"Indeed." She raised her sword again for the next attack. It never came.

The Wyvern's gang had surrounded the remaining half dozen men. One by one, they dropped to their knees in surrender, looking more relieved than defeated. Bull disarmed them while two others were tied together. Hawke and Wren were nowhere in sight.

"Check the bodies," Harpy ordered. "Has anyone seen Hawke or Wren?"

She spotted one of the captives peering back at the cave and nodded at him for Remus's benefit.

He signaled to his twin.

Romulus regrouped the men, readying to advance on the cave. Their number had been reduced to a dozen, not much of a loss compared to their counterparts. Two men agreed to stay behind with the captives.

Only half their horses remained, and they were forced to double up until they reached the cave entrance, where they dismounted. A horse could be as much a liability as a boon in such close quarters. Their mounts would stay behind.

Pistols were loaded, and swords were drawn as they stalked into the rocky cavern. The entrance was narrow, allowing only two men abreast. They had to use their lamps and makeshift torches to find their way. Romulus and Remus, followed by Harpy and Bull, led the group again. The rest trailed in similar pairs.

Bull's torch rose high overhead, giving no hint to the ceiling above. If she had seen the sky, she would think they were in a large crack in the cliff face instead of a cave. The air was moist and full of salt but old like mildew.

The twins fanned out when they reached an open area that appeared to be living quarters of a sort. Blankets were strewn along the walls. Cooking pots were stacked near an old campfire, which still burned on ember logs. A goat stood tied off to the side, bleating at them when they approached. An opening branched off to the right of the living area. She stared after the torches that disappeared inside.

"Find anything?" she called after them.

Remus appeared in the opening. "There's nobody in there, but the Wyvern will be happy to know there is a stockpile of brandy and tobacco."

"Is there any other exit?"

Romulus shook his head as he joined them.

"And you didn't see anyone flee the cavern? Could someone have snuck past you before the fighting?"

Romulus and Remus glared at her. Romulus folded his arms across his chest.

"All right." She threw up her hands. Bull's torch shone the furthest, and she beckoned him to follow her into the adjoining room. She came up short when she spotted the barrels.

"Bull, help me with these lids."

The twins had followed her and soon caught onto her idea. Other men worked through the room with them, searching the barrels at a rapid pace. Sure enough, Bull made a surprised grunt, and Harpy angled to see a sun-bleached head and blue eyes staring up at her.

Bull clenched his fist in that cloud of hair, pulling Hawke out as he kicked his feet at him. Bull threw him to the ground before Harpy's feet.

"Hello, Hawke," she said.

"Miss Wolcott." He greeted her with the bow of his head, still managing to sound civilized.

"Why did you think hiding in a barrel was a good idea? You know we would have taken them."

The men were gathering around them, having finished their search of the barrels without locating Wren. They listened to the exchange in silence, uttering the occasional cough or snort of disgust.

"Of course, but you would have had to come back for them." She screwed her lips up. "Hmm. I see your point."

"I mean you no offense, Miss Wolcott. This was business to me, nothing more." The man sounded so reasonable, so cultured. She wanted to slap him.

"Oh? So kidnapping me and Maggie was business to you?"

"Not my normal line of work, but it paid well."

"I'm sorry if I take this personally. I find it hard to look past being beaten, manhandled, and almost killed. I am human, after all."

He raised his hands as though to ward off her words. "Whoa. That wasn't my doing. My men were instructed to be civil. Daniel took a dislike to you when you stabbed him, and he had his own group of Wyvern rejects handle your kidnapping. I can't say I blame him, but his humiliation was long overdue. Did you kill him?" His voice was conversational. He could have been talking to her at a garden party.

Harpy cocked her head at the calm man who had been hiding in a barrel just moments before. "No, but whether he lives has nothing to do with you."

"What of Riley? Have you located him yet?"

She sighed in response.

He nodded in understanding. "He was late returning. You probably scared him off."

"What of Maggie? Why take her? She did nothing to you. A stupid mistake to kidnap the Wyvern's own sister."

"Yes, I agree with you there. The plan would have been suicidal if it hadn't turned out exactly as we expected."

Her jaw worked, mouth opening and shutting as she looked for a response to this confusing statement. "What do you mean? You failed."

He gave a dry laugh. "No, we succeeded. I see you haven't worked everything out. Let me enlighten you. Who do you think hired me?"

She squinted, processing each of his words in turn. "I... I don't know."

He smirked, clearly enjoying the moment. "Riley."

Her body stilled. Impossible. "But Riley is in love with Maggie."

"Yes. Exactly. What better way to win love than to rescue your maiden in distress? Maggie was never supposed to get hurt. A quick kidnapping and rescue. Love and the resulting marriage. The happy couple would live out their days at Rycroft House with a story to tell their grandchildren."

"How do I factor in this?"

He snorted. "You are just like Rycroft. You can't seem to understand that not everyone loves you. I don't think Riley cares one way or another about you. Daniel, however, figured if he got rid of you, he would be let back into the pack."

"Why didn't he just kill me?"

"Bait. Riley couldn't just tell everyone where Maggie was being held. He had to motivate Rycroft to follow a trail. Your trail. Daniel decided to use you. I think Daniel had bigger plans for you in the end. He's a sick man. I won't mourn whatever became of him." He took in a breath and released it as though he deflated. "I can't say his plan was reasonable, but he had enough coin to make his presence tolerable. Honestly, I'm glad he was never able to carry out his twisted ideas."

To Harpy's surprise, she believed everything Hawke had told

her. He had nothing to gain by lying, and he seemed worn of the whole matter. Daniel had brought this man's entire operation down. She might have felt sorry for the smuggler if he hadn't caused her so much trouble. Perhaps they should return to Daniel and help dish him out to the magpies.

"What do we do with him?" Remus interrupted her morbid thoughts.

She shrugged. "Bull found him. I suppose he can decide. I find myself feeling lenient toward him. I wouldn't trust my mind with this. In any case, we should head back soon. Perhaps our new friend here knows where Wren flew off to?"

Hawke grunted. "I always hated Rycroft's insistence on fake names."

"What of Hawke?"

He glared at her, and a frown etched over his brows. "My real name."

Her face lit up in her brightest smile. "How fortunate. Now where would Wren perch his pretty self?"

"I believe he probably returned to his nest," Hawke supplied in a dry voice.

"Indeed? And where, pray tell, is that?" She fluttered her lashes above a sweet smile.

His clever blue eyes narrowed at her in exasperation. "Where his hen is in her coop. Rycroft House."

The simplicity was like a blow to Harpy's head. Hawke had to be mistaken. Wren would have to be suicidal to return to Rycroft House under any circumstances. Maggie would never love him after what he had done. Mrs. Johns might defend her grandson, but Harpy got the impression breaking the Wyvern's trust was unforgivable. Loyalty was part of what made him a powerful leader. A breach would be difficult for him to overlook.

"Fine. We will return to Rycroft House." Harpy turned her back on Hawke, a dismissal and insult. "Romulus, I want an inventory of this cave. Bull, have you come to a decision?"

The burly man stepped forward. "The rock." A man of few

words, Bull got right to the point.

"Excellent choice. I'm sure Daniel would like some company." Harpy left through the cave's exit without another word, finding Glue where she had left her. She patted her horse, waiting for the rest of the men to join her. She sent Outback to see to the captives and assess their injuries.

Outback hesitated to move. "Miss Harpy?" the rugged man said in a low, respectful voice.

She gestured for him to continue.

"What do you plan for them? If you mean to kill them, I'd rather not sew them up."

"I think, Mr. Outback, I mean to release them. They are looking for quick pay as much as any of the Wyvern's men. Unfortunately, they chose the wrong side, but I don't see what else we can do unless you want to butcher them?"

He shook his head.

"I thought not. Hand them off some coin to buy their loyalty and mention the possibility of a job. Be done with it. I will let you judge if any of them are going to be a problem for us."

They waited long enough for Romulus and Outback to rejoin them before setting off. One of the men had found a few of Hawke's horses grazing above the cliff, but some still had to ride double. Since Harpy was the smallest one there, she offered to ride with Remus once again.

At Bull's insistence, they left Hawke tied on the other side of the trail from Daniel. The traitor looked no different from when they had left him. Yet the magpies had increased in number, going from four to thirteen. However she figured it, the number reflected on Daniel and not Hawke or the Wyvern's gang. In the end, she decided fate frowned on the wicked, and left the men to their dues.

Hawke appeared calm as they deserted him, but Daniel went back to his muffled yelling from behind the scarf. Harpy borrowed a knife from Remus, leaving it at Hawke's feet. He nodded in understanding, no words needed. His stare was fixed on Daniel in an angry scowl. In their own way, Hawke and Harpy had mutual respect. Once he was free, Daniel would be bird food, but he wouldn't come after Harpy. She had proven herself a difficult enemy. She would leave him in peace if he stayed out of her way.

Their return journey started at a steady pace, becoming more hurried the more she thought about what lay ahead. By all accounts, Wren was traveling alone. The numbers at Rycroft House would spell certain defeat for him. Once she factored in Wren's deadly force added to him taking the household off guard, her hands tightened on the reins.

The Wyvern was in no shape to fight, nor did she believe he would resort to battling his childhood friend straightaway. Jackal and Bear would be formidable opponents if they saw the danger coming. That left Maggie, her brother, Carrington, Greymore, and whoever else had arrived in their absence. Uncertain abilities against uncertain numbers surrounding Wren's arrival.

Then there was Mrs. Johns. Her loyalty would be split between her grandson and her loving employer. An easy choice for some, but the Rycroft family had been like her own. As old as she was, she could still be trouble for either side. The best scenario for everyone was to take Wren out of the fight, alive and unscathed. Harpy had no idea how that was possible.

Her mind fought through points and counterpoints until Rycroft House loomed before them, and she set Glue off at a dead run to meet whatever fate had dealt in response to their own wicked ways. She could blame nobody but herself.

CHAPTER TWENTY-TWO

UPON LYNETTE'S ARRIVAL, her first priority was seeing to Maggie's safety. She took the stairs two at a time. Her feet skidded to a halt outside Maggie's door, but before she could knock, it was flung open to reveal her friend staring at her with a confused expression.

Maggie's brows were raised. "What is it? Has Max's wound reopened?"

"No," Lynette said through gasps of breath. "I needed to be sure you were all right. Riley might be coming for you."

"You can see I'm well. Did you just get here?" Maggie gestured for her to follow into the room.

Lynette took up a seat, grateful to be sitting on anything other than a saddle. "We just came in. Has there been any word of Riley?"

"No, but I think he'll prove the least of your problems."

She worried her lip. "The least of my problems? We're in danger."

"For now, we're alive, and I intend to stay that way." Maggie frowned. "Didn't you see the carriage in front of the house?"

Lynette shook her head. "I came in the servants' entrance at the side of the house and straight here first."

Maggie sighed. "I'm afraid nobody can keep quiet in this house, and your brother caught word of some nonsense.

Anyway, he sent for your parents. I was just going down to greet them when you rushed at my door like a rabid boar."

Lynette groaned, dropping her head into her hands. "I don't suppose you'll hide me?"

Maggie folded her arms over her chest and tapped her toe against the floor.

"No?"

"I swear, you are just as determined to avoid problems as my brother. Unfortunately for him, your parents got to him first."

Lynette gawked at her. "What do you mean? Isn't he in bed? Did they barge in on an injured man to lecture him on taking me out into the great, bad wilderness? Not that I wouldn't expect as much."

"Max insisted on meeting them in the drawing room like a proper master of the house. He is doing well, putting up a brave front. I keep telling him to go back to bed, or his wound might reopen. I had to go up and change, or I would have defended you. Speaking of changing, you really should get out of those men's clothes." Maggie sniffed, examining Lynette's not-so-glamorous appearance.

"Right, go on ahead without me. Tell them I'll be down in a moment. Make some excuse for me—that is, if they don't already know where I was."

Lynette followed her out into the hall, but her heart clenched when she thought about leaving Maggie open to attack once they parted. Foolishness. The house was full, and the likelihood of Riley getting in and out of there was next to nothing, or so she told herself.

In the meantime, she washed and groomed the best she could without the benefit of a bath, but her mind wasn't on getting ready. She stumbled about, forgetting what she was doing more than once. Twice she stopped in her work to stare out the window, wishing and dreading Riley would appear to end her madness.

She fidgeted as she changed into a gown of sapphire, a bit

fancier than was expected of her, but Lynette thought it best that she overplay her femininity. The dress was cut low and tight and emphasized what little curves she possessed.

Her hair was the most challenging part, as she had to conceal the loss of length. She squinted in concentration as she settled for a twisted updo and weighed it down with small paste gems, hoping to distract from the lack of volume. It would have to do. For the first time, she wished she had the help of a lady's maid. Perhaps her parents would see it in their best interest to get her one now.

Once Lynette had decided she could no longer postpone the inevitable, she made her way down the stairs to whatever doom she faced. She mourned the loss of her men's clothes, which were much easier to move around in, but she especially missed the weight of her two swords on her waist. At least when she had them, she felt safer. She doubted she would ever get the chance to wear them again.

Jeffrey's shouts came from the drawing room, as well as the muffled hysterics of her mother. Maybe it wasn't too late to run off? Glue could probably take another turn through the country.

Lynette shut her eyes, taking a deep breath before pushing open the door.

Jeffrey was on his feet, held back by Carrington and Hugh, with a pinched expression on his face as he tried to attack the unconcerned, reclining Max. Carrington and Hugh looked worn as though they had been at this for some time. Howell wore a wide, amused grin, sitting off to the side of Max and Maggie, who seemed thoughtful but concerned.

Beyond the commotion, Lynette's father sat staring at Max, emotionless. Her mother was babbling incoherent words through her tears. Greymore attempted to console her with little noticeable effect. All eyes turned as Lynette entered. She avoided looking toward Max for fear her expression would give her away.

"At last, you decided to show yourself," Jeffrey fumed, meeting her halfway as she meant to sit near Maggie.

"Good day to you too, Jeffrey," she said through a pleasant smile.

He grunted. "Is that all you have to say? Your family comes to see you after months of your absence or even a letter in your hand. You've barely said anything to me since I came here, and you don't even bother to stay put for one day."

She attempted to move past him, ignoring his lecture. He grabbed her arm in an iron grip before she could take a step.

"We know all about what's been going on. The people you have been associating with. It ends now."

She blinked up at him, his huge frame dwarfing her own dainty figure. Her brother could mean anything. "What are you talking about?"

"Your riding off in your men's clothes without an escort. You've compromised yourself in the worst way. Hopefully there won't be any unforeseen consequences. Mother is beside herself trying to think of a man willing to marry you before the story gets out."

She caught herself before she could laugh in his face. Was he implying she might be pregnant by one of the men in the house? Fair enough. Her family seemed only to grasp the surface of her actions, but she wasn't about to help them out.

"How can you do this to me?" her mother wailed, facing her but not meeting her eyes. "My baby. How can my baby be a trollop? We raised you right. I thought it would be Delia, not my little girl. To think you gave yourself to this man." She went back to her unchecked sobbing.

Lynette froze. How could her mother possibly know? She must have used her overactive imagination to concoct such a possibility, but her mother rarely hit the mark.

Carrington flinched, watching his mother-in-law insult his wife but not bothering to offer her any comfort. Indeed, Greymore had stopped trying to soothe her. Mr. Wolcott was scowling now at Max, ignoring his wife's comments.

"I'm sure you don't mean to imply Miss Wolcott is unmarriageable now. Mr. Rycroft has been nothing but hospitable to her since he rescued her from the accident," Hugh said through clenched teeth.

She'd never thought Hugh would be so loyal to her. Carrington and Greymore were both nodding along to his words. Maggie gave her an encouraging smile. Howell's amusement seemed to reach a new level. She continued to look anywhere but at Max.

Her mother thinned her lips. "Of course that's what I mean. We'll have to confine her at Briarwyck before considering taking her home. If she's carrying some bastard, she might be better off in a nunnery. We'll give the child up, obviously."

Lynette's face froze in openmouthed horror. Her chest was like a vise, cutting off all possible defenses from her lips. The world spun around as her mother humiliated her in front of everyone. She toppled before she knew what was happening. Strong hands righted her into a chair. Her misty gaze cleared to reveal Max stooping over her, his brow creased with worry.

Maggie draped an arm over her shoulders, pulling Lynette down to lean into her.

She sensed more than saw Max stand, turning to face her family.

"No, you won't," Max said in a stern, unwavering voice.

Lynette dared a glance at her mother, gauging the woman's response. Her mother was frowning at Max, mirroring her father's continued expression. To her credit, she seemed uncertain how to continue.

Her mother spoke, voice quivering, "We are grateful for your hospitality and for taking in our poor dear when she needed aid, but you needn't trouble yourself any further. We'll relieve you of her, placing no more blame at your door."

"But I do trouble myself, and I am to blame for this mess." Max widened his stance, blocking Lynette off from her family.

"Don't be ridiculous. This is a family matter and doesn't concern you. Come, Lynette, we need to get you back to Briarwyck. With any luck, word won't spread to New York." Her mother got to her feet.

How many of them understood what he was saying was not just the concern of a host?

Max cleared his throat. "Yes, a family matter." He mumbled something she didn't catch before raising his voice again. "I can't allow you to take any possible child from me."

The room fell silent.

Maggie tightened her grip on Lynette.

There was a moment in which the people in the room were absorbing his words. It all had been painfully obvious to her, of course. She wished there weren't so many people here. Most of them were family or dear friends, but she would rather have had this conversation alone with her father.

The first to move was Jeffrey, springing forward to land a blow to Max's jaw but narrowly missing as Max jerked back nearer to Lynette. It took Carrington, Hugh, and Greymore to hold Jeffrey back as he squirmed toward Max.

"I'll kill you," Jeffrey spit out, grasping toward Max.

By this time, Lynette had gotten to her feet with the help of Maggie. "Jeffrey, please stop. This is just as much my fault. If you're going to blame anyone, blame me."

Jeffrey dropped his arms, glowering at the men around him as they backed off. He met Lynette's eyes. "Netty, you're too young. He took advantage of you."

She scoffed at his words, pulling herself up to her full height, making her head parallel to his shoulders. "I'm not a child. I'm nineteen, and in case you haven't noticed, I'm already out. You would see me a spinster if you had your wish." She glared at her mother. "And you, mother, you'd see me married to the first eligible man who would have me."

Her mother's face somehow grew paler despite her features already being colorless. "Well, certainly not him." She indicated Max with her tear-soaked handkerchief.

To everyone's surprise, Mr. Wolcott gained his feet, meeting Max toe-to-toe and eye to eye. "You'll have to understand our

Netty is precious to us. She is the baby, as my son and wife so ardently called her. But," he said, eyes roaming over Max with little concern, "Netty is also a grown woman now. You seem like a reasonable enough man with the means to take care of her. What do you intend to do about it?"

Lynette's heart caught in her throat as Max spun to face her. His hazel eyes shone in a way she hadn't seen at any other time except when they'd been in bed together. The room was heavy with expectation.

He pulled her hand to his lips, not taking his eyes off hers. "Miss Wolcott, I know I said I could never marry, but the thought of your leaving is more painful than this bullet hole in my leg. I mean to do right by you, and if that means we must marry, then I am prepared to do it. Will you have me?"

"No." Lynette snatched her hand away as though she had been burned.

Max narrowed his eyes in confusion. "Why not?"

"I'm not going to marry someone who's being shamed into it. I don't care if that means I'm ruined. Better to be ruined than have a doomed marriage." She wanted more than anything to accept him, but she couldn't be the one to chain him into a marriage he didn't want. They might be happy for a time until he grew to resent her for trapping him. She didn't want any man that her parents threw her way simply because it was the expected thing to do. Misery was founded on the expected.

She let the tears come as she fled the room, not bothering to check her speed as she raced across the floor, skidding along the slick surface. She nearly tripped in her rush to escape. Her eyes were a blurred mess as she pushed toward the kitchen, meaning to leave through its exit to the stables.

She was blinded by the time she reached the kitchen entrance, opening the door to collide with a solid mass making its way out of the room. Her body fell back only to be steadied by a long-fingered grip. A gasp thrust from her lips as she recognized the bony frame of Riley.

"I didn't think you would come back," she stammered, stuck in place as much from fear as from his grip.

"My whole life is here. Much as yours is." He gestured back toward the drawing room. He had dried out, and the smell of whiskey no longer radiated off his body. His eyes were clear once again.

She shook her head. Her life was no longer anywhere, and he was cast out just as much as she had become. "Why did you do it? You betrayed this family and your friends. You betrayed me."

He let out a long breath, loosening his grip on her shoulders. "Your arrival gave me the idea. A blind fool could see how you and Max stared at each other. I wanted that with Maggie." He paused, closing his eyes.

She didn't speak, hoping her silence would prompt him to continue.

"The night I went to send word to Briarwyck, I got to thinking...and drinking. I'm not proud of the idiotic plan I made, but once it started, I couldn't get it to stop. The plan was like a living thing I released on the world. Too many people wanted something of it. After a while, it wasn't me in control, and no amount of alcohol could make me forget what I had done."

"Then why didn't you tell me? I could have helped you," Max said as he approached behind her.

"I got your sister kidnapped, Max. Then Daniel joined us, and in my drunken state, I allowed him to kidnap your woman. Hell, I encouraged him to kidnap her. I was a jealous fool out to make everyone as miserable as I was. Now I've ruined everything. All my chances with Maggie, my friendship with you. My grandmother doesn't want to talk to me."

"I doubt Mrs. Johns will cast you off," Max said in an uncertain tone.

"She told me I wasn't her family and threw me out of the kitchen. How is that not disowning me?"

Neither of them spoke as they watched Riley falling apart before them. Lynette was rooted in place in case he resorted to anger in his heightened state.

"You're making me wish I had put an end to Daniel. The man will be a rock in my shoe until I'm sure he's gone." Her hand went to her side before she realized she wasn't wearing her blades.

"Indeed, you should have, and you would have been well justified. Some of the things he said in his drunken fits…" Riley trailed off, shaking his head. "That man isn't fit to breathe the same air as you."

Lynette smirked at him. "It's kind of you to notice, but you're a bit late."

"Can the two of you forgive me? I don't deserve it. My grandmother won't have me near the house, but I want things settled." He looked behind Lynette at Max.

Max placed his hands on Lynette's shoulders, tugging her out of Riley's soft grip. He pressed her back against him in a protective embrace. "I think I can forgive the insult to our friendship. For me to forgive you for kidnapping Maggie and Lynette, they will have to forgive you first."

Riley nodded and gazed thoughtfully toward Lynette, his blazing red head tilting to consider her.

"I don't know." Lynette paused. "I'm more upset with Daniel than you, but I cannot pretend you didn't cause me pain. Not to mention the old wounds you helped reopen. Maybe in time, I'll forgive you. You'll have to live with my answer. I don't think Maggie will have a kinder response. Why don't you find her? She's in the drawing room with some of the other people you hurt."

CHAPTER TWENTY-THREE

R ILEY LED THE way into the lion's den, pushed and prodded to face the consequences of his actions. His face was downcast and worn. Lynette took comfort in his distress and was gladdened to know he was facing the room this time, and not her.

The first to react was Hugh, having been the only one to recognize him out of the immediate household. Hugh's alarmed shout alerted Greymore to the man's presence, who drew a pistol Lynette did not recall seeing. A ripple of weapons being drawn went throughout the room until everyone was armed but the women and Riley.

Max brandished a blade, pointing it at each of them. "I would appreciate it if you didn't put holes in the furniture. Most of it is imported from France and Italy, and I'd rather not have to replace it."

Maggie snorted.

The drawing room door opened behind them, causing Lynette to jump. She dared a glance back at Mrs. Johns, Jeremiah Rycroft, and another, older man she hadn't met. They stared at the scene before them with round eyes.

"Max, what is the meaning of this? Why are so many armed people here? How could you bring this down on your sister?" The graying man studied his adopted son with the silver-gray eyes of the Rycroft family. He was barrel-chested with a deep, commanding voice that left no room for argument.

Max stiffened at the words, lowering his blade as he met the man's eyes.

"Bloody hell. The Travers are here. You have some serious explaining to do."

Carrington lowered his pistol, offering the man a stiff bow. Hugh followed his example as Carrington addressed the man. "We mean your daughter no harm. You can rest easy knowing our father has promised not to renew his chase. I'm deeply sorry for any wrongs he has caused you and yours."

Henry Rycroft snorted, an echo of his daughter's earlier action. The resemblance was striking. "That's very well coming from you. No offense, but I'd rather hear it from the man himself. Finding everyone in my home prepared to do battle is not reassuring either."

Riley stepped forward, bowing to Mr. Rycroft. "This is my doing. You needn't blame Max for this mess."

"Indeed? Well, Mrs. Johns will know what to do with you." Mr. Rycroft gestured to the older woman, who scowled at her grandson. "Maggie, are you safe?"

"Of course," she said. "But, Father, I think you need to reconsider your position with Riley. After all, he was the one who had me kidnapped."

"What? Our Riley?" Mr. Rycroft stared at the boy who had grown up in his house, playing with his sons. Howell and the Travers men had moved to flank the door, trapping Riley inside. Greymore took up a position near Maggie.

"What's this? Kidnapped?" Mrs. Wolcott screeched from her silent state. "Lynette, we need to get away from here this instant." She rose to her feet, pulling her husband along in her unsteady gait. Jeffrey joined his parents in their advance to retrieve Lynette.

Max placed himself in front of Lynette before they could get their claws in her. His hand still grasped the hilt of his sword. She would have fled again if it had been an option. Too many bodies were between her and the door. She cursed herself for wanting to see what would become of Riley once he entered the drawing room.

"My boy, what are you playing at? Who is this girl? Let her go with her parents," Mr. Rycroft said, his face growing scarlet. "We have enough problems to deal with as it is."

Max didn't move. "Father, allow me to introduce you to Miss Lynette Wolcott. These are her parents, Mr. and Mrs. Wolcott, and their son, Mr. Jeffrey Wolcott. Miss Wolcott, my father, Mr. Henry Rycroft. I believe you know everyone else."

Mr. Rycroft was scratching his head, studying the Wolcott family. "A pleasure. How did you come to know my son?"

Mr. Wolcott stepped forward, ignoring his wife's murmurings. "Our other daughter is married to Lord Carrington. She is expecting her first child, an opportunity we didn't want to miss. We came to bring Lynette back after your son rescued her from highwaymen."

A strangled, choking laugh escaped Mr. Rycroft's lips. "Max rescued her from highwaymen?" He gave Max a sour look and cleared his throat. "A story for another time, perhaps. You'd best be on your way, then. We wouldn't want you to miss the birth of your first grandchild." He turned to Max, who kept his place before Lynette. "What is the matter with you? Go on."

Max stood his ground, addressing his father. "Not yet. Sir, may I speak with you alone?"

"Fine, but we need to deal with Riley first. Lord Carrington and Mr. Travers, would you be so kind as to restrain him? Not too tight—I still consider him like a son to me. Mrs. Johns, have you had your say?"

Mrs. Johns said something in Romani and nodded. She placed a hand on Riley's shoulder, forcing him into a kneeling position, where she pecked him on the forehead. Her hand combed through his hair before Mrs. Johns said something else, bringing tears to Riley's eyes. She left the room without another word.

Riley's head rested on his chest while the men tied his wrists.

He didn't say a word to anyone. Maggie weaved through the room to the man who'd had her kidnapped. He went still when she stood before him, eyes trained on the carpet.

"It wouldn't have worked. We can't choose who we love. I think..." She gulped, seeming to catch her own words. "I think I can forgive you, not for you, but for me. Go in peace, Riley. You have a hard path ahead of you." Maggie swept out of the room. The clank of the door behind her sent an echo. Riley never looked up.

Riley was guided out into the yard between Carrington and Hugh. The rest of the company trailed behind, Max keeping Lynette tightly to his side. When they neared Mr. Rycroft's newly arrived carriage, Carrington reached out to open the door, and Hugh pushed him inside without fanfare.

Max stood slack, staring past the cliff face that bordered the back of the house. His skin was ashen as Lynette came to join him. She laced her hand in his and leaned against him, not saying a word.

They were left in silence except for the clamoring from the magpies along the roof and the crashing of the waves below. Max melted against her, bringing her into his arms in a warm embrace. When she met his gaze, she thought he might cry. Tears waited beyond his eyes, but they never surfaced.

She understood now that Riley had been more family than friend. All Max's life, the definition of a sibling had been blurred. Maggie was his favorite, but they were not related by blood. The Travers brothers were his half brothers, but they were only now recovering from being his enemy. Then there were his Rycroft half brothers who seemed to barely be present in his life while he protected their own half sister.

Riley had been by his side from the beginning. They shared love for Maggie, though love of different sorts. By all means, Riley may have become more of a true brother to him by law if things had gone differently. If romantic love was not such an elusive emotion, falling away from the grasp of the deserving,

Riley might have been a better man.

Lynette faced back toward the house. The yard was deserted by everyone except Mr. Rycroft and her own father. Max seemed to grasp the situation as well, having calmed his breath in her arms. They waited for their fathers' approach, Max's arm comforting them both around her shoulders.

"Could this be?" Mr. Rycroft asked without preamble. His voice was just above a whisper. He stood studying Lynette with a spark in his silver-gray eyes.

Max gave him a short nod, squeezing Lynette's shoulders as he kissed her hair.

"I thought you might never find anyone. Maggie kept telling me otherwise, but you know what a romantic she is."

"Just wait a minute. My daughter has already refused to marry him. There won't be any forcing her to do anything, and that goes for your mother too, Netty," her father interjected, thrusting out his chest.

"Well, I can't say I blame her, but may I ask why?" Mr. Rycroft asked, staring between her and Max.

She gazed up at Max, who closed his eyes, waiting for her response. Her eyes snapped back to Mr. Rycroft. "I don't want Max to be forced into marriage to me. It's the right thing to do, I know it is, but I can't make both of us miserable because of one night."

Mr. Rycroft's eyes flickered open wider, and he considered his son anew. Beside him, Mr. Wolcott waited, allowing matters to unfold as was his way.

Max dropped his arm from Lynette, pulling back to better see her face. "Would you be miserable?" His voice was barely audible over the crashing waves.

Her lips trembled as she spoke. "No, I would be miserable seeing you so unhappy."

"Father. Mr. Wolcott. May I talk to Miss Wolcott alone? I think I deserve that much at least."

The two fathers exchanged looks and retreated over the lawn.

Max waited until they were gone and took her hand, leading her away.

"Where are we going?" she asked as she fought to keep up with him.

"For a ride," he said, shrugging.

He must be joking. Yet the stables were coming up in front of them. She fought to pull her hand away, but he tightened his grip and continued to pull her forward.

"This isn't funny, Max. My family is waiting for me. Whatever crazy idea you have, it needs to stop now."

He didn't say anything.

"Max. This dress is not suitable for riding. I really hate sidesaddle. Max, stop." She lost her shoe somewhere in a sunken heap of mud, and she kicked off the other to keep up with him. The shoes had only been worn once since she had bought them in London, before her fated trip to Devonshire.

At last, she lost her footing, unable to keep pace with him. She fell forward in front of the stables, where he took her after he lifted her into his arms.

"Won't you speak to me?"

"Love, I can't believe you think I would let anyone shame me into anything. The only time I'll be miserable is when you're not by my side." He put her down in front of Hermes, readying his horse to go. She watched, slack-jawed, as he secured the saddle, blanket, and bags over the stallion.

"Since I don't think I can persuade you, should I ready Glue?"

He shook his head. "Your horse is exhausted. Hermes will do." As usual, his horse appeared ready to take him to the ends of the earth if he so chose.

"Where are we going?"

Instead of answering, he hoisted her headfirst over the horse. She shrieked as he hopped up into the saddle. He steadied her in place with one hand as he urged Hermes forward. Hermes flew over the yard and into the countryside before Lynette could so much as take a breath.

209

"Max, what on earth are you doing? Take me back."

She flopped uncomfortably on her belly, and it wasn't long before her back grew cramped. To his credit, he didn't try to grope her while she bounced about. His focus appeared to be on speed and distance while keeping her firmly in place.

She gave up on pleading, watching the underbrush rush past them. From her position, she couldn't tell which direction they were going or even how much time had passed. The ground stayed much the same, ruling out the coast but nothing else. At least they were not near the bogs, but they hadn't been traveling long enough for her to be sure that wasn't where they were headed.

The shadows beneath them grew long. It had been late when they'd left, and it must be near sunset now. Her parents and Jeffrey would be frantic. She wished he would return to Rycroft House soon or, at least, let her take a break. Max would be a dead man when they got back.

He didn't stop Hermes until it was well into the night, and she suspected he only did so because they didn't have the benefit of light. He jumped out of the saddle as though they hadn't been riding for hours and pulled her down to sway on her feet.

"Where are we? This isn't Rycroft House."

"Yes, I'm aware of that," he said dryly. He brought his lips lazily down to hers, making her toes curl in the dirt.

She nestled into his body, her hands lacing behind his neck. She deepened the kiss until a low moan crept into her mouth. Her lips drew away as she sought out his eyes. He was staring down at her with naked want and something warmer.

"We need to get back," she said without much enthusiasm.

"We aren't done talking yet," he replied, keeping her close as the stars shone around them.

She tilted her head back. "We haven't done any talking. You have made it impossible."

He chuckled, kissing the revealed part of her neck. "Exactly." He wandered his mouth along the skin, leaving a whisper of fire behind his lips.

A gasp escaped her, dying off in the wind. "More of that."

He nipped at her tender flesh, sending a rush of pleasure between her legs. She clasped his shoulders, afraid he might pull away. When he did, she whimpered in disappointment.

"Talk first," he said, keeping her in his arms but at a safe distance from his lips.

"Why did you bring me out here? We could have talked just as well back there. My answer is still the same." She could just make out his features in the night. His eyes never left her.

"Give me a second," he said, releasing her as he rustled through his saddlebags. "I keep supplies on hand in case I need to make a quick escape from Rycroft House. It has saved me on countless occasions." He pulled out a small lamp, which he lit without too much fuss. He set it down on the ground. "I wanted to see you."

He studied her eyes in the low light. "That's better." He took her hands in his, kissing them both in turn. "Lynette, sweet, as I said before, I am not being forced into anything. I want to marry you."

She shook her head. "No, you don't. I'm damaged, spoiled goods."

He scoffed. "Yes, by me, but that has no weight on my decision."

She studied the ground. "Please, you don't understand—the things I did in New York. Max, I've killed a man. I was responsible for the death of a second man. I can't elaborate any further without giving away others, but be assured I am broken."

"Oh, sweet." He let out a low laugh. "You aren't broken. You're the strongest woman I know next to Maggie. The Wyvern has killed too. So if you're broken, then I am. We will complete each other." He guided her chin up, forcing her to meet his gaze.

His hazel eyes were lit with warm brown from the lamp, rousing a comforting feeling deep in her chest. "Marry me. I can't think of anyone I would rather be with. You aren't going to chain me down. You're going to set me free."

"You don't want to marry me," she protested, lost in his knowing eyes.

A playful smile tugged at his lips. "Love, haven't I been telling you all along? I've never wanted anything more. I love you."

The corner of her mouth twitched up. "Even when I stab your men and order everyone around?"

His body shook in her arms as he erupted in full-body laughter. "Especially when you stab my men and order everyone around. You're my Harpy."

"In that case, I have some ideas about ways we can improve the efficiency of brandy redistribution."

"Is that so? Redistribution, is it?" He shook his head. "We can talk about it later. Is that a yes?"

Her lips broke into a smile, making her eyes well. "Yes, it's a yes."

He kissed her, unable to hold himself back any longer. He grinned back at her, a captivating rogue in his happiness. "You're sure you want someone like me? You could do much better. I'll give up being the Wyvern if you want. I could take up farming or trade with my brothers."

"Don't you dare." She slapped his arm playfully. "I love you the way you are. I'm not marrying a farmer. Besides, half the country seems to be smuggling. It would look odd if we didn't. Suspicious, even."

He nodded sagely. "Of course, you're right."

"Max, we must head back. Everyone will be looking for us, and Riley needs to be dealt with." She paused, realizing how insensitive that must have sounded. "I'm so sorry. I know what he means to you."

He gave her a grim smile. "In time. We need to grasp this now while we have the chance. I'd like to think Riley approves."

She eyed him with a quizzical tilt to her head. "What do you have in mind?"

"Why, my love, I'm kidnapping you."

CHAPTER TWENTY-FOUR

L YNETTE STARED AT Max with a blank expression. The man must have lost his mind. A wide, half-crazed grin spread over his face as he watched her blink back her confusion. She could not have heard him correctly.

"Haven't we had enough kidnapping for a lifetime? Don't you think our families will come looking for us?"

He captured her against his chest, breathing in the scent of her hair. "Sweet, this will be the most enjoyable kidnapping. It will make you forget all other kidnappings. As for our families, I'm sure they will. Why do you think I ran Hermes into the night?"

Her fingers played along his jawline. "Oh? I thought maybe you wanted to get me alone."

A laugh rumbled through his chest, shaking her against him. "That too." He kissed the top of her head before releasing her and going back to Hermes. He made the horse comfortable, unsaddling him and giving him water from what looked like a flask made for humans.

She giggled at his doting on the horse. He would make an excellent father. Where had that thought come from? Oh well; it was only a matter of time.

Max had made a pile of the saddlebags, and Lynette rummaged through the things he had brought. She found a scratchy rolled-up blanket to serve her purpose and laid it out in the least rocky area she could find. The arrangement would still have her wake to aches all over her body, but she didn't intend to sleep much.

"I'm afraid I didn't pack any food. There is some brandy, but I will have to find some sustenance for us on the way." He came to join her, carrying the lamp. He looked down at the blanket with a half smile. "You are thinking ahead, I see." He set the lamp down off to the side.

"Not too far ahead, I hope."

In answer, he took her face in his hands, kissing the tip of her nose. She made a gurgling sound in exasperation, causing him to chuckle. His lips met hers as he laughed, forcing her to laugh along with him.

"We need to get you out of this dress. I'm afraid it's ruined."

She looked down at herself, seeing the wrinkles and dirt smudges from their journey. He was right. It couldn't be salvaged. The fine sapphire fabric wasn't fit as a cleaning rag. Still, he tugged carefully on the garment, being sure to avoid ripping what was left of it. He worked on undressing her, one piece of clothing at a time.

He grunted as he got past the gown to her skirts. "This is an awful lot of fabric. Aren't you hot?"

She rolled her eyes. "You have no idea. Would you like some help?" Her hands moved to the ties at her back, but he slapped them away. "You're going to lose my pins." She sighed. There was no helping it in the wilderness.

He ignored her comments, working now at her stays. "I should have forced you to change before I kidnapped you, but I think it would have lost the effect. What would people think of me if I didn't properly kidnap you?"

She narrowed her eyes. "They would think you're normal. A horrible thought, I know." Her shift and muddy silk stockings were all that remained of her clothes. Her stockings would have to be thrown away too. A pity; they had been imported from

France.

He guided her to stand above the blanket, and he knelt in front of her. He lifted her shift over his head, disappearing from view. When she peeked under her shift, he removed her garter with his teeth. He glared up at her, pulling the shift back over his head.

"What are you doing?" she asked through suppressed laughter.

He tossed the stocking off, throwing it behind his shoulder. The soft texture of his lips graced her thigh, and he worked on the other stocking. He seemed to be losing his patience, opting to guide the stocking down with his hand.

"Take this off." His voice was muffled under her shift. He gave it a sharp tug.

She tsked at him, throwing the undergarment after the rest of her clothing. Her body was bared to his wandering eyes, sending a thrilling shiver down her spine. He watched her with that look she had come to identify as adoration. The soft glow of the lamp and the faint light of the stars were all that guided them.

He yanked at his own clothes with less finesse, having to lean back to remove his boots and breeches. Yet once again, he refused her assistance. A shower of clothing rained here and there, making her laugh, the sound echoing off the land.

The flame of the oil lamp flickered in the faint breeze, casting shadows along his toned body and accenting the pulse along his neck as he urged her closer. He guided her to seat herself, straddling his thighs as he sat with legs out in front of him. His hands slid along her back as he teased her lips, licking and nipping the sensitive skin.

She let her hands travel over the grooves of his chest, savoring the feel of the coarse hair between her fingers. She gave his nipple a light pinch. He moaned, deepening his kiss to possess her, to claim her.

She cried out for release, but he continued to torment her, moving from her lips to take the tender flesh of her breasts. His hands worshipped her chest while he suckled one of her nipples. She arched into his mouth, letting a moan-like cry escape into the wilderness.

His hand slid between them, cupping her mound with his palm. He caught her hips in his hands as she rocked to meet him, gliding her along his lap to slide himself just inside her. Her legs wrapped around his back by instinct, pushing him deeper.

Her already tender breasts rubbed against the rough hair of his chest with their embrace. Her gaze held his, their breath mingling with their joined bodies. They moved together. He set the rhythm with gentle pressure to her back, rocking her back and forth along his length.

His heart beat against her skin, or was it hers?

Their lips met, almost as though their bodies were locking in place or perhaps making them whole. A sense of contentment spread through her. Her body ran on a fount of power, making her come alive in his arms. She knew then she loved Max with every part of her, and she couldn't imagine what life would be like without him. Never wanted to imagine.

Her body tremored, and their pace increased. She became lost to coherent thought, surrendering herself to the friction between them and the heightening warmth enveloping her.

Her hips thrust over him, sending shock waves between them. She clenched herself tightly around him. A scream of pleasure went up into the night from deep in her throat. He burst inside her, moaning against her ear and intensifying her orgasm until she collapsed against him.

They panted in each other's arms.

The moon came to peek out at them, a wash of light picking up the colors around them. The darkness had cocooned them into eternity, creating the illusion of them being the only two people in the world. There was no time, no thought inside that darkness. Nothing else mattered, just Lynette and Max and the fiery bond between them.

She was near exhaustion when Max laid her down across the

blanket. He settled down by her side, on his back, drawing her against his chest. She let out a contented sigh as they stared up at the stars twinkling overhead.

Her eyes caught a flash of light reflected from the metal at his throat, and she reached up to the locket he always wore. He closed his eyes, his breath even. Her fingers fiddled with the clasp until it gave. A lock of hair fell out into her hand. She clasped it in her palm as she examined the portrait of Mary. The stunning hazel eyes Mary shared with Rycroft were just visible, as was her shining black hair. A hint of auburn shone under the painter's strokes—a small, oval masterpiece in detail.

She squinted at the miniature and down at the hair in her hand. Her gaze jumped to Max's face, and he looked back at her with a small smile.

"This is my hair," she finally said.

He nodded, stretching his arms around her.

"I thought I discarded all of it. When did you get this?" She sighed, and a tear rested on her cheek.

"Not all of it. I found that shortly after you chopped it off." He ran his hand over her loose hair, picking out what was left of her paste gems. The gems mirrored the stars as they shone against his skin.

"But that was...right after our first kiss. You've kept my hair since then?" It seemed like a lifetime ago. So much had happened since that night. Not all of it bad. Some of it had been beautiful, breathtaking.

"Yes. I've worn it since we discovered you'd been kidnapped. This time, it will accompany your kidnapping." He took the lock of hair back and secured it safely away next to the portrait.

"About that, why exactly do you need to kidnap me? I've agreed to marry you." She walked her fingers down his chest, reaching his navel, where he caught her hand.

He watched her hand. "Not yet, love."

She stuck her lower lip out at him. "Well?"

"Well? Didn't you have reservations about marrying me?"

She nodded and rested her head back down against his chest.

How she could have had any reservations was beyond her. The sincerity of his love for her was plain to her now as hers was for him.

"So my kidnapping was successful."

"Max, I don't understand. We can go back now."

He ran his hand through her hair. "Not so. How many parents would let their daughter marry their kidnapper? We will proceed as planned."

"What do you mean by that? What are you planning now? Why is it you always tell me only some of what runs through that twisted head of yours?"

A dry laugh vibrated beneath her as it ran through his chest. "Oh, I love you. I can't bear for you to see the things this twisted head comes up with. You'd run away screaming. Haven't you already guessed? We're going to Gretna Green. I mean to marry you before anyone gets a chance to dash you off to Briarwyck."

She closed her eyes. "Mmm... Scotland. I've never been there."

"You will, love, and we will return to explore later. Perhaps we can find business there for the Wyvern. For now, we must make a swift return, or my likeness will be up everywhere, and people will call for my head."

She giggled, lulling herself into sleep. "They already do," she whispered into his chest.

A blazing sun woke her from a deep sleep. She rubbed her eyes, letting them adjust. Max was already up, saddling Hermes. He peered back at her, the smile like a permanent feature etched into his handsome face.

"Ready to go?" A joke. She lay naked against the blanket, aglow in the sunlight.

"I thought maybe you'd like to release some urges before we left." She patted the blanket beside her.

His eyes darted away as he shook his head. "We woke too late. They could be on our trail."

She stretched to her feet, and he came to assist in dressing her as best he could. They opted to leave her hair down and left the stockings to the animals. At least this time, he let her ride sidesaddle in front of him. Yet the result of such riding kindled a desire between them that would not be ignored.

The first time, he almost took her atop Hermes until Lynette started to fall off the horse. After that, they had to take breaks to make love beside the road. As indecent as she now appeared, Max left her after one such incident to find her proper clothes and food for them to eat. She'd donned her new garment, a pale-green riding habit that was not as fine as her dress but was far more comfortable and easier to put on. She'd left the sapphire gown on the side of the road.

They passed by other travelers on occasion, every time making her grateful for the riding habit. More than one passerby gave them knowing glances the closer they got to Gretna Green. Lynette found herself blushing at the attention. They would be remembered. There was no help for it.

Night was falling by the time they reached the small village. Max pointed toward the first building they found, a blacksmith's of all things. The long, stout structure stood out like a light against the coming darkness. She'd heard of the runaway marriages, but at the time, they had sounded absurd to her. Now she wouldn't have it any other way.

When they approached the door, a jovial man greeted them with a wave of his hand, ushering them inside. He led them into a long room lit by the fading sun through the window and the large open door. An anvil sat near the center, drawing her attention.

"You have payment?" the man mumbled to Max in a faint Scottish accent.

Max handed him a purse and nodded to Lynette when she raised a brow at him. His superstition was rubbing off on her. She wasn't about to get married with fake coin. The man's eyes widened when he glanced inside, more than enough payment for the ceremony. Max must have been in a charitable mood.

"Witnesses? Ring? I'm afraid I sold my last ring this morning. You'd be amazed how many couples forget these things."

Max grew pale, turning to Lynette. "I'll be half a moment."

He bolted out of the shop like the smuggler patrols were on his heels.

She smirked after his retreating form.

The man beside her gave a dry laugh and craned his neck to yell over his shoulder, "Megs, we got us another! Get the lass some flowers. They've more than paid for it."

A grunt came from the room beyond and then rustling. Some moments passed before a smiling, heavyset woman bustled into the room, carrying a small but vibrant bouquet of bluebells tied with streaming ribbons of blue and white.

Megs presented the flowers to Lynette. "I picked these just this afternoon. We tend to get couples rushing in after sundown with the devil on their heels."

"Thank you. They're lovely."

Megs's eyes widened, and she addressed her husband. "An American. We don't get many colonists here. The boy sounded a bit English, or was he another American?"

"Max grew up in Devonshire, but he's traveled extensively," Lynette supplied, growing increasingly anxious about the groom's absence. Had he changed his mind and left her here? How hard was it to find a ring in a wedding destination? Her foot tapped with impatience, and the couple looked at her with knowing smiles.

"It's just that we are in a bit of a hurry," she said by way of explanation for her rudeness.

Megs shrugged. "Aren't you all?"

At last, Max returned, pulling a small, bespectacled man behind him. "I had to bribe the jeweler to come as a witness. I'm afraid nobody else seems to be out."

The couple chuckled together at the jeweler's annoyed expression. "You needn't worry. My old man was having a bit of fun with you. I can serve as a witness if you like," Megs said as she gestured to the anvil. She took one of each of their hands, joining them to place them on the anvil, and stepped back to allow her husband to take her place.

He took their names before beginning. A faint smile tugged at his lips at their impatient answers. After all, he had already been paid, and what did it matter to him if they didn't get through with the ceremony?

"Max, do you vow to love and cherish Lynette?"

"Yes, of course," Max said, meeting Lynette's eyes. A thrilling rush filled her chest.

The blacksmith cleared his throat. "Do you, Lynette, vow to love and cherish Max?"

"Yes," she managed, her voice catching over the word.

"The ring," the blacksmith said, gesturing to Max.

Max fumbled through his waistcoat pocket, fishing out a gold band. He lifted her hand from the anvil, placing the ring on her finger. She looked down at the intricate floral design, admiring the work of the jeweler. The jeweler beamed at her as he snuck away from the ceremony, but she didn't care.

"A posey ring," Max said. "The engraving says, 'Love till you die, and so will I.'"

"It's perfect." She took his hand in hers on the anvil once again.

Her eyes were locked with his. In the corner of her eye, the blacksmith raised his hammer, swinging it toward their hands. Lynette almost flinched away when Max squeezed her fingers, reassuring her she would always be safe in his hands.

The hammer tapped them, another trick of the blacksmith, who seemed to wish them yet more anxiety. "You are now forged anew. Kiss the lovely lass."

Max obeyed, leaning into her lips almost shyly. His touch was soft but sure as he pulled her into his embrace. The bluebells were pressed between them as they shared their first kiss as husband and wife. A sweet, grassy aroma erupted from the flowers between them as their kiss turned to smiles.

An exasperated grunt came from somewhere behind Megs. "What am I going to tell your mother?"

Her father stood beyond the room with a sullen, hopeless hang to his body.

CHAPTER TWENTY-FIVE

MR. WOLCOTT WAS followed by Lord Carrington and Mr. Rycroft as they pooled into the room. The three men were equally solemn in their demeanors. They didn't appear to mean Max any harm, or at least, not yet, since no weapons were drawn.

Max clutched Lynette tighter to him, his eyes focused on the newcomers. His stance widened similarly to the one she had learned.

"Hello, sir, whatever is the matter?" Max asked his father. "I thought you approved of the match."

Mr. Rycroft snorted. "A settled match in a church, not a kidnapping."

"I was a perfectly willing accomplice." Lynette threaded her hand with Max's.

Carrington took a step forward and raked a hand through his hair. "Not by the servants' accounts. They said you were forced on Hermes and taken away like a spoil of war."

"What servants? Mrs. Johns wouldn't say anything like that," Max said, anger lacing his voice. "I don't recall having any other servants at Rycroft House."

Mr. Rycroft's face twisted into a frown as he considered his son. "He means your men. I don't see any reason to beat around the fact. They were upset about your taking Miss Wolcott. Howell was beside himself with anger. The rest of them were grumbling about it in the drawing room. They seem to have taken a liking to your new wife here. I don't believe they appreciated being left out of the ceremony."

"Nor does your mother or brother. I don't know how your sister would feel about this whole mess. If you put her child in danger from stress, your mother will never forgive you," Mr. Wolcott said.

Lynette wouldn't forgive herself either. The child meant everything to Delia and Carrington, a chance for an heir or a daughter to adore. Lynette couldn't see any way around what she and Max had done. For them, this was the only real choice to be made. Their family wouldn't see that now, but in time, they would understand it was the most logical decision.

"Fine. I kidnapped her. We're married now, so what do you intend to do about it?" Max asked with an air of indifference. She knew it was an act by the way his arm clung to her back.

"I've convinced them to let you go. In the interest of any future children and the happiness of Lynette, nobody intends to take legal action. However, it seems there is an idea for a second ceremony to appease your families. I'm sure both parties can agree on Lynette's dowry before the ceremony takes place," Carrington said in that commanding way about him that had earned the love of her sister. She had admired it once, but in the present circumstances, she wanted to scream and kick him out the door. She appreciated his help with Max, but he was turning her beautiful day into a business transaction.

"I don't need a dowry," Max said in an offended tone. "I leave it up to my wife if she wants another ceremony."

Lynette cast her gaze about in annoyance. "No, this fine blacksmith has done the job. We don't need another wedding. I know the rest of you might think this union is about you, but clearly it's not. Max and I will do just fine without your leading strings."

"But, Netty, your mother will be hurt if she hasn't a wedding to plan. I don't blame you myself. Weddings are a bit too much work for me. I can't speak for your sister. Jeffrey will get over it," her father said as if by rote.

"I'm sorry, Papa, but Mama is part of the problem. I am deeply sorry about causing Delia any distress, Carrington," she said, leaning into Max for comfort.

Carrington dipped his hand into his overcoat, causing Max to stiffen in response. Her brother-in-law smirked at the action, handing Lynette a folded letter addressed to her in her sister's neat hand. "That arrived for you just as we were leaving. I didn't read it, of course. Perhaps you will find some answers there. She couldn't know much about this."

She turned the letter over in her fingers, uncertain what to do. Max came to her rescue.

"You must read it. Take it over by the window there, and I will have a talk with our fathers."

Her head was already bent to the letter while she found a chair to suit her purpose. The letter was dated after her parents had set out to Rycroft House.

My dearest Netty,

Do not be distressed by our parents' arrival. I wanted to warn you, but they arrived at Briarwyck sooner than expected. They mean well, as do we all. I know you don't mean me ill by your absence, and do not let Mother tell you otherwise. She thrives in other people's distress, and I will not have you be another victim of hers.

I have watched you over these past months and know you have become unhappy at Briarwyck. Whatever it is that is keeping you at Rycroft House, hold it closely. I'm told you have been behaving improperly with a man, though I was refused any further details. Is it Mr. Max Rycroft? I can only guess. He is much like his brothers and quite handsome. Abigail assures me he is mostly harmless, though a bit of a liar and thief. I'd keep that in mind.

Don't let duty hold you back. I almost lost the man I love because I felt obligated to keep those close to me safe. Well, you

*know the rest. I hold no such restraints over you. I don't need
another hen clucking at me at all hours. For the sake of your
own happiness, follow your heart. Have some adventures for me
and then come back and tell me all about them so that I will not
be so miserable confined at home.*

Your devoted sister,
Lady Dee

Lynette read the letter two more times before returning to
the men who led a discussion about her dowry. Max leaned
against the wall. A slight narrowing of his eyes showed his
irritation at the conversation. Carrington appeared to be
mediating while the two fathers were doing most of the talking.

"The boy said he didn't care about the dowry, and I've been
assured your son is well equipped to take care of my daughter,"
Mr. Wolcott said, always the shrewd businessman, even when it
came to his children's wellbeing.

"Max doesn't have any head for business, but Lord Carrington has already stated that your daughter's dowry is quite
substantial. In his best interest, I must object," Mr. Rycroft
argued. From what she knew of Henry Rycroft, he had come
from a humble background of minor merchants and made his
fortune by his own toil. Of course he wouldn't want Max to pass
up her fortune.

While the discussion became heated, Lynette tugged Max's
arm and led him out into the night air. Carrington's eyes followed
their exit, and she placed a finger to her lips, a plea written on her
face in hopes he would understand. The side of his lips tugged up,
but he nodded to her to be off.

As they reached Hermes, Max finally spoke, "Where are we
sneaking off to? We needn't return in any secrecy, and we'll be
alone soon enough."

"Max, do you really want to discuss the business of marriage?
I'd rather not be around while they settle the matter."

"Of course not. I'd rather impale myself on my sword than

talk about money with my father. Why do you think I haven't bothered with the family business?"

She gestured for him to mount Hermes, following him up as she had countless times in the past day. "I thought you were a thief. There couldn't be much room for that."

He let out a disgusted sound as he took up the reins, leading them forward without a destination. "You'd be wrong. Trade is thievery as much as smuggling. You haven't answered my question. Hermes needs a direction."

"We're going to see the *Mary*. I need a honeymoon, and I can't do that if we stand around here. Besides, if you don't get my dowry, we'll have to make money somehow. We might as well get started with our imports. I wouldn't mind going to France while we're at it."

He chuckled, putting Hermes into a trot. "We'll find a place to spend our wedding night, and first thing tomorrow, I will lead you into a life of shady business dealings and backstabbing."

"I love you, my flying worm."

He kissed the side of her neck as they left Gretna Green behind. "I love you too, my Harpy."

About the Author

Mae Thorn enjoys being romanced and terrified – a combination not normally found in books so she writes them. Her favorite stories include kickass women and the men they fall for. She writes historical romance and fantasy.

When she isn't writing she battles for equal access for those with hearing loss, discovers hidden records as a volunteer archivist, geeks out about Legos, torments her feline minions, and watches bad movies.

Mae holds a Bachelor's degree in English from the University of Utah and a Master's degree in Library and Information Science from San Jose State University.

She lives near Salt Lake City, Utah with her cats; Church, Shadow Moon, and Sabrina.

Website:
Maethorn.com

Twitter:
Twitter.com/maethornwrites

Facebook:
Facebook.com/maethornwrites

Instagram:
Instagram.com/maethornwrites

Pinterest:
https://pin.it/15qQIQ6